PROTECTION & SECU[...]

PASS

SERVICES

PRAISE FOR FREYA BARKER

Freya Barker writes a mean romance, I tell you! A REAL romance, with real characters and real conflict.

~Author M. Lynne Cunning

I've said it before and I'll say it again and again, Freya Barker is one of the BEST storytellers out there.

~Turning Pages At MidnightBook Blog

God, Freya Barker gets me every time I read one of her books. She's a master at creating a beautiful story that you lose yourself in the moment you start reading.

~Britt Red Hatter Book Blog

Freya Barker has woven a delicate balance of honest emotions and well-formed characters into a tale that is as unique as it is gripping.

~Ginger Scott, bestselling young and new adult author and Goodreads Choice Awards finalist

Such a truly beautiful story! The writing is gorgeous, the scenery is beautiful...

~Author Tia Louise

From Dust by Freya Barker is one of those special books. One of those whose plotline and characters remain with you for days after you finished it.

~Jeri's Book Attic

No amount of words could describe how this story made me feel, I think this is one I will remember forever, absolutely freaking awesome is not even close to how I felt about it.

~Lilian's Book Blog

Still Air was insightful, eye-opening, and I paused numerous times to think about my relationships with my own children. Anytime a book can evoke a myriad of emotions while teaching life lessons you'll continue to carry with you, it's a 5-star read.

~ Bestselling Author CP Smith

In my opinion, there is nothing better than a Freya Barker book. With her final installment in her Portland, ME series, Still Air, she does not disappoint. From start to finish I was completely captivated by Pam, Dino, and the entire Portland family.

~ Author RB Hilliard

The one thing you can always be sure of with Freya's writing is that it will pull on ALL of your emotions; it's expressive, meaningful, sarcastic, so very true to life, real, hard-hitting and heartbreaking at times and, as is the case with this series especially, the story is at points raw, painful and occasionally fugly BUT it is also sweet, hopeful, uplifting, humorous and heart-warming.

~ Book Loving Pixies

FREYA BARKER

PROTECTION & SECURITY
PASS
SERVICES

LOCK & LOAD

PASS Series

ALSO BY FREYA BARKER

STANDALONES
WHEN HOPE ENDS
VICTIM OF CIRCUMSTANCE
BONUS KISSES

ARROW'S EDGE MC SERIES
EDGE OF REASON
EDGE OF DARKNESS
EDGE OF TOMORROW

PASS SERIES
HIT & RUN
LIFE & LIMB
LOCK & LOAD

ON CALL SERIES
BURNING FOR AUTUMN
COVERING OLLIE
TRACKING TAHLULA
ABSOLVING BLUE
REVEALING ANNIE
DISSECTING MEREDITH (MARCH 2021)

ROCK POINT SERIES
KEEPING 6
CABIN 12
HWY 550
10-CODE

NORTHERN LIGHTS COLLECTION
A CHANGE OF TIDE
A CHANGE OF VIEW
A CHANGE OF PACE

SNAPSHOT SERIES
SHUTTER SPEED
FREEZE FRAME
IDEAL IMAGE

PORTLAND, ME, SERIES
FROM DUST
CRUEL WATER
THROUGH FIRE
STILL AIR
LULLAY (A CHRISTMAS NOVELLA)

CEDAR TREE SERIES
SLIM TO NONE
HUNDRED TO ONE
AGAINST ME
CLEAN LINES
UPPER HAND
LIKE ARROWS
HEAD START

ISBN: 9781988733593

Cover Design: Freya Barker
Image:
JW Photography
Josh Sargent & Morgan Boyd

Editing: Karen Hrdlicka
Proofreading: Joanne Thompson
Formatting: Christina Smith

LOCK&LOAD

PASS Series

CHAPTER 1

Hillary

"HEADS-UP. SOMEONE'S on the warpath."

I shove the last of my salad in my mouth as Linda slides across from me in the cafeteria booth.

I groan while I'm chewing. I know exactly who she's referring to.

Four years I've worked with the woman and I still can't figure out why she ever became a nurse. Karla Velky is one of the most miserable people I've ever encountered. She's my boss and hates my guts. Also a mystery, although, I have a sneaky suspicion that may have had something to do with me dating Bill Shearer for those unfortunate four weeks.

Dr. Sugarlips, because the man could kiss—for a urologist anyway. Too bad he was all about the hunt for another notch in his stethoscope. Unbeknownst to me, Karla had been his *catch du jour* before me and had not quite gotten over it. Or him, so it seems.

"What's she on about now?" I ask, already rolling my eyes in anticipation.

"She was looking for you earlier and wasn't happy when I told her you were on your dinner break. I thought she'd bust a vein. Said you should've been back on the floor twenty minutes ago." She takes a huge bite of her pizza slice.

"Twenty-five minutes ago I still had my fingers in the entry wound of the GSW that came in off the street. What does she expect? For me to tell the patient; sorry, can you stop bleeding for half an hour so I can take my break?"

Annoyed, I pick up my salad container and my water bottle and shove the chair back as I stand.

"Leaving already?" Linda looks up at me, grinning.

"You know you're enjoying this way too much, right?" I accuse her, which only makes her grin wider as she nods affirmatively.

"What can I say? It's been a slow night for me, I could use a good mudslinging to distract me."

She wiggles her eyebrows and I shake my head, unable to stop the smile on my own face.

"You're incorrigible. What would your wife say about that?"

"Maggie? She'd be pissed I didn't tape it. She loves a good wrestling bout as much as I do. Just last night we found a good one on YouTube. Female mud wrestling, look it up."

Linda and her wife, Maggie, are probably the most unconventional couple I know; unapologetically hedonistic and always up for a good time of one kind or another. In comparison I'm dull and uninspired, which is fine by me; I can find better things to do with my time than watch a bunch of busty women go at it in a tub of sludge.

"I'll pass," I tell her, which sets her off laughing again.

That's another thing about them; they laugh all the time. Somehow, in the sometimes heartbreaking and gut-wrenching work we do, Linda is able to find the humor.

I'm envious of that. I have a tendency to absorb some of the misery around me and find it difficult to shed it at the end of my shift. I'm also more duty driven, my focus always on what I should be doing, rather than what I'd like to be doing.

Now that's getting a little old. Working two jobs so I can finish paying off my student loans has been my sole focus for the past ten or so years. I'm so close to being free of that burden I can taste it, but as they say, the last mile is the longest.

I'm going on thirty-six, feel at least ten years older most days, and there are times I worry life may have already passed me by. Six more months of working two jobs and then I can tell Karla she can shove her schedule up her ass.

My fairly new second job at the homeless shelter my friend, Rosie, runs is what I'll focus on full time then. I'll still be caring for people—something that is ingrained in me—but I'll be able to see the long-term impact of my work. You don't really get that kind of gratification in the ER. We patch them up and send them off, rarely seeing the results of what we do.

Karla has her office door open when I attempt to sneak by.

"Where were you?"

The nasal pitch of her voice grates on me, but I try to plaster a smile on my face when I stop and turn. She's in the doorway to her office, a hand on her hip, and a scowl on her face.

"On my dinner break. Linda mentioned you were looking for me so I cut it short."

She looks pointedly at the watch on her wrist.

"Short? According to the schedule you should've been back almost half an hour ago."

I take a deep breath in before answering. I've learned it doesn't help my case if I lose my cool.

"Actually, I was busy with the gunshot wound that came in earlier, so I went on break later." When she stays silent, only glaring at me, I quickly add, "I was assisting Dr. Bogosh, feel free to check with him."

Her lips press into a tight line. She does not get along with Kevin Bogosh, one of our second-year residents.

"I will."

She's about to disappear into her office when I stop her.

"Why were you looking for me?"

From the glint in her eyes I know I'm not going to like what's coming.

"Supply room is running low on a few things. I need a full stock count so I can order."

I open my mouth to protest, I was in the supply room earlier and supplies looked fine to me, but think better of it. This is her game; every so often she puts me on some grunt job that'll take more hours than I have left in my shift to finish, so she can get her jollies off. It's just easier to give her what she wants so she's off my back for a bit.

There are about four hours left in my shift. If I put my shoulders into it, it can be done in that time.

Make that five hours. Around ten thirty, four victims of multiple-vehicle accident came in and it was all hands on deck for a while before I could finish up the task.

It's a little after one in the morning when I climb behind the wheel of my car and force my eyes open for a little longer. Monday is my double day. I start at the shelter from seven thirty until one thirty, then half an hour to scoot home to change and wolf down something to eat before heading to the hospital for my ten-hour shift starting at two. It's a really long day, but luckily I only have one double-shift day a week.

I live in an apartment building halfway between the shelter and the hospital. A one-bedroom apartment on the top floor of a two-story building, just up the street from Lincoln Park. It takes me five to ten minutes going to either location, depending on traffic.

When I pull into the parking lot behind the L-shaped building, I notice two of the lights are out again. I'll have to notify management tomorrow. It's not the first time that's happened and since I get home when most people are already asleep in bed, I'd rather not traverse the lot in the pitch dark.

I grab my bag and get out, locking the doors of my 2006 Honda Civic. Keeping a close eye on my surroundings, I make my way to the outside stairway leading up to my apartment.

Halfway up the stairs I hear a noise from the street—it sounds like a muffled scream—and peek through the brush blocking part of my view. It takes me a moment to register it's a woman, who appears to be struggling with two attackers. The one person goes down when I notice one of the others raise something over their heads, bringing it down sharply.

I find myself already running back down the stairs when the sound of a wet thwack has my stomach roil. My feet keep moving despite the massive stop sign my brain registers. Just as I burst through the bushes onto the sidewalk, I hear another strike.

"Hey! Stop it!" I yell at the top of my lungs, as I see one of the two men bend over the victim. "Leave her alone!"

Both of their heads swing in my direction and I see they're not men.

They're boys.

Radar

"Let's go, Phil."

My new rescue, an aging furball of an undetermined breed I normally would've walked right by, blinks those pleading dark brown eyes at me. She already knows she has me by the balls.

That became clear the first time she blinked those heavily lashed peepers at me. I'd been looking for a good-sized rescue—a big, manly dog—to keep me company, since the kind of work I do is mostly solitary and often has me by myself in the office or at home. Three weeks ago my boss, Yanis, walked into my office, thinking I was on the phone because I'd been talking for a while. Turns out I was talking to no one, and I didn't even notice it.

Do you know how scary it is to turn forty and find out you're already walking around, mumbling to yourself? The crew at the office thought it was hilarious, but it rattled me. So I went to get a dog, and instead came home with Philomena, a nine-year-old fluffy thing on stumpy legs.

"Let's go, lazy bones," I prompt her again when she stays curled up on my couch, despite the leash in my hand.

She won't stop bugging me for her morning walks, can muster up at least some excitement over the ones during the day, but at night, after the sun goes down, Phil is out.

Even when I clip on her leash and set her on her feet on the floor, she drags her little ass. The outside air perks her up a little as we start our nightly walk around the block.

I found this place last month, after my previous one became too small for my computer equipment. That had been a tiny one-bedroom, and the only place

I ended up being able to sit was a stool by the kitchen counter or my bed. Every other piece of furniture had been repurposed to hold my stuff.

The new apartment has two good-sized bedrooms, one of which I spent some time organizing so I could fit every piece of equipment behind that one door, while the rest of the place is big enough for me and Phil to actually live in.

Nice neighborhood, even though I really couldn't care less where I live. My work is my passion and both have me glued to my computer screens for the most part. Dimas had tried to sell me on buying a house. I can easily afford to but pass on the responsibility of looking after a property. I don't want the headache. For what? I don't garden, I don't even really cook, except the bare necessities, and I don't have a family. Except for Phil, of course.

No, this place suits me just fine.

We round the corner when Phil suddenly stops in her tracks, her floppy ears as perched as they can get, and one front paw lifted halfway in the air.

"Hey! Stop it!"

A few feet in front of me a woman comes flying out of the hedge and suddenly I notice a small group farther down the street. Two guys—one with a baseball bat—standing over someone on the ground. The damn woman runs straight for them, still yelling.

Shit.

All I wanted was to take Phil for a quick pee and roll into bed. It's been a long fucking week already and it's only Monday. Instead I find myself running to stop some suicidal chick from getting her head bashed in by a bunch of hoodlums.

By the time I get to her, she's on her knees beside the victim, a woman judging by the clothes. Her face and head are a mess.

"Call 9-1-1," I snap at the woman attending to her, without paying her too much attention. "And hang on to my dog."

I drop the leash and take off after the two attackers I see darting around the next corner. By the time I get there, all I see is a car starting up about halfway down the block. I just manage to pull my phone from my pocket and snap off a few shots as it peels away from the curb. I could only make out half the license plate—QLK—but hopefully I'll have a few images I can clean up.

Not much I can do on foot to catch what looked like an older model Corolla and sounded like it was souped-up, so I turn and start jogging back.

Phil is sitting on the sidewalk, looking at me as I approach, her tail wagging.

"Good girl," I mumble, before crouching down beside the foolish guardian angel tending to the victim. "Did you call?"

She reaches for the beanie covering her hair and as she swivels her head to look at me incredulously, her curls bounce free around her face.

A memorable face I've seen before a time or two.

"Hillary?"

CHAPTER 2

Radar

"YOU SAID YOU had pictures?"

One of the detectives, Crystal Bissette, draws my attention with her sharp tone. She and her partner, Manuel Garcia, showed up about fifteen minutes after the injured woman was whisked off in the ambulance. I don't think she likes me much. For the past eight months PASS—the security company I work for—has been involved in the 'cleanup' of the Grand Junction Police Department, at the behest of Chief of Police, Chris Underwood, after evidence of police corruption in the department was uncovered last year.

My eyes were on Hillary—who is being questioned by Garcia—almost exclusively. I know her as a friend of Rosie who is married to Hutch, one of my colleagues at PASS. She was first introduced to me at their wedding, and I've seen her at one or two gatherings, but we never actually talked. I'm not sure why, other than she's perhaps a little intimidating. Can't quite put my finger on it.

Almost immediately when I came running back, the ambulance and a police cruiser arrived at the scene and things were moving fast after that.

"Yes." I pull the pictures up my phone and hand it over. Bissette studies the screen closely.

"It does look like a Corolla," she confirms what I told her. "Can't really see the color, though."

"It's probably black, maybe a dark navy," I volunteer.

She hands me back my phone and a card.

"Email them to me?"

"Sure. Are you done with me?" My gaze is already drifting back to Hillary, her face mostly obscured by the curls gleaming where the glow from the streetlights hits them.

"You'll both need to come in tomorrow to look at some mug shots."

My eyes snap back to the detective.

"I told you I didn't really get a good look at them, mostly from behind."

"Yes, but you were still able to give descriptions of height, clothes, and footwear with great detail. You may recall more than you realize."

I'm not sure whether having me sit in a small room for hours, sifting through pictures of repeat offenders, is some petty revenge for the in-depth scrutiny we put everyone in the department through, but there's not much I can do about it. On the plus side, Hillary will have to do the same, so perhaps we can coordinate our efforts. Only makes sense, since we're apparently neighbors.

"Fine."

Garcia seems to be done with Hillary as we start walking their way. The two detectives step away—comparing notes, I'm sure—leaving Hillary and I standing on the sidewalk.

"That wasn't smart."

She slowly turns her head to look up at me and I notice her eyes are a dark brown, almost black. If they weren't currently shooting flames in my direction, making me doubt the wisdom of opening my mouth, I might've commented on their deep color.

Unfortunately I'm not smooth, and normally not particularly tuned in either—which is why I tend to stick to computer screens—but I have no trouble reading the indignation on her face.

"Excuse me?"

The sharp rise of her voice on the last syllable confirms it only took me three words to piss her off. *Nice going.*

Even as I start justifying my comment, I already know I'm only digging the hole deeper, but I can't seem to help myself.

"The smart thing to do would've been to call 9-1-1. Not running into a dangerous situation in the middle of the night, especially when you're outnumbered. They could've easily turned on you."

Her eyes narrow and her head tilts slightly to the side, like she's looking at something particularly distasteful. I snap my mouth shut but the damage is already done.

"It's Radar, right?" I nod affirmatively. "Well, Radar, if you think I'm gonna stand by and let a couple of punks beat a woman to death with a baseball bat, you're out of your mind. I'm an ER nurse, I work at a homeless shelter, you think I sit and crochet doilies all day? *Puleeze*, spare me your chest-pounding, sexist, alpha bullshit. I've got no time for that."

She waves a dismissive hand, turns on her heel, and starts walking toward the apartment building. I glance over at the detectives, who obviously heard me being told off—Garcia shooting me a sympathetic shrug—before I quickly stalk after her. Phil struggles to keep up with me on her short legs.

"Go away, Radar. I've had a long fucking day and I need some sleep," she fires off, without turning when she hears me close in.

"Just walking you to your door."

I fall into step beside her, catching the roll of her eyes.

"I've managed to find it by myself for years now," she snarks.

If she thinks her attitude is any kind of deterrent, she's dead wrong. I grin as I climb up the stairs and walk right up to the door behind her. Normally, I don't care about my neighborhood or who lives next door, but I can't deny discovering Hillary is right around the corner in the same apartment complex is a perk I didn't expect.

"You can go home now." With her key in the lock,

she turns to look at me before glancing down at Phil, who dropped down at my feet. "Is he okay?"

"She's fine. A little dramatic because she doesn't like her evening walks," I explain. "She'd rather be in bed. She's a morning girl."

"I see." If I'm not mistaken, that's a smile tugging at the corner of her mouth. "I thought she was a boy with that name. Not exactly the kind of dog I'd have picked for you."

"Me neither." I look down at my feet where Phil's head is now resting on my boot, her eyes blinking up at me. "More like she picked me. As for her name, it's Philomena, and no, I didn't choose that either. She came with it. She's a rescue."

Hillary bends down to pet Phil when the little hussy rolls to her side right away, flutters her ridiculously long eyelashes, and offers herself for a belly scratch.

When Hillary glances at me, this time it's with a hint of a smile that immediately turns into a jaw-breaking yawn.

"Sorry," she mumbles behind the hand she slammed over her mouth.

"You should get some rest," I prompt her. "What time should I pick you up tomorrow?"

"Sorry? Pick me up?" She's about to open her door when she swings back around.

"Mug shots at the police station. Didn't they ask you to come in?"

"Well, yeah, but…I can get myself there. I have a shift in the morning first."

"So what time is good?" I persist.

"The police station is a couple of blocks from the shelter," she starts. "I'll stop in on my way home. It would be ridiculous for you to go out of your way."

She's going to think I'm some weird stalker if I push any more, so I let it drop, but not before I share, "Not exactly out of my way, since it appears we're neighbors."

Without waiting for a response, I bend down, scoop my lazy dog under one arm, and head down the stairs.

I cross the parking lot to my side of the complex, and am about to head up the stairway to my place, when I turn to glance back and see her outlined in the window of her apartment, watching me.

Hillary

"Hey, Hillary."

Brad, our resident cook, is carrying a tray of muffins into the dining room as I'm fixing myself another coffee.

A disabled veteran, Brad had a hard time adjusting to civilian life and ended up on the streets. He was one of the shelter's first residents when Rosie opened the doors last year, and as I'm told, almost immediately took over the kitchen.

He's now officially on staff and a good cook, feeding every hungry mouth; something he says makes him feel useful.

"Banana walnut muffins?" I ask, sniffing the air.

"Last time I checked."

I ignore his snippy response—he prefers the solitude of the kitchen to dealing with people—and smile at him, snagging a muffin to go with my coffee.

I walk back to my office and sit at my desk, groaning when the flavors of my first bite hit my taste buds. It's the first thing I'm putting in my stomach, aside from the gallon of coffee I've already consumed today. The need for caffeine is high, since I didn't hit my bed until about quarter to four this morning. I almost flung my alarm through the window when it went off just two and a half hours later, after a restless sleep.

That poor woman's face; even with all I've encountered in my years in the ER I've never seen that kind of damage on someone who was still breathing. Hell, she even tried to talk through the mangled mess of tissue and bone. I wasn't really sure what she said, like I told the police, but it sounded like *school*, which made no sense under the circumstances.

Unfortunately, when I called the hospital this morning to check in on her I was told she didn't make it through the night. My heart feels heavy as I keep going over what more I could've done. Not the first time that's happened, and I'm sure it won't be the last. Another challenge that comes with the job.

I'm just finishing up the last report of the day when Rosie walks into my office and sits down.

"What the hell happened?"

"What do you mean?"

She leans forward and wags a finger in my face. All five foot nothing of her. I'm not a giant by far, but

I feel like one next to my friend.

"I can't believe you didn't say anything this morning and I had to hear it from Jake."

Ah. My new neighbor, the one I was caught watching last night, must've been flapping his mouth.

"Radar," I conclude out loud.

"Whatever," she dismisses. "Are you nuts? Throwing yourself into a dangerous situation like that? You could've gotten hurt."

"I didn't. I'm fine."

"But you could've," she insists, and I can see the concern on her face.

Great, now I feel guilty.

"I'm fine," I repeat. "And you know you would've done the same thing. Not that it matters," I add dejectedly. "The poor woman didn't make it."

"I heard." Her tone is instantly sympathetic. "Jake mentioned she lived in the building across the street? A teacher?"

For a second I wonder where the hell he got that information, then I remember what he does for a living.

"I didn't know who she was," I admit. I don't tell Rosie; even had I known the woman beforehand, the likelihood of me recognizing her would've been slim to none. But now I know she was a teacher, the word she uttered makes a little more sense. Which reminds me I should get to the station and meet up with Detective Garcia.

"I should get going." I get up and shrug into my

coat, slipping my purse over my shoulder.

"Are you sure you're still able to babysit Thursday?"

"Off course," I assure her. "Been looking forward to having that little angel to myself for the night."

Thursday is a day off for me and I can't think of a better way to spend it than with Tessa. Rosie and Jake need a little break and I don't have to go into work until Friday afternoon.

DETECTIVE GARCIA LOOKS up when I'm shown to his desk.

"Ms. Glenwood, thanks for coming in. I just have a statement for you to sign, and then I'll take you to a quiet room so you can look at some pictures."

"Before we get to that, I assume you've heard the victim didn't make it?" When he pulls his eyebrows into a frown I quickly add, "I'm an ER nurse, remember? I checked in this morning and was told she passed away."

"Yes. Unfortunately Sandra Elliot died."

"And she was a teacher."

He registers surprise. "Yes, she was."

"Right, and last night I mentioned to you she mumbled 'school.'"

"You said it sounded like it might have been 'school,'" he corrects me. "Are you telling me you're sure now?"

"It makes sense now, it didn't last night because I had no idea who she was. Had I known she was a teacher at the time, I wouldn't have doubted it was what I heard."

"I guess that's reasonable." He shoves a document across his desk. "If you want to make that adjustment on your statement, go ahead, but please initial it."

After I read and sign, he leads me into a small room with a computer on a table and two chairs. There, for the next hour and a half, I flip through grainy images until my eyes get blurry from the intense staring at the screen, without recognizing anyone.

"I'm sorry, I wish I could've been more helpful," I tell Garcia when he walks me to the lobby.

"Not to worry, this is usually a long shot anyway." He pushes open the door. "You have my card, please contact me if you think of anything else."

"Of course."

I have to admit I'm a little disappointed. It would've been nice to point my finger at a picture of those animals, but I guess it's not that simple.

A dark gray truck pulls into the parking lot just as I slip behind the wheel. The only reason I notice is because of the tall man behind the wheel. I recognize the glasses and longish hair escaping the dark beanie and flopping over his forehead.

For a moment I consider getting out to say hello, but instead I end up ducking low, pretending to look for something in my purse.

Tempting, but too close on all fronts.

CHAPTER 3

RADAR

"I'LL STOP BY Home Depot on my way."

"Faucet in the kitchen's leaking as well."

"I'll have a look at that tomorrow night as well, okay, Dad?"

My father is quiet on the other end, probably looking around his six-hundred-and-twenty-square-foot mobile home to see what else needs fixing. There's a lot, the place has been falling apart around him.

I grew up in Montrose, where my dad did thirty years with the police force before retiring at fifty-five. He and my mother got a few good years of traveling in when she was diagnosed with breast cancer, and in a matter of eighteen months she was gone. That was thirteen years ago.

Dad couldn't bear to stay in the house they'd lived in most of their married life and sold it, buying a mobile home instead. Big enough for him, he'd claimed at the time. For years he'd been able to manage the upkeep by himself and until recently he refused any help, despite his arthritis slowing him down.

I'm heading down there this weekend to start on some repairs. Apparently the winter hasn't been kind on the roof and he has a few leaks. I'm not exactly a handyman—my brother, Hugh, fits those shoes—but I can find anything I need to know on Google or YouTube.

"Meeting in five." Yanis, my boss, sticks his head around the door of my office. I give him a thumbs-up.

"Dad, I gotta get ready for this meeting, but if you think of anything else, just gimme a call, okay?"

"Bring some donuts," he grumbles. "None of that fancy stuff, though. Don't care for the sprinkles."

I grin because he tells me the same thing every time. I always bring him donuts, and except for that one time, years ago, when I thought I'd broaden his horizon with a fancy assortment, they're always the regular ones.

"Gotcha, Dad. Gotta go. See you tomorrow."

By the time I have my notes and laptop gathered for the meeting, I'm the last one to walk into the conference room.

"Sorry," I mumble, as I take a seat beside Bree Graves, our only female team member.

The only one missing is Shep Kirwin, who is somewhere in South America providing security for a corporate executive. Shep and Kai Olson have taken over a lot of the international travel assignments since joining PASS full time last year. The rest of us—Jake

Hutchinson, Yanis Mazur, and his brother, Dimas, Bree, and myself—tend to stay closer to home.

Plenty of work right here in Colorado with a pretty full roster of steady clients, which is why we have these meetings twice a week. In part to brief on the ongoing jobs, but also to discuss possible new projects.

"Where are we on the GJPD report?" Yanis starts, referring to our in-depth investigation of the local police department. "The chief is expecting to see something on his desk on Monday."

"I'll have mine ready before the weekend," I promise.

"Bree? What about the psychological profiles?"

"About done," she answers him, without looking up.

I've been responsible for digging into backgrounds, looking at financials for any irregularities, and flagging anything that looked off. Bree would draw up a profile based on employment records and the info I provided, and Jake and Dimas would take on the investigation and sometimes surveillance of those officers.

We uncovered sixteen of the hundred and thirteen sworn officers who looked to be engaged in some criminal activity or another. A little over fourteen percent of the entire department. That's pretty substantial for a relatively small force. Add to that the nine civilian employees who fit those same criteria, and you have a problem on your hands. Or at least,

Chief of Police Chris Underwood does.

In order for him to use the information we uncovered to clean up his department, we have to make sure every piece of evidence is substantiated in our report for each of the names on that list.

Arguably the least favorite part of any project for any of us is the writing of reports, but Yanis insists on it.

"Mine is ready, I'm just waiting on Hutch for his part," Dimas announces, and all eyes at the table turn to Jake who throws up his hands.

"Hey, you'll have mine on your desk sometime this weekend."

"Famous last words," Dimas mumbles, earning him a sharp elbow in the ribs from his best friend.

"Just you wait until you're up at all hours with a teething baby," Jake throws back at Dimas who grins, having succeeded in rattling Jake's cage. "If I had eight hours of sleep this entire week I'd be surprised."

"Maybe you guys need a break?" Bree suggests carefully.

"We do. We're going out for dinner, a movie, and we'll hopefully get some sleep tonight."

"Where's Tessa gonna be?"

"Rosie's friend, Hillary." My ears perk up at the mention of her name. "She offered to keep her overnight. Nothing fazes that woman, not even a screaming baby," Jake adds.

We move on to new business, but my mind isn't in it. A few times Yanis has to call my name when I'm not paying attention.

"What's the matter with you?" Bree asks, following me into my office after the meeting.

"Me? Nothing."

Unfortunately Bree is like a human lie detector and narrows her eyes on me.

"You lie for shit."

I drop down in my chair and lean back.

"Fine. It's that attack outside my building," I give her part of the truth. "I can't leave it alone. The cops aren't in a sharing mood, and I can't find anything on that license plate when I started digging. I'm starting to wonder if I saw it wrong."

"They don't have any suspects yet?"

"None they're sharing with me."

"Yeah, tell me about it. We're persona non grata with the GJPD for the time being." Bree sighs and I know she's had her own issues with the department. She's the one who maintains contact with law enforcement, and I can't imagine these past months have been easy. "Are you sure of what you saw?"

"Positive. QLK. You can even see it on one of the pictures, although the last three digits are not quite clear. I'm pretty sure the first one is a six, then a three or maybe a five, and a one."

"Show me."

She rounds my desk and looks over my shoulder as I pull up the image I've been trying to clean up.

"See? QLK."

She leans closer and squints her eyes at the screen.

"Is that the original?"

"No, I've been working on this one. Sharpened the edges."

"Can I see the original?"

I pull up the second one and display them side by side.

"See this?" She grabs a pen and points at the tail of the Q. "That's dirt. See how gritty and uneven it is compared to the rest? You're looking at an O."

For fuck's sake.

She's right. I can't unsee it now and yet when I look at the second image I cleaned up, it's clearly a Q. Or maybe I turned it into one because that's what I believed.

"Not all is as it seems, even when you're staring right at it," Bree says sagely before walking out of my office.

An hour and a half later I send off a list with three possible license plates, along with their respective DMV registrations, to Detective Bissette.

I don't hear anything back.

Assholes.

HILLARY

I SLEPT IN this morning.

Don't know how long it's been since I've vegged in bed until eleven, but I did this morning. It was necessary.

Talk about the week from hell. One thing after another, and all of it messing with my sleep. To top it all off, Karla decided to flex her muscles again last night. I'd been tending to a five-year-old with seizures, who'd been brought in by his frantic mother, when she sent in another nurse to take over because I was needed elsewhere.

A homeless guy had come in with diabetic sores on his feet and lower legs that had been horribly neglected, and Karla insisted I look after him since working at the shelter I should be 'used to the stench.'

It wasn't the first time she played that card. In fact, I'm pretty sure I've been looking after the homeless people coming in on our shift since I started at the South Avenue Shelter. Don't get me wrong, I don't mind—there are far worse things than a bit of dirt and body odor—but I don't appreciate being pulled away when I'm helping other patients to do it.

I'm getting tired of it and I went home last night thinking maybe I should see if I can get on another shift. Unfortunately, that would mess with my routine at the shelter. Still, her constant poking at me is starting to take its toll, so I needed those extra hours of rest this morning.

As a result, I didn't get the jerk pork I had planned for today going on time—I like to have it simmering all day—so I had to run to the store before Tessa is dropped off for something quick and easy to throw together.

I try to eat healthy when I have time to cook, especially when you end up at the hospital cafeteria three nights a week. Today I have no idea what to make, though. I'm standing in the middle of the produce section, finding not a single iota of inspiration. *Damn*, I'd really been looking forward to that pulled pork.

I watch a woman grab a premixed salad from the cooler at the end. That would be easiest, I guess. Maybe I can cook some fish to go with it.

My basket is pathetic when I step up to the checkout. A bag of baby greens, a can of tuna—because I couldn't decide on what fish to buy—half a loaf of bread, a jar of peanut butter, and a tub of mint chocolate chip ice cream. My guilty indulgence. I feel a binge coming on.

I shove the first spoonful in my mouth about an hour after Jake and Rosie dropped Tessa off. Poor thing has been loudly unhappy ever since. Rosie had warned me beforehand she was fussy because she's teething.

"Hush, little one," I placate her with a mouthful of mint chocolate chip as I bounce her on my arm. My entire shoulder is soaked in tears and drool.

With my free hand I shove the tub back in the freezer when I spot the reason I opened it in the first place. A teething ring Rosie put in there before she left. I hope to God it's cold enough.

Tessa clamps her gums on the cold surface and immediately stops crying, when a knock sounds at the door. Shit, I hope it's not one of my neighbors complaining about the noise.

"What are you doing here?"

I'm surprised to find Radar on my doorstep

carrying a six-pack of beer and a large pizza, which smells amazing.

"I come bearing sustenance," he says, squeezing past me through the door.

I open my mouth to protest the invasion, but words get stuck in my throat when he bends his head down. I'm not sure what I was expecting, but he ends up kissing the top of Tessa's head.

"I'm surprised she's quiet," he says, moving directly to my kitchen where he drops the box on the counter. "Jake says he hasn't slept in days." He opens the fridge door and shoves the six-pack inside before he turns around and sees me staring. "Sorry, did you want a brewski now?"

He's about to dive back into the fridge when I repeat, "What are you doing here?"

That seems to startle him.

"Oh, well Jake mentioned you were looking after Tessa. I figured you'd have your hands full, so I brought dinner. And beer. And an extra pair of hands so you can eat." He lifts his and wiggles his fingers.

I'm not sure what to say to that. It's terribly invasive and presumptuous, but at the same time awkwardly thoughtful and kind of sweet.

"That's…nice of you."

He shrugs. "Not really. I'm a bit of a health nut and this gave me a valid excuse to skip cooking and eat pizza."

The admission makes him even more appealing. He lifts the lid of the box and suddenly freezes, looking at me with such abject panic on his face I almost laugh out loud.

"What?"

"Please tell me you're not a vegetarian, because I got an extra large meat lovers."

I let the laugh escape and Tessa suddenly tilts her head back to stare at me, her bite ring momentarily forgotten.

"Meat lovers pizza is my favorite."

That earns me a grin.

"Perfect. Hand me that little terrorist and grab yourself a beer and a slice. You can eat first."

I'm surprised at his confidence as he takes the baby from me.

"You've done this before?" I ask, pulling a few plates from the cupboard and grabbing some paper towels.

"My brother's brood. He's got two boys I used to babysit before he took his family to Alaska."

"Wow. That's a ways from Colorado."

I grab a couple of beers from the fridge and hold one up for him. He nods and answers me as I set a bottle in front of him.

"Yeah, it is, but it was always a dream of his. Three years ago Hugh was offered a job as a project manager, working on the construction of a new hotel outside of Anchorage. He's a civil engineer. Leslie, his wife, was willing, and since his boys were only two and four at the time, they figured the timing was perfect."

"You must miss them."

He shrugs, bouncing a little when Tessa starts fussing.

"We FaceTime. They fly down for Christmas. It's all good."

I load two slices on my plate and take a bite of one.

"Oh my God. This is so good," I mumble with my mouth full and catch him smiling at me. "What?"

"You didn't think I'd show up with just any pizza, did you?"

He turns to the travel crib Jake had carried in, and I'm about to warn him I tried putting her down earlier with little luck, but when he lays her down I see she's fast asleep, the teething ring still clutched in her little fist.

CHAPTER 4

RADAR

"JUST A QUICK ONE around the block, Phil."

She looks at me with those woeful eyes, when I clip on her leash, and waddles reluctantly outside when I open the door.

Of course the dog had been fast asleep when I walked in after sharing pizza and a beer with Hillary. I made sure not to overstay my welcome, in particular since I basically invited myself in. Had I given her an inch, I'm almost positive she would've turned me away.

Previously she'd come across as so self-assured, in control—aloof, even—but she wasn't any of those tonight. Babies can be disarming like that, unintentionally stripping away the layers until the person underneath the veneer is exposed. I learned that much from my nephews, who had been able to wash off the thick grief covering my father with their mere presence.

Maybe that's why I picked up the pizza and beer,

to see for myself if that would be true for Hillary. I'm glad I did. Seeing her slightly rattled made her more human, more approachable.

There were no in-depth conversations, mostly small talk, but we did briefly discuss Monday night's events. She'd heard from one of the neighbors there would be a vigil held for Sandra Elliot Saturday night outside the building and she planned to attend. I mentioned I wouldn't be able to since I'm going to be in Montrose, helping my dad.

Phil picks a spot on the grass of the berm to do her business, and I quickly get rid of the evidence before turning her back to the apartment. I'm eager to get to my computer.

I managed to finish up my portion of the report for the police chief this afternoon, but I'd like to do a little more digging of my own on those license plates. I have a feeling the detectives on the case are not inclined to share their findings with me, and I'd like to get started tonight.

The dog curls up on the couch again as soon as we get home. I grab a beer from the fridge, walk into my office, and boot up my computer. Both my laptop and desk unit are hooked into the PASS network, so it's easy to access the information I pulled up earlier.

The first DMV record I open is for an eighty-four-year-old woman, Candace Miller, who lives in a seniors' community just a few blocks from here. The car is a 1998 dark green Corolla. I'm pretty sure the car wasn't green, but I know how colors can sometimes get distorted under streetlights. I know for a fact it wasn't a woman her age running away, but it's possible someone else was driving her car. Maybe a grandchild?

With a little digging I discover Ms. Miller, a retired pharmacist, has no living relatives. No siblings, no kids, and no grandkids. Doesn't mean she doesn't know anyone she may have lent her car to, but there's no way for me to find that out right now. I close that one and pull up the next file.

This one is for a black, 2016 vehicle, owned by one Karl Manheim. He turns out to be a forty-seven-year-old tow truck driver with an address in Clifton, on the east side of town. The car is a newer model Corolla than I thought, but when I discover he's a widowed father of two teenage girls, fifteen and seventeen, I dig a little deeper anyway.

I quickly jot down their names and start scanning social media. Both girls look to have Facebook accounts, and both appear to be students at Central High School. I open a new tab and look at the school's staff roster, but unfortunately Sandra Elliot's name is not on there.

Remembering the two dark figures running ahead of me, I had the impression they were male, but I could be wrong. It's worth looking into, though.

The last file I flagged is for a 2004, graphite gray Toyota. It's one of three vehicles owned by Bernard Briscoe, a name I recognize as a city council member. He's also the owner of a catering company servicing

Grand Junction Regional Airport. Aside from the Toyota, he owns a Porsche Cayenne and a Lexus IS 350. The old Corolla must stand out like a sore thumb in the driveway of his mansion near the Redlands Golf Course.

Interesting.

It looks like Briscoe married a woman by the name of Ingrid Loman ten years ago and his new wife came with a son.

Twenty minutes later I call Bree.

"Do you know what time it is?"

I glance at the clock indicating it's after midnight. *Shit.* I was too excited to check before I dialed.

"Sorry."

"Where's the fire?"

"I need a favor."

"Now?" She doesn't sound too pleased.

I swallow the urge to say yes. Given the hour it's unlikely anything will be done with the information before tomorrow anyway.

"I guess tomorrow morning will do," I concede. "I found the car."

"What car?"

"The one involved in the attack on that teacher. I've been doing a bit of digging and I'm sure we're looking for Jeremy Loman. He's sixteen and attends The Christian Academy, a private school where Sandra Elliot was a teacher."

"No shit?" She definitely sounds more alert now.

"You'll never guess who his stepfather is…"

"I give up."

"Bernard Briscoe."

"The councilman?"

"That would be him," I confirm.

It's quiet for a few beats on the other side.

"How are you sure it's him?" she finally asks.

"Because I scoured the kid's social media and found pretty damning evidence."

"Like what?"

"Like a picture of him holding a bloody baseball bat. I'm pretty sure he's one of the kids I saw."

"You're shitting me. Have you called this in?"

"No. That's where you come in. I'll send it to the detectives on the case, but I don't think I'm a fan favorite with either of them, seeing as they haven't even acknowledged the initial information I sent them. This is gonna cause ripples, and I think Chris Underwood should be informed."

"And you want me to do that."

"You *are* our law enforcement liaison."

I grin when I hear her growl.

"Can't call the man out of bed, but I'll get hold of him first thing in the morning."

"You're a treasure, Bree."

"Whatever. Can I get back to sleep now?"

"Sure thing. Sweet dreams."

I hang up, put all the information in an email, and shoot it off to Bissette. Then I turn off the lights and head to bed.

Tomorrow morning I'll stop by Hillary's place to

give her a heads-up.

HILLARY

"DID YOU SLEEP?"

I glare at the far too handsome, freshly showered man on my doorstep. I'd be tempted to slam the door in his face if not for the extra steaming takeout cup he's holding out. After a restless night with only a couple of hours of sleep, it's not a good day to find out your coffee tin is empty.

I snag the offered cup from his hand and take a gulp, burning my mouth and trying to ignore the smirk on his face. None too graciously I leave the door open as an invitation for him to follow me inside. I hear it close and Radar tails me into the kitchen.

"I'm taking that as a no."

Poor Tessa only managed to nap for thirty minutes or so at a time before she'd wake up crying again, until she finally crashed at four this morning and she's been asleep ever since. I almost cried myself when my internal alarm woke me a little after six. I tried falling back to sleep, but instead I ended up listening to Tessa's breathing from the travel crib I'd set up beside my bed until the doorbell rang.

"Tough night," I mumble with my lips already pursed for my next hit of coffee.

At that moment a familiar angry squeal sounds from the bedroom, followed by hearty crying, and I groan. I'd hoped to grab a shower so I could feel a bit more human before she announced herself, but I guess it'll have to wait until after Rosie picks her up.

With a deep sigh I set my cup on the counter and start walking toward the small hallway leading to my bedroom, when a hand lands on my shoulder.

"Finish your coffee," Radar says behind me. "I can get her."

He doesn't wait for my answer and brushes past me into the bedroom. I should probably object to him invading my space or something, but I just don't have the energy. The feeling of relief is quickly doused by a wave of guilt as I return to the kitchen and grab my cup.

I love that baby to death, but I have to admit there was a time or two last night when I wanted to bang my head against a wall. My lack of sleep is showing when I managed to be annoyed at the fact there hasn't been a peep from her since Radar walked into my bedroom.

Grabbing a bottle from the fridge for her, I drop it in the warmer Rosie brought over. Then I pop a few slices of bread in the toaster. I turn when I hear Radar walk in.

It should be illegal for someone to look that good this early in the morning. His dirty blond hair is still wet and curling at the ends where it hits the collar of his shirt. Despite his tall, lanky frame, the shirt he's wearing stretches enticingly over his surprisingly muscled shoulders and biceps. Thick veins curling around his arms suggest more strength than you might've given him credit for at first sight. Not as much of a nerdy geek as he might appear. Even the brown eyes behind the heavy frame of his glasses are beautiful on closer inspection.

I'm suddenly aware of my own rumpled state and tug the threadbare robe closed with one hand, while the other reaches for what I'm sure is an unruly mop of hair.

"Did you find everything okay?" I try for a friendlier tone than I greeted him with and am rewarded with a mesmerizing grin. The ping of my toaster provides a good distraction and I busy myself slathering on jelly.

"Yup," he says from close behind me.

His long arm stretches around me to pluck Tessa's bottle from the warmer, and I try not to shiver at his proximity.

Get a grip.

Shoving a bite of toast in my mouth, I turn around to see him casually perched with a hip against the counter, Tessa in the crook of one arm reaching eagerly for the bottle he's holding up for her.

"Have you eaten?" I ask, belatedly reminded of my manners.

"I have. I'm sorry for barging in so early," he continues. "But I wanted to talk to you before I head off to work."

"About what?"

I pull out a stool and sit on the other side of the counter with my toast and coffee.

"I was looking into some stuff last night when I got home." He one-handedly manages baby and bottle, while pulling a phone from his pocket. It takes him a minute to find what he's looking for before he holds up a Facebook page for me. "Do you know him?"

He hands me the phone and I look at a picture of a kid, an older teen, flipping the bird at the camera obscuring part of his face.

"Who am I looking at?"

"Check out his latest post, see if you recognize him in the photo?" He answers with another question.

I scroll down until I see the same kid wearing a black hoodie pulled over his head, brandishing a baseball bat in his hands. Even without the blood caking the wood of the bat, I would've known who he is.

"How did you find him?"

Scrolling back up I look at the name; Jeremy Loman. The name doesn't ring any bells.

"Partial license plate. I left a message for the detectives, so I hope they'll be in touch at some point, but I wanted to make sure you're aware."

I study him with unveiled curiosity. Interesting that he's taken it upon himself to investigate, and even more so that he feels the need to warn me.

"Why?" I regret my question the moment it leaves my mouth, because it clearly makes Radar uncomfortable, unless it was my close scrutiny that put the blush on his face. "I mean, it's awesome you were able to find him, but why the warning?"

He shrugs. "Figured you should know, that's all. The cops have to conduct an investigation by the book and God knows how long that can take. Didn't want you to walk around without knowing who to steer clear of."

It didn't really cross my mind that I could be a target of any kind, but I guess it's possible. He's just being cautious, and to be honest, kind of sweet.

"I appreciate it. Sorry if I was a bear," I apologize quickly. "Lack of sleep will do that to me." I glance at the calm baby snuggled in the crook of his arm. *Now* she's quiet, the little traitor.

"I have a little time, why don't you grab a quick shower? It'll make you feel better."

I smile my gratitude, because that too was thoughtful of him.

"It's okay, I can wait until Rosie picks her up. I don't have to work until two."

"What time is she picking her up?"

"Rosie said she'd be by after nine."

"It's barely seven thirty now. I can handle this little troublemaker for a bit. Go on," he urges me.

The truth is, a shower will make me feel better. Decision made, I shove the last piece of toast in my mouth, nod at Radar, and dart toward my bedroom.

I take a little longer than anticipated, determined to wrangle my hair into submission, and when I step out of the bedroom, I'm surprised to hear more than one voice from the living room.

"You're early," I tell Rosie when I see her sitting on my couch, a sleeping Tessa on her shoulder.

Rosie swings her head around at my voice, a smile

on her face.

"Missed my little peanut."

"Did you guys have a good time last night?" I ask, my eyes drifting to Radar, who is perched stiffly on the armrest of my wing chair.

"The best," Rosie says, as Radar gets to his feet.

"I should get going."

"Yeah, of course," I mumble, feeling a little awkward with my friend's curious eyes darting between us. I'm not sure what she's thinking, finding me in the shower with Radar looking after her child at this hour of the morning, but I can see the wheels in her head spinning. "I'll walk you out."

I can feel her eyes burning on my back as I follow Radar to the front door.

"Thanks," I tell him as he steps outside. "For the coffee, for the heads-up, and for the shower," I ramble.

He turns around, grinning, as he taps his index finger on the tip of my nose.

"Any time."

The simple touch makes my knees weak and I grab on to the doorpost when he turns away. I watch him walk toward the stairwell, his gait limber and confident, and try not to stare to hard at the flex of that tight ass.

Trouble

CHAPTER 5

RADAR

"YOU HEADING OUT?"

Yanis sticks his head in the door, just as I'm packing my laptop in my backpack.

"About to."

"Big plans for the weekend?"

I look up. Yanis isn't one for idle chitchat so the question is out of character.

"Heading down to Montrose, helping my dad with some repairs. Why?"

"Got a call from Underwood. They picked up that kid you told them about."

By the time I got in this morning, Bree had already put in a call to the chief of police. I never got a response from either Garcia or Bissette to the email I sent, so I figured they had things in hand and focused on other work I had waiting.

"Oh yeah? Good."

"His father walked in ten minutes later with his lawyer, so they're not getting much. They've been trying to get more info from the kid's social media accounts but apparently those were deactivated this afternoon. Underwood is asking if there's any way you'd be able to still access those."

I straighten up and face my boss.

"It's technically possible. Deactivated accounts are just hidden, not removed. A warrant should be enough to get access." Yanis raises one eyebrow. "You want me hack into them?"

"Underwood does. Briscoe and his lawyer have already made it difficult for the GJPD to get a search warrant for the house and car."

It's tricky. In fact, it's unlikely you'll be able to get in and out without being detected, which could bring a whole different set of issues. Unlikely, but not impossible.

"Does he realize that even if I could get in, none of what I uncover can be used as evidence?"

"Course he does. He's confident he'll get the warrant signed eventually, but he's in a hurry to get something to work with before he has to let the kid go."

I guess I could have a look tonight; Dad goes to bed early. I share as much with Yanis.

"Want me to shoot it straight to him should I find anything?"

He shakes his head. "Send it to me, I'll find a way to get it to him discreetly."

Discreetly is a better word than covertly, I guess. It doesn't escape me that this is, at the very least, an unusual request by a chief of police who just spent the past almost year trying to clean up his department. I swing my pack over my shoulder and turn off my desk light.

"You recognize the irony here, right?" I challenge my boss, who grins in response.

"Sure, but there's a difference between breaking the law for personal gain, or bending the rules for justice."

Now it's my turn to grin and shake my head. I've done both breaking and bending, but then I'm not in a public post.

"I'll be in touch," I say as I step out of my office, closing the door behind me.

"Have a good weekend."

Yanis claps me on the back and disappears into his own office. I lift my hand to Bree and Dimas, who look up when I pass, and tell Lena—our office manager—I'll see her Monday, on my way out the door.

I swing by my apartment to pick up my bag, my tools, and my dog, make a quick stop at the hardware store to get a few supplies, and am on the road by five.

"ANOTHER BEER, SON?"

Dad pushes himself out of the chair.

He'd waited for me with dinner, even though he always eats early, and insisted he take me out for a good steak. Of course we had our customary argument over the bill, but I let him win this one. It was already close to eight when we got back to the trailer. Despite the cool weather, we've been sitting outside on his minuscule deck, prioritizing the work that needs doing.

"I'll pass, Dad."

The roof is at the top of the list. No use doing anything else unless the trailer is waterproof, which is currently not the case, judging by the water stains on the ceiling. I hope it's something I can fix, or else I'll have to get a contractor.

I watch my father shuffle his way inside; a little concerned he seems to have slowed down even more. He doesn't like it when I ask about his health—gets his back up easily—but I'm going to poke the bear.

"When's the last time you saw Doc Childs?" I ask when he walks out, a fresh bottle in his hand. He glares at me, but I don't back off. "Looks like you're hurting."

"I'm fine," he grumbles, lowering himself in the chair. He stares straight ahead, takes a deep tug on his beer, inhales deeply, and finally turns his eyes on me. "Last week. Body's going to shit."

"How so?"

"Got the gout." He rubs a hand down his lower leg while taking another drink from the bottle.

"Hate to say it, Dad, but drinking beer doesn't help."

I imagine it's not easy for a man like my dad—

who's always been strong and active—to be forced to slow down in any way.

"That's what that quack said. Gave me a list of stuff to avoid. Bunch of bullhicky."

"Childs is hardly a quack and you know it." I get a grunt in response. "Did he prescribe something?"

He huffs. "More pills. Bathroom is starting to look like a damn pharmacy."

"Maybe lay off the beer for a bit, give them a chance to work," I suggest carefully.

"Fucking hate getting old. Each time I visit the damn doctor, another little pleasure is taken. Can't work with my hands no more, can't eat the good stuff 'cause I gotta watch the cholesterol, and now I've gotta give up my beer." To underline his displeasure, he tosses the remainder of his bottle back and moves to get up again.

"Where are you off to?"

"Bed. I'm tired," he grunts, moving to the door.

I feel bad. Dad is only seventy-three, retired from the force eighteen years ago with great hopes of enjoying the rest of his life. Then Mom died just five years into his retirement and his life has never been the same.

I lift my feet off the railing and follow my father inside, catching him on his way to the bathroom.

"When you've got this thing licked, and the weather gets a little warmer, why don't you and I take off into the mountains for a weekend? Get some fishing in. Haven't done that in a while."

His bleary eyes turn to me. He looks old and I make a mental note to give my brother a call as soon as Dad's in bed.

"Sure," he says with a sad smile that makes me feel guilty.

Life gets so damn busy; I tend to forget time is running out on some things.

"Then that's what we'll do. Maybe I can convince Hugh to join us?"

He nods. "That'd be good. Night, Son."

"Night, Dad. Love you."

"Back atcha, kid," he mutters, as he slips into the bathroom and closes the door.

HILLARY

I'VE BEEN DEALING with a difficult resident this morning.

The man was found by the back door of a convenience store, bleeding from a cut to his head and his face bruised and swollen, but he wouldn't let EMTs come close. Instead he insisted he be brought here.

I patched him up with a couple of stitches and an ice pack for his face, but he won't tell me what happened and even at my urging, he refuses to get checked out at the hospital. I'm worried he has a concussion or worse.

"I just want to make sure you didn't crack your skull, Jeff," I push. "You could have a bleed we can't see, your brain could be swelling and we wouldn't know it until it's too late."

"I'm fine," he grumbles.

"How long were you out there?" I try a different tactic to get some answers. I checked the log and noted he hadn't signed in last night, as all residents are required to do, which means he'd been gone all night.

He shrugs. "Couple of hours, I guess."

I wonder if perhaps he couldn't remember, which might indicate he'd been out at least for some time.

"Were you on your way here when it happened?"

A deep groove appears between his eyebrows as he tries to remember. Could be he was too drunk last night, judging by the alcohol fumes still coming from his pores. There is a strict no alcohol policy at the shelter, but that doesn't mean the guys don't drink while they're out on the streets. Not much we can do about that.

Many of our residents use the shelter for a roof over their heads and a sure meal, but like to maintain their freedom during the day. They know they have to be in by eleven at night, or they'll find the doors locked, and if they don't show up more than one night they could lose their bed.

"Must'a been."

It's like pulling teeth.

"They hit you from behind?"

It's a wild guess, but one that pays off when his eyes—bloodshot but sharp—flash to me.

"Damn cowards," he grinds out between clenched

teeth. "Punks. Still got one of them. Came at me with brass knuckles and I broke his damn arm."

Pride. It doesn't matter what their life circumstances are, most of these veterans still have pride.

The brass knuckles have me concerned; it implies intent.

"I think you should make a report to—"

"No cops," he repeats what he told me earlier, as he gets to his feet.

Also not a surprise, these men have a healthy distrust for law enforcement and in some cases with reason.

"I can't force you, Jeff, you know that. However, if there is a group of punks, as you call them, out there targeting people—"

"They were punks," he interrupts me as he walks to the door and opens it. "Kids. More than one. But I still ain't talking to the cops." Then he disappears into the hallway.

I go over the conversation in my head while I clean up the medical supplies, but it's not until I sit down to write up a report something jumps out at me.

He mentioned breaking the arm of one of his attackers.

We had a pretty busy shift last night—four victims of a car accident brought in at the same time—but I recall the patient with his arm in a homemade sling I'd led to a cubicle before the end of my shift. He was brought in by his mother, who claimed he'd fallen out of bed. The boy himself had been tight-lipped. I took a quick glance at his forearm and could tell from the distinct deformation he'd need ortho. I put a call in for the surgeon before I left for the night.

It would be a long shot, but I can't help wondering whether the kid really fell out of bed. That's something you see with younger children, but not with big, hefty teenagers.

On a whim, I pick up the phone and dial the direct line for the emergency room. A familiar voice answers.

"Hey, Maureen. It's Hillary. I'm just checking in on a patient from last night—I forget his name—a sixteen or seventeen-year-old kid, brought in just before the end of my shift. He had what looked like a spiral fracture of his right forearm, and I put in a call for the orthopedic surgeon before I left. Could you have a look?"

"I saw Dr. Brandall leave just a few minutes ago. Let me have a look." I hear the rapid tapping of keys before she comes back on the line. "Curtis Philips. Displaced spiral fracture of radius and ulna, right arm. Brandall had him in surgery early this morning and it looks like he's back on the orthopedic wing to recover."

I contemplate popping over to the hospital after my shift here and pretend to be checking in on him. Maybe if his mother isn't there, he might be a little more forthcoming on what happened. It's unlikely the two incidents are related, but even if the boy has nothing to do with the attack on Jeff, I'd still be curious to know how he got that injury. His mother's story he fell from his bed sounds a bit far-fetched. Had I been a little sharper last night, I would've picked up on that sooner. Just because the boy is man-sized doesn't necessarily mean he can't be the victim of abuse.

"CURTIS?"

The dark-haired kid turns his head to the door. I notice he's alone in the room when I walk in.

"Yeah?"

He sounds a little groggy, not unusual after general anesthetic. Its effects can linger.

I move closer to the bed and pull up a stool so I can get eye level with him.

"I'm the ER nurse, Hillary, remember me from last night?" He nods ever so slightly but doesn't lose the suspicious expression on his face. "You came in at the end of my shift and I was gone before the orthopedic surgeon came in. I wanted to check and see how you were doing. I see you had surgery?"

"Yeah."

Still monosyllabic but a little more relaxed.

"Are you feeling okay?"

"Sore."

"I bet." I indicate his bandaged arm. "Every so often try to wiggle your fingers a little. Get the blood flowing, it helps with healing."

I watch him wince as he tries to follow my

suggestion, and I notice the swelling and abrasions on his knuckles.

"Are you right-handed?"

"Yeah."

"That's gonna suck. How long do you have to be in the splint for?"

"Dunno."

He sounds sleepy and his eyes drift out the window.

"Your mom said you fell out of bed…" His focus snaps back to me. "Does that happen often?"

"No."

His response is very clear, very firm, and very defensive. Like it would be a sign of weakness if he did.

"But you fell out of bed last night?" A grunt is all I get this time, but he squints his eyes on me. He's not liking the questions and I want to know why. "Looks like you did some damage to your hand as well." I point at the scraped up knuckles just visible under the edge of the removable splint.

"Can I help you?"

A woman's voice sounds behind me and I turn to find his mother standing inside the doorway, a bakery bag in her hand. I get up from the stool and smile at her.

"Hi, Mrs. Philips?" I hold out my hand. "Hillary. I'm the ER nurse who first looked after you last night. I popped in to see how your son is doing."

Hesitantly she takes my hand, but her eyes drift beyond me to the hospital bed.

"Yes, I remember now," she says in a timid voice.

She sounds more like a victim than a potential abuser and when I turn to look at her son, I catch him glaring at her. *Interesting.*

"I should probably get going," I announce, figuring I've overstayed my welcome as it is. "Glad to see he's doing okay. Hopefully they'll let you take him home soon." The woman forces a smile and nods as I move past her. I turn when I get to the door. "Get better soon, Curtis."

I wasn't really expecting a response, but the cold stare he gives me follows me all the way to the nurses' station where I have a quiet conversation with the charge nurse.

CHAPTER 6

Hillary

"WE'D LIKE YOU to have a look at these pictures."

Detective Garcia slides a sheet of paper with three images on it toward me. One of them is the same as one of the shots Radar showed me on Friday, the one with the kid flipping the camera the bird.

"Does he look familiar?" the female detective asks with an edge to her voice.

They both showed up at my door this morning. At first I thought it was Radar again, getting me out of bed on a day I don't have to, and I yanked the door open only to find the detectives outside.

On a Sunday morning at eight thirty. *Who does that?*

After the heads-up I got on Friday, I'd expected to see them a lot sooner. I may have been a bit prickly getting caught in my ratty robe again. Garcia was apologetic, but Detective Bissette looked at me disapprovingly, her lips pressed shut.

I pick up the sheet of paper and look closely at the

other two images I hadn't seen before. One shows the boy fishing off a dock somewhere, and the other is clearly a school picture.

"He looks familiar in this one." I point at the one with the obscene gesture. "Pretty sure he was one of them."

"Pretty sure?"

Bissette's tone is getting to me.

"Yes," I snap. "I'm as sure as I can be from a grainy image. The other two pictures you have here don't even look like the same kid."

They don't. He looks like a wholesome kid in those, instead of the defiant punk in the last one.

"She's got a point," Garcia mumbles, coming to my defense. "How about these? Recognize any of these?"

Another two sheets are placed in front of me, with seven images in total. I don't recognize any of them.

"Sorry, it's hard to tell from these pictures. Both of them had hoodies pulled down over their heads, and the second guy's face was mostly in shadow. I saw them run off, though, so maybe if I could see them move..."

"We're working on that. We have this young man in custody," Garcia says, pointing at the kid I identified. "Still trying to piece together who he may have been with."

"We can take her to the station. See if she can pick him out of a lineup?" Bissette turns to her partner and talks about me like I'm not there.

"It'll take us a while to get a physical lineup together, I don't want to waste her day."

"Wouldn't take that long."

"Excuse me," I interject, done with being talked over. "I'm right here. I'll gladly come to the station whenever you're ready for me, but I'd rather not waste my Sunday waiting around. I have stuff to do."

The detectives share a look, Bissette's is one of annoyance while Garcia's is admonishing.

"We'll try to get something set up for this afternoon, would that work for you?"

"Sure. Give me a call."

Bissette is the first one out the door, while Garcia lingers behind.

"Sorry about that. We just caught another case yesterday morning, very similar. It wasn't an easy scene."

"I'm sorry," I immediately soften. "Is it related?"

He shrugs. "If we hadn't had the only suspect in Sandra Elliot's case in custody at the time, I would've said yes. There were no witnesses in this latest attack."

"Did they survive?" I ask, even though I can already guess the answer.

"No."

"Garcia! Are you coming?" his partner calls up from downstairs.

"Best get going. I'll be in touch."

He flashes a cocky smile, instantly upping his already handsome looks, and heads toward the stairs.

Nice guy, very good-looking, and if I'm not

mistaken he was just flirting a bit. Unfortunately, I'm not in the market.

That doesn't explain why my eyes are drawn across the parking lot to the apartment on the other side, hoping to catch a glimpse of dirty blond hair and glasses.

Radar

Dad is standing in the doorway, waving as I back out of his short driveway.

I got a lot done over the weekend, despite the rocky start that left me with a few cuts and bruises. The roof is patched and hopefully it'll hold up under the next rainfall, a new faucet is installed in the kitchen, and I gave the trailer a good cleaning since it had clearly been a while.

I'd spoken to Hugh, who was on board for a fishing trip but had to get back to me with possible dates. That seemed to perk Dad up, but he still looks a bit lost and lonely watching me drive away.

As soon as I leave Montrose behind me, I dial Yanis' number to update him.

"What've you got for me?"

Typical Yanis; no wasting time on niceties and straight to the point.

"Went through all the kid's online contacts, focusing on local ones. Pared it down to a shortlist of sixteen friends, then I went over each of those accounts with a fine-tooth comb to find commonalities. School, soccer team, family, all your standard stuff. Nothing jumped out at me. No pictures of bloody baseball bats."

"Fuck. We need to find something."

"I wasn't done," I comment. "I noticed Jeremy making quite a few references to gaming on his profile, mostly violent games. Two names off the shortlist consistently interacted on those."

"Jesus," Yanis mutters.

Wouldn't be the first time kids got swept up in violence as a result of certain types of games they play online. There is a disturbing amount of evidence to support that.

"Yeah. I'm on my way back now, but will dig into that angle a little more when I get home."

"Good, because I just spoke to Underwood and unless we can come up with something concrete, he'll be letting the kid go," he informs me.

"No pressure," I comment sardonically.

"Lots of pressure. GJPD caught what looks like another random attack early yesterday. Stabbing. Victim is a thirty-two-year-old waitress at the Station Diner downtown. Found in the alley behind the restaurant with multiple stab wounds to the head. Dead."

"Any indication the cases are related?"

"Other than both victims were rendered unrecognizable, no. Underwood has a gut feeling, though."

"Shit. And I guess Jeremy Loman has the perfect alibi, being in police custody."

"Bingo. We need leads. Let me know what you

come up with."

"I will," I respond, but the line is already dead.

It's coming on two when I park outside my apartment. Before I go in I take Phil for a quick walk, because once I sit down in my office time has a tendency to disappear and her bladder can only hold so much.

I pull my beanie over my ears against the cold wind. I lucked out with sunshine yesterday, making it feel much warmer, but today is overcast and it cools down right away. Phil doesn't seem to care, taking her time and sniffing every blade of grass she passes.

"Come on, girl, I need to get busy."

A little tug on her leash and she reluctantly follows me back across the parking lot when I hear a car door slam. I recognize Hillary walking away from the silver Honda Civic and call out as I jog over to her.

"Hey," she greets me with a smile that doesn't quite reach her eyes.

"Everything okay?" I find myself reaching out to put a hand on her shoulder.

"Honestly? Today's been a bit of a shitshow. I think I need a nap."

"Work?"

She shakes her head. "No, well not just work. Technically it's my day off but the cops showed up on my doorstep at the ass crack of dawn, then I got a call from the hospital wanting me to come in for a meeting, and finally I received a summons to the police station for a lineup and was verbally assaulted for the effort."

"Wow. That's a lot," I mumble, as my brain tries to process her list of complaints. "What did the cops want?"

She crouches down and gives Phil the attention the dog was begging for. Her head is level with a part of my anatomy, which is suddenly on full alert. I slightly angle my hips in an attempt to hide the evidence of my attraction to her.

"They wanted me to look at some pictures of their suspect, like you predicted they would, and wanted me to come to the station to see if I could pick him out of a lineup. I just got back."

She slowly lifts her head, but her eyes get caught partway up my body. *Shit*. Then they shoot up to my face, a flush deepening her dark skin as she rises to her feet.

"Who verbally assaulted you?" I ask, ignoring the fact my cock is now painfully straining against my zipper.

"Not sure—he didn't introduce himself—but I think it was the kid's father. He looked familiar."

"Probably his stepfather. Councilman Briscoe."

"Could be." She shrugs. "Anyway, Detective Garcia intervened. Now I have just a few more hours to salvage what is left of my super-shitty Sunday off, and I plan to do that curled up on my couch with a tub of ice cream watching mindless TV."

I was going to ask about the meeting at the hospital she mentioned but decide to save that for later, when I plan to knock on her door with takeout from that Thai place down the road. A girl can't live off ice cream alone.

"Enjoy," I say instead, and unless I'm imaging things, there may have been a hint of disappointment flashing in her eyes.

"I will."

With a big smile she turns and heads toward her apartment. I do the same; I have work waiting.

IF NOT FOR Phil starting to whine for food, I would've forgotten all about my plans to pick up some Thai for two.

I'd been up to my eyeballs sorting through a few years' worth of posts, trying to find anything that jumped out at me. Recurring names, references to particular games, repetitive hashtags, and suggestions of violence. I already filled a few pages of my notepad with scribbles and have a file folder on my desktop full of screenshots, but with every potentially interesting piece of information comes another line of investigation to pursue.

At least I was able to shoot off a couple of names of interest—in particular one of Jeremy's gaming buddies—in an email for Yanis.

The smells coming from the paper bag holding two generous servings of Pad Thai assault my nose, causing an involuntary rumble in my stomach as I lift my hand to knock on her door.

"Why am I not surprised anymore, finding you on my doorstep bearing gifts?" She shakes her head teasingly and I'm glad to see her smile light up her eyes. "Oh my God, is that what I think it is?"

She grabs the bag from my hand and sniffs it as she turns and heads for the kitchen. I recognize the silent invitation and step inside, closing the door.

She's already pulling down a couple of large bowls from the cupboard when I walk in.

"Wanna grab a couple of beers?" she asks without looking, as she busies herself serving up the food.

Another thing to like about her; she doesn't make a fuss about me showing up and simply goes with the flow. Easy and laid-back, inviting me to be the same.

"Guess the ice cream didn't fill you up then?"

I sit down at the table across from her, sliding a bottle her way. She's already chewing her first bite, moaning at the taste. I'm ridiculously pleased she chose chopsticks instead of forks for the Pad Thai. Tastes much better that way, in my opinion. Something else we seem to have in common.

"Forgot I finished the tub last night," she admits after swallowing. "I was about to order in when you showed up so conveniently. This is perfect." She deftly grabs another bite but pauses it halfway to her mouth. "Aren't you hungry?"

"Starving." I realize I'm still staring at her and pick up my chopsticks.

The gnawing in my stomach starts to wane when

I'm two-thirds through my dinner, but the hunger I feel for the woman across from me stays.

"Oh my God, I'm so full." Hillary sits back and folds her hands over her stomach. "I ate too fast."

The last word has barely left her lips when it's followed by a hearty belch. She looks mortified and slaps her hand over her mouth, her eyes almost bulging out of her head. I throw my head back and burst out laughing.

"I'm so sorry!"

I don't want her to feel uncomfortable and decide to share a talent usually reserved for locker rooms and frat parties, burping on command.

"There," I announce after. "Now we're even."

Hillary

"Did you know in some cultures it's good dining etiquette to burp after a meal?"

I grin at him in disbelief.

Radar keeps surprising me. In a very good way. He's making light of what was an embarrassing moment, not only by letting out a burp that was far more impressive than mine, but by passing it off as good manners. If he had tried to pretend nothing happened I would never have lived the embarrassment down. Now, I'm laughing about it.

Another mark in the plus column for this man.

"I'll take your word for it."

"It's true, look it up. It's considered the highest compliment to the cook."

He grins at me and something warm settles in my chest. A little unnerved at the unexpected feeling, I get up and gather the dishes.

"Want another beer?"

"No thanks. Gotta keep a clear mind. I have some more work to do tonight."

"Do you usually work on Sunday?" I ask, running water in the sink for the dishes. Radar gets up, walks over, and grabs a dishtowel off the hook.

"Depends. I was in Montrose helping my dad with some repairs this weekend but cut my visit a little short because of some work stuff that came up. It happens. What about you? You mentioned something earlier about getting called in?"

He takes the dripping bowl from my hand before I can set it in the dish rack, the tips of his fingers brushing my skin.

"It was about something that happened yesterday."

I explain to him about the kid coming into the ER with the spiral fracture. Then I relay Jeff's story the next morning at the shelter and finally my visit to the hospital.

"There was something off about that boy and his mother. The story they told didn't really match his injury, so I talked to the charge nurse and we decided to call in Child Protective Services. Today I got called in to explain my request to the case worker."

I don't mention the reprimand I received from the director of nursing. He wasn't happy I took it upon myself to visit the patient instead of alerting one of the hospital's social workers.

I notice Radar's hands stopped moving and when I look over his eyes are on me, angry.

"Why would you stick your neck out like that?"

"I didn't stick out my neck, I followed hospital protocol. Besides, I want to help Jeff."

"You said Jeff doesn't want any help, and I don't give a fuck about Jeff. This is about you putting yourself in the middle of a potentially volatile situation. Again."

Definitely angry.

"Well, I do give a fuck about Jeff, which is why I went to see the boy." I lift my chin an inch and match his angry glare. "And I'd bet my last dollar that kid was involved."

"Yeah?" He leans in close, his eyes shooting fire. "What good is that knowledge if your buddy doesn't want to file a complaint? All you did was risk your own neck."

I open my mouth to respond before I realize I don't really have an answer for that. Sure, CPS can investigate, but their only interest is the well-being of the child. My mouth snaps shut. He's right, it was a knee-jerk reaction I didn't really think through and now I have a reprimand on my otherwise flawless employment record. Karla Velky will have a heyday with that.

I don't like being wrong and I suck at admitting it. Instead I try staring him down until he tosses the towel on the dish rack and wipes his hands on his jeans.

"I've got work to do," he grumbles, heading toward the front door.

"Wait!" I call out, hurrying after him. "I…uhm… thanks for dinner," I finish lamely, feeling like an idiot as I stare at his rigid back.

He turns slowly but he no longer looks pissed, more…exasperated. Lifting his hand, he taps my nose with his finger.

"What am I gonna do with you?"

The next moment he's out the door.

CHAPTER 7

RADAR

I FEEL LIKE a stalker, peering through the blinds in my kitchen at the parking lot below.

It's the second day in a row I've been standing here, waiting for a glimpse of Hillary getting into her car.

I caught a glance of the schedule she'd tacked on her fridge door Sunday night and memorized it. Her hospital shifts run from two until midnight, but on Monday, Tuesday, and Saturday she spends her mornings at the shelter. Yesterday she had one after the other and didn't pull into her parking spot until twelve forty-five. I waited up.

She needs someone looking out for her. At least, that's how I justify my behavior.

I could've spit nails Sunday night; I was so pissed at her for being careless. With the news about a second victim dying in a very similar attack to the first fresh in my mind, her recklessness rubbed me the wrong way.

She's a woman alone, a beautiful one at that, and should be more careful.

I see the lights flash on the Honda before Hillary walks into sight. She opens the door and pauses, turns her head and seems to be looking straight up at my apartment. Then she slips behind the wheel and I let out the breath I was holding before I watch her drive off.

Close call. I let go of the blinds and go to fill my travel mug with coffee for the road.

It's been a long while since I've felt drawn to a woman to the point of stalking her. Middle school, when I used to walk to school, going out of my way an extra block just to pass Penny Richard's house, on the off chance I could catch a glimpse of her. Penny was two years older—a lifetime at that age—a cheerleader, and probably had no idea I even existed. I was a skinny runt with an overbite, and the beginnings of what would be a raging case of acne in my teenage years. I'd been heartbroken when she graduated and left for college. She'd never spoken a single word to me and I'd felt secure in my secret adoration of her.

At forty, I've not lacked for female companions—even had a few relationships—but I never found myself at the verge of being obsessed with a woman since Penny. Until now, that is.

Lena and Jake are the only ones in the office when I walk in.

"Where is everyone?"

Jake looks up from his desk.

"Kai left for Colorado Springs this morning, Bree and Yanis are meeting with the chief of police, and Dimas took a personal day. Morning to you too," he adds sarcastically.

I choose to ignore him and focus on something else instead.

"They're seeing Underwood? This about our report?"

Jake shrugs. "Probably. I wasn't really paying attention."

He rubs both hands over his face and I notice he looks like he didn't get much sleep.

"That little princess of yours still wreaking havoc?"

He groans. "You have no idea. How can something so little produce so much noise?"

"Can't help you there, but I'm sure it won't last forever."

"Fuck, I hope not. Rosie and I have taken to sleeping in separate rooms, taking turns with Tessa, so the other can sleep a little. That better fucking not last forever."

I grunt sympathetically, clap him on the shoulder, and head to my office.

I feel bad for him. He went from an uncomplicated, independent single life a couple of years ago to this. I'm not saying his wife and daughter aren't worth it, but it's got to be a hard adjustment.

Or is it? I mean, look at Dimas, a consummate bachelor, who barely seemed to notice the loss of that status the moment Willa hit his radar not that long ago.

Makes you wonder if it isn't so much about giving up the single life but has more to do with meeting the right person.

An image of Hillary floats to the surface and I shake my head trying to clear it. Too soon for thoughts like that. Although, I should probably remind myself of that next time I stand at my kitchen window, waiting for a glimpse of her.

I boot up my computers and dive into the high security network I'm setting up for a software company in Salt Lake City. We promised them the framework by the end of this week and if they approve, I'll have to head out there to install and instruct. It's my least favorite part of jobs like this since it requires dealing with people but has to be done.

My little side investigation of Jeremy Loman will have to wait. Despite Hillary's positive identification of the boy, and what little circumstantial evidence I brought to the table, the DA didn't feel there was enough there to charge him. Underwood reluctantly had to let him go yesterday.

The morning is almost gone by the time the boss sticks his head into my office. I'd been buried so deep in what I'm doing, I didn't even hear them come back.

"Conference room. Lena is ordering lunch."

He doesn't wait for an acknowledgment and I quickly finish what I'm doing, before picking up my laptop, and following him down the hall.

"What's up?" Jake asks when he walks in right behind me.

"I'll get to that," Yanis says, turning to me. "How far are you with the MadTex account?"

"Should be done with the design for the framework today. It'll take me another day or two to build it."

"How long to install?"

"At least a day on site, maybe two. Why?"

Yanis nods at Bree who takes over.

"Underwood asked us to come in to discuss our report. He's planning to clean house but anticipates blowback. Timing sucks, given he's dealing with two murders that look to be connected, so he's—"

"That's confirmed?" I interrupt. "They have evidence they're connected?"

"Nothing concrete," Yanis responds, "but other than the murder weapon, the cases seem eerily similar. Both women attacked—what appears to be randomly—late at night in front of their homes, two suspects seen running from the scene."

"So there are witnesses for this latest one?"

"One. An elderly man with insomnia, living around the corner, spotted two people running down the sidewalk and getting into a light-colored pickup truck around the time of the attack. Wasn't able to make out model or license plate."

My fingers are already flying over my keyboard, searching through social media posts of some of Jeremy Loman's friends whose profiles I saved.

"What are you looking for?" Bree wants to know, coming around the table to stand at my back.

"Looking for connections," I mumble, as I discard

the first kid and move onto the next one. "We know it wasn't Loman, he was in custody, but we never found the second guy. Jeremy posted a selfie with the baseball bat, if the cases are connected, maybe some other kid did something equally stupid."

"Bit of a stretch," Jake comments, but he still leans over to peer at my screen.

"Maybe, maybe not. Loman is an avid gamer and so are some of his buddies. It's all about the competition with those kids. Some of these violent games can make them feel invincible."

"He's got a point," Bree agrees with me. "Plenty of recorded cases of violence that would support that."

"Where's the fire?" Dimas walks into the conference room, shooting his older brother a fiery look. "I was having a fan-fucking-tastic and well-deserved—if I may add—day off with my wife when you called."

"Underwood needs some backup," Yanis says unapologetically before explaining the situation to Dimi. "I need Radar to finish the MadTex contract, so we need you on the computers in the meantime."

I'd rather be working on this instead of a boring security network, but it's a big contract bringing in a nice chunk of change for PASS, so we can't exactly blow it off. Besides, next to me, Dimas is the most at home with technology—that doesn't mean I have to like giving this case out of hand. I'm into it up to my neck already.

"Show me what you've got," Dimi says, crowding

out Bree behind me.

Twenty minutes later I'm in my office, the door closed, determined to crank this system out in record time. There's no way to avoid the trip to Salt Lake City, but if I can get the system built as soon as tomorrow, head up there on Thursday, at least I can have this off my plate by the weekend.

I don't mind working around the clock if I have to—wouldn't be the first time I missed some sleep—but it means I won't have time to watch out for Hillary.

And I really like keeping an eye on her.

Hillary

"Rather you than me."

I throw Linda a dirty look as she slips through the curtain, before looking back at my patient.

"I'm going to need you to slip out of those track pants, Mr. Thompson."

Mark Thompson—a thirty-three-year-old construction worker—shoots me a pained expression. The poor guy walked into the ER ten minutes ago with complaints of groin pain. He'd been cupping his junk and was walking bow-legged when I showed him to the cubicle.

"When did you first experience discomfort?" I ask him, as he gingerly slips his pants down.

I try not to get distracted by the fact he's going commando and is packing or react to the clearly distended and deep purple testicle.

"When I got out of the shower after work," he

grinds out through clenched teeth.

"What time was that?"

I don a pair of gloves and gently palpate his scrotum, but still his whole body clenches. His left ball is rock hard. Mr. Thompson may well have a testicular torsion, which means time is of the essence before irreparable damage is done.

"A little before seven. I was getting ready for a date."

I'll leave it to the surgeon to explain there likely will be no 'dating' for the upcoming few weeks at least. This guy will likely need surgery and fast. It's a quarter past ten now. After six or so hours the testicle starts dying off and he stands a good chance of losing it.

I pull the sheet up to cover him and remove my gloves.

"I'm going to call in a doctor to have a quick look at you. Hang in there, okay?"

He grunts, sweat beading his forehead from the pain.

Slipping through the curtain I rush to the nurses' station.

"Who is the urologist on call?" I ask Linda, who is working on one of the computers.

"Your favorite guy; Bill Shearer."

Of course. Isn't that just my luck.

"Can I have the phone?" Linda lifts the phone on the counter, a smirk playing on her lips. "You're enjoying this a little too much," I accuse her.

"Been a slow week, I can do with some action around here," she teases with a shrug.

Over her shoulder, in the small office behind the nurses' station, I catch Karla eyeing me.

Just wonderful.

In the twenty minutes it takes Bill to get here I have a Doppler and the portable ultrasound ready outside the cubicle.

"Couldn't do without me after all?" he smarms, as he walks up with a smile I'm sure he thinks is far more effective than it really is.

I slide the notes I made in Mr. Thompson's chart to him without a word. Luckily he's enough of a professional to give it his full attention until Karla, who must've spotted him, comes rushing out of her office.

"Hey, Bill, what brings you in so late?"

He looks up from my report. "Hillary called me."

Her eyes immediately swing my way, her dislike evident.

"Patient with a testicular torsion," I explain what Bill failed to clarify. For some reason he seems to enjoy fueling the flame. *Bastard.*

"I see," she responds sourly. "Well, if you need a hand."

The last is directed at Bill, who raises an eyebrow as Linda—who's been listening with rapt interest—chuckles softly.

"Thanks," he says, "but I'm sure the patient's… *care* is safe in Hillary's hands."

The comment is dripping with double entendre and I almost feel sorry for Karla, whose lips pinch in a tight line. If I wasn't sure it would cost me my job, I'd have slapped that arrogant smirk off his handsome face.

Ten minutes later Mark Thompson is on his way to the OR, looking a little shell-shocked. Men don't always handle the idea of anything sharp that close to their prized possession well. Wait until he hears he'll have to abstain from sex for the next four to six weeks.

Poor guy.

The final hour or so of my shift is filled with the usual late-night emergencies: a twenty-two-year-old drunk driver hitting a tree, a dehydrated cancer patient after a night of vomiting, and a child with a persistent nosebleed.

By the time I pull the car into my parking spot, I'm bone-tired. Luckily tomorrow is Thursday, my day off. Other than some laundry and a quick trip to the grocery store to replenish my food supply, I have nothing on the schedule. Maybe I'll cook something nice.

I glance up at Radar's apartment, which is as dark as it was last night. I haven't talked to him since Sunday night and the only time I saw him was yesterday morning.

I wonder if he'd appreciate a home-cooked meal.

CHAPTER 8

Radar

"GO HOME."

I blink my eyes open to find Bree glaring at me in the doorway, Phil peeking in between her legs.

It takes me a second to get my bearings. I'm lying on the cot in the locker room at the office. It's there in case one of us works late. On some contracts our hours don't exactly run eight-to-five and in the past days I've become intimately acquainted with the all-too-thin mattress.

I glance at my watch and see it's already after four.

Shit.

Today is Sunday.

Since Tuesday, this past week has gone by in a blur. Bree was kind enough to take care of my dog while I put my nose to the grindstone to finalize the system for MadTex. I put the final touches on it Thursday morning, grabbed a change of clothes I keep in my locker, and drove to the airport to catch a flight to Salt Lake City. Of course, what should've been a one-day thing turned into almost three due to a few glitches streamlining my system to their network, and I didn't get back until last night.

Instead of going home, I came straight to the office when I heard from Dimas he'd come across something that might be of interest. He's a good tech, but not a hacker. That's my specialty.

He'd been looking at my gaming angle and came across the name of a game he hadn't heard of before; *Lock&Load - Revenge*. I'd never heard of it either and was no more successful than Dimi had been trying to find more information. Usually, when a new game hits the market it'll get written up in gaming blogs, but no one even mentions this one.

What I did find were a few references to it on social media posts, and I spent most of the night and this morning taking down names of anyone who made mention of it, until I got so tired I couldn't see straight. I tried a shower to wake up but that didn't work, so laid down for what was supposed to be a catnap, one hour tops, but turned into four.

I swing my legs over the side and plant my feet on the floor, raking my fingers through my hair.

"I've got work to do." Even my voice sounds rough as I lift my head to look up at Bree, but my eyes get stuck on my dog's big, pleading ones. Her body is almost gyrating as she strains against the leash. "Come here, girl." I pat my leg and Bree reluctantly lets go of her.

"You don't deserve her," she grumbles, and I don't

disagree as Phil's compact body circles around my legs, her entire back end wagging.

I don't deserve her, but I'm not going to admit that to Bree.

"You're just saying that because you want her."

"So? At least I'm around to look after her."

I snort, because more often than not it's her gone for days, sometimes weeks, at a time on a contract.

"Until your next case takes you out of town." I pick up my dog, who insists on giving me a tongue bath, and get to my feet. "Besides, she loves me best," I tease her.

"Only because you spoil her."

I grin and lift Phil away from my face but that doesn't stop her from trying to lick me.

"No more than you," I fire back. "Tell me you didn't let her sleep in your bed?" Bree doesn't answer and is suddenly very interested in the toes of her boots. I start laughing. "See?"

"Whatever. You need to go, Boss's orders. You've been burning the candle at both ends all week. How long since you've been home?"

It shouldn't surprise me Yanis keeps close tabs on who's in the office at any given time. I installed the monitoring system myself.

Fuck, it's been five days. I have food I'm sure is growing legs in my fridge and I really need to wash a load. I can grab some groceries on the way, cook a meal, get my laundry started, and do some work from home.

"Fine," I grudgingly concede and with my dog under my arm, head to my office to grab my laptop.

MY ARMS ARE full of groceries when I spot the note stuck under my front door. I dump the bags on the doorstep, grab the note, and unlock my door. Phil pushes the door open and makes a beeline for the kitchen to her empty food bowl. A quick glance at the note reveals tidy feminine handwriting and Hillary's signature. An invitation to dinner for six. I take a quick glance at my watch. Five thirty. The day is looking up after all. After feeding Phil, putting the groceries away, and starting a load of laundry, I quickly hop in the shower.

My brother and I were raised never to show up empty-handed, so in lieu of a bottle of nice wine or something, I grab the apple pie I just picked up at the grocery store. I only feel a small pang of guilt when I spot my laptop discarded on the coffee table as I walk out of the apartment.

There's a decent breeze blowing and with the sun sinking lower in the sky, it's pretty chilly. I pull my beanie down to cover my ears when I cross the parking lot to the other building. A hint of nerves builds as I approach her front door. I haven't seen her in a week—or rather, she hasn't seen me—and the last time we didn't exactly part on the best of terms. I distinctly recall chewing her out and I haven't contacted her since.

If I ever had any game at all, it seems to have gone out the window in my dealings with Hillary. Maybe the fact she's a friend of Rosie's has me fumbling; if I fuck up I'll piss off a lot of people. I could still head home, dive into my work, and pretend I never saw the note.

I almost turn around when the door suddenly swings open, revealing a surprised Hillary, a garbage bag in her hands. Backlit, her untamed hair is like a halo around her shocked face and I'm so busy taking her in—the extra large T-shirt revealing one silky-skinned shoulder, and gray leggings hugging her bottom half—it takes me a second to clue in to the fact she was clearly not expecting me.

"Radar? What are you doing here?"

She sounds less than pleased I'm here.

"I, uh, got your note?"

Her forehead crinkles when she pulls her eyebrows together.

"Note?"

"About dinner? Look," I add quickly, trying to divert from the awkward moment, "I may have misunderstood..."

"The note? I left that on Thursday."

Definitely not happy.

Shit.

I lift an apologetic hand. "My bad. I've been out of town for work. I just—" Maybe this wasn't a good idea after all. The potential for complications is all too real.

I start turning away, feeling like the moron I am when she grabs my arm.

"I was going to have leftover beef stew. There's plenty for two," she offers with a tentative smile.

Fuck. How am I supposed say no to that?

"I brought dessert."

The grin widens.

HILLARY

I HAVE TO drag my eyes from his retreating back as he takes my trash down to the dumpster.

I'd been so sure I'd made a mistake inviting him when I didn't see or hear from him these past days. In fact, I thought maybe I'd misinterpreted his interest and he was doing his best to avoid me. I was pissed, disappointed in him and myself. If I'd just bit the bullet and asked Rosie for his number, I might've known he wasn't even around.

Leaving the door open, I rush to the kitchen, drop the pie on the counter, and pull the large container of stew I made last night out of the fridge. I quickly dump the contents in my casserole dish and shove it in the oven, turning it on high.

Truth is, I was going to make a tuna salad for dinner but got carried away cleaning and lost track of time. I hear the front door click shut as I dive into the freezer to grab a French loaf. Suddenly nervous, I busy myself wrapping the bread in tin foil, keeping my back turned. I hear his footsteps closing in and my hands shake a little as I try to focus on tearing off a piece.

"Hillary…"

A shiver runs down my spine when I feel his breath brushing my skin.

"Hmm."

The rough pad of a single finger strokes along my skin from the base of my neck down my exposed shoulder. My hands still and my body instantly responds with a shiver.

"Look at me?"

I take in a deep breath and turn. I knew he was close, but I still suck in a breath when I discover how little space there is between us. His glasses do nothing to hide the intensity in his eyes.

"What?" My voice cracks a little and I swallow hard when his eyes drop to my mouth.

"Let's clear the air," he says, forcing his gaze back up to meet mine. "I'm sorry you thought I stood you up on Thursday."

"I didn't—" I start denying when he shakes his head sharply.

"You did," he insists. "I could see it all over your face when you opened the door. Had I been around, I would've been here in a heartbeat." The slight burn of the hurt feelings I've been carrying around these past days eases as he takes a step closer. I can feel the heat from his body. "To clear up any possible further misunderstandings; I like you. I'm not particularly good at this but I'd like to know you better." My heart melts at the sincerity in his words and the hint of vulnerability in his expression. "Say something."

"Okay," I finally manage.

"Okay?" I nod to confirm, my eyes never leaving his. My breath catches as he reaches up and brushes a finger over my bottom lip. "If you don't want me to kiss you, now would be the time to tell me," he mumbles.

Instead, I lift my arms and slip them around his neck. The brown of his eyes darkens, as he hooks an arm behind my back, and pulls me flush against his front.

"I've got nothing to say."

My whispered response is drowned when his mouth slants over mine and I can't stop the groan from deep in my chest.

Holy shit.

I can already tell this man is going to obliterate my defenses. All it takes is the light brush of his tongue along the seam of my lips for me to welcome him inside. Not good at this, my foot. I can't remember the last time I was kissed so thoroughly my toes curled. Maybe never.

The fingers of his hand pressing against my lower back dig into the swell of my butt. I find myself shamelessly rubbing against him, my own fingers tangling in the long hair brushing his neck.

My nerve endings are on fire—from zero to blazing inferno—and I moan down his throat. Immediately his hands move to my hips. I embarrass myself by tightening my hold as he pulls back.

"Sorry," I mumble, releasing him instantly and dropping my head down to my chest.

Too much. Too soon.

"Hey…"

He hooks a finger under my chin to lift my burning face. I catch a satisfied grin stretching his swollen lips before I get to a pair of smiling eyes.

Jesus. The man is lethal.

"Glad I'm not the only one getting carried away," he whispers, kissing the tip of my nose before taking a step back.

I wrap my arms around my body, the sudden chill hitting my chest. Or so I tell myself.

"There's beer in the fridge," I share for something to fill the sudden silence. "I'm just gonna pop this in the oven. Dinner won't be long."

Turning to the counter, I finish wrapping the bread and quickly shove it in the oven. By the time I feel some of the burn leave my face, I have bowls and cutlery set out, and Radar is sitting at the kitchen table, taking a sip from a beer. He placed a second one on the table across from him.

"I'm gonna need your number," he says, setting his bottle down and pulling his phone from his pocket, holding it out to me.

I can't quite place the look on his face as I take it from his hand and punch in my digits. His fingers stroke the back of mine when I give it back. Then he saves it and types something before tucking it away. The sound of a message coming in has me automatically turn toward the coffee table where I dropped my cell earlier.

"That's me. So you have my number as well."

"Ah." I busy myself setting the table. "Why did you stop?" I ask when I sit down across from him, unable to hold back the question circling around my head.

"I told you, I'm not very good at this."

I snort and mumble, "Could've fooled me."

"I mean pursuing someone," he says with a cocky grin.

I find the fact he seems plenty confident in his physical abilities but not his social skills, fascinating. Damn, the man has the whole hot nerd thing down to a fine art.

"Trust me, you were doing fine," I share honestly.

"Good to know." He smirks and reaches across the table to grab my hand. "But I meant what I said earlier; I want to get to know you better. I didn't come here to fuck you on the kitchen counter. At least not the first time."

Yowza. Not sure whether it's the vivid image he creates in my mind or the crass words he uses, but I'm suddenly on fire. I stand up abruptly, pull my hand from his and escape into the kitchen. His soft chuckle follows me.

"Hungry?"

"Starving," he confirms, and I don't look back to see if he's wearing that smirk.

I can hear it in his voice.

Over dinner we manage to fall into an easy conversation; mostly about things like work, family, a little history. It's not until we're in the kitchen washing dishes—he insisted on drying again—that he brings up the cause of the disagreement we had last week.

"The guy at the shelter, Jeff, any luck trying to get him to file a report?"

I shake my head. "No. He won't budge." I peek at him over my shoulder. "Didn't really expect him to."

"Me neither. Why don't you give me the kid's name? I have to get going and do some work tonight anyway. I can see if there's anything I can dig up."

"You don't have to do that."

I'd be lying if I said I wasn't disappointed he's leaving.

He tugs free a curl that got stuck in the corner of my mouth.

"It's not a big deal," he says, hanging up the towel.

I follow him to the front door where he turns toward me.

"His name is Curtis Philips," I share.

He tugs me into his arms and I go willingly, lifting my face. This kiss is too short, but he pecks my lips twice more before letting me go. That's sweet, as is the little tap on my nose before he opens the door and steps outside.

"Don't forget to check your messages," he reminds me before heading down the stairs.

As soon as I lose sight of him, I duck inside and make a beeline for my phone.

Unknown number: Wonder if you taste that sweet all over?

Sweet Jesus.

My cheeks flush and my body tingles.

Before common sense sets in, I fire off a message back.

Me: Only one way to find out.

The response is almost immediate.

Unknown number: Now that's just cruel.

I'm still walking on clouds an hour later when I peek out my kitchen window one last time before turning off the lights and heading to bed.

I've just put my head on the pillow when my phone beeps on the nightstand.

Unknown number: Sleep tight, Lady.

He must've been checking too.

I'm smiling when I doze off minutes later.

CHAPTER 9

Radar

I PUSH MY chair back from my desk and run my hands through my hair in frustration.

For hours last night and most of today I've been trying to find information on that game Dimas saw referenced; *Lock&Load - Revenge*. He's working on an ever-growing list of people who make mention of the game on social media, while I've been fruitlessly looking into the game itself.

Nothing. There isn't a single piece of information I can find. No actual product, no manufacturer, no gaming blog reviews, no press release, and no mainstream distribution. I'm starting to wonder if it even exists. If it weren't for the dozen or so social media mentions Dimas found referring to levels of the 'game' reached, I wouldn't be looking. As it is, I may have to venture into the more obscure layers of the internet to find information.

The dark net is a dangerous place for a geek like me. It's only a portion of the onion that makes up the deep net, which is equal parts disturbing and fascinating. It wouldn't be the first time I succumb to the temptation to discover all. It can become an addiction; crack to a former hacker.

It's creeping up on six. If I'm going to dive in, I'm gonna need some fuel and possibly a lifeline. I get to my feet and Philomena groans in protest from her bed under my desk.

"Have a minute?"

Dimas looks up from his laptop when I walk into the general office space. We're the only ones left.

"What's up? Find something?"

"Not a whisper." I sit down at Bree's desk and turn the chair to face him. "What about you? Any more luck?"

"We're up to eighteen names." He flips through his notebook and settles on one of the pages, turning it toward me. "I was able to get locations on eight of them."

I glance at his scribbled notes. Jeremy Loman graces the top of the list, right here in Grand Junction. Of the other seven names, one more is local, one is from Palisade, one is in Tulsa, and the other three are from Saginaw, Jacksonville, and San Luis Obispo.

Whatever their connection, unfortunately it's not geographical. That might've made things a little easier.

"Did you print out the new posts you found?"

He hands me a stack of printouts and I go through them, looking for any more information than the previous ones. A hashtag catches my eye on one of them.

"Did you notice this? H10:30?"

Dimas glances over and shakes his head.

"What does it mean?"

"Open up a new browser window and enter it. Let's see what comes up."

I lean forward as he types the hashtag into the search bar.

"A headset?"

My eyes scan the page on the screen. "Aviation headset," I clarify. "That doesn't make any sense. Keep scrolling."

"It's also a medical code," he says, clicking on one of the links leading us to a page of ICD diagnostic codes. "For acute conjunctivitis."

"Why would a fifteen-year-old hashtag pinkeye?"

Dimi has no answer either. The hashtag has to have something to do with the content of the post. We're just not seeing it.

"Are you ready?"

Both of us turn at once to see Willa, Dimi's woman, walk into the office. He gets to his feet to greet her and I turn my eyes back to the screen, giving them a little privacy.

"Hey, Radar," I hear her say on a soft chuckle, indicating it's safe to look at them.

"Willa, how are you?"

"Good. Better if I can get this lug to come with me so we can make our reservation at Engine 36."

She names one of Grand Junction's most popular restaurants. "I put on a dress and everything."

I hadn't noticed, but now I do.

"You look great."

"Get your own damn woman to ogle. This one's mine," Dimas grumbles, slapping his laptop shut and grabbing it and his phone off the desk. "Lock up, will you? See you tomorrow."

I lift a hand at Willa, who winks at me before Dimas slings a proprietary arm around her shoulders and steers her out of the office. My thoughts immediately drift to Hillary. I wish things weren't so hectic, I wouldn't mind taking her out for a proper date one of these days. Maybe Thursday?

As if conjured up, a message comes in on my phone when I head back to my office after making copies of Dimi's notes and printouts.

Hillary: OMG just read back my text from last night. Sorry, didn't mean to be a tease.

I sit down in my chair and drop the copies on my desk so I have my hands free.

Me: Not complaining.

Hillary: You were last night, calling me cruel.

Me: Still not a complaint. Nothing wrong with ramping up the anticipation.

Hillary: Anticipation?

Hillary: NVM I get it. *Facepalm*

I chuckle and find myself relaxing into the banter. I feel a lot more confident on a keyboard than in person.

Me: Although the anticipation was already pretty high when you opened the door in that outfit.

Hillary: Those are my ratty old lounge clothes

Me: Worked for me.

Hillary: You really that easy to please?

Me: Only one way to find out.

I watch the dots dance on the screen but it takes a while before her response comes.

Hillary: Touché. You have me flushed in the middle of the hospital cafeteria. People are staring.

Me: Because you're beautiful.

She sends back a blushing emoji and I send her a smiling one. This may well be the first time I've ever used an emoji. I'll never be able to live it down if the guys find out.

Hillary: I should get back to work.

Me: Me too. Still at the office. Talk later?

Hillary: I'll be late.

Me: Tomorrow then.

Hillary: Do you like butter chicken?

Me: Doesn't everyone?

Hillary: 6-ish?

Me: I'm there.

Phil stands up and stretches before propping her front legs against my knee. Her big round eyes plead with me.

"Let me guess, you're hungry." She answers me with the wagging of her tail. "Fine. Let me shut this off and we'll head home."

I shove my laptop and my work in my backpack, clip Phil's leash on, and make my way through the office, flicking lights off as I go. I toss my pack in the truck and follow the dog to the berm where she quickly relieves her taxed bladder. Then I help her up in the passenger seat, where she spends the drive home with her nose up catching the stream of chilled breeze coming in from the slightly opened window.

Once home, I get her fed, make myself a fried egg sandwich, and take my plate and a beer into my office. There I spend the evening expanding on the list Dimas made. By the time Phil comes to alert me she needs to go out, I have twelve new names added, complete with locations.

Sixteen names in total at some point used the hashtag H10:30 on a social media post. Definitely a connection, but the meaning escapes me.

For now.

Hillary

AN ELBOW HITS me in the jaw and I wince as I struggle to get the arm under control.

Two nurses and an orderly, and still we can't seem to subdue the patient who stumbled into the ER five minutes ago, bleeding from a gaping wound to his abdomen.

"Someone call security!" Linda calls over her shoulder, while trying to hold down the other arm.

James, one of our orderlies, threw himself on the man's thrashing legs, and manages to pin at least his bottom half to the stretcher.

Instead of security, Dr. Sugarlips walks in.

Wonderful.

"What's going on here?" His authoritative voice grates on my already frazzled nerves.

"A sedative maybe? Some restraints?" Linda sneers sarcastically.

If anyone dislikes Bill Shearer more than I do, it's

her. That one month I lost my faculties and dated him, despite her warnings, almost cost me our friendship.

I finally get the patient's arm under control when Bill returns with leather restraints, the surgical resident and a security guard right behind him. In minutes they have him secured and I go in search of the syringe the patient knocked out of my hand. I find it in the corner of the room, which looks more like an abattoir right now. The bed, the floor, and my scrubs are covered with his blood and I'm afraid if we don't act fast, he'll bleed out under our eyes, but Linda and the resident are already working on him.

He smelled like he'd soaked in alcohol and rather than place him in a cubicle and stink up the entire floor, I'd escorted him to a room. He'd already been agitated when I tried to have a look at his injury, but the moment he saw me with a needle he became combative. It didn't take me long to clue in to the fact alcohol wasn't the only thing he was high on. Luckily James and Linda were walking by and heard me yell when he whaled on me.

I pick up the dirty syringe and drop it in the sharps container mounted to the wall, before raising my hand to my throbbing face. Shit. He got me good, busted my lip, and I can already feel the swelling under my left eye where he clocked me with his elbow.

"You look a mess." Bill is standing far too close, scrutinizing my face. I flinch when he lifts his hand and carefully palpates my cheekbone and eye socket, but he doesn't even notice. "Come with me."

Without waiting for my answer he grabs my arm and steers me ahead of him, out of the room into the hallway, where we bump into a sour-faced Karla. Just my luck.

My escapades last week involving CPS have landed me at the top of her shit list, and I know she's waiting for me to make one misstep so she can be up one side of me and down the other.

"I hear you weren't able to control your patient without manhandling him?" I press my lips together before something flies out that could cost me my job, but Karla isn't done. She gives me a once-over with a look of disgust before she continues, "Even a hint you did more damage than good and you can pack your bags."

With that she steps around us and into the room. Bill's chuckle in my ear has my skin crawling and I jerk my arm from his hold.

"Hillary, Hillary, have you not been playing nice?"

"Enough, Bill," I snap. "You know damn well why she can't stand the sight of me and you are *not* helping. Grow up."

I'm not interested in hearing what else he may have to say and slip into the linen closet to grab a clean pair of scrubs. He's standing in the same spot when I step out, but I pointedly ignore him and head for the washroom at the end of the hall, locking the door behind me.

Flicking the light on, I check my face in the mirror. *Oh man...* My left eye is swelling shut and you can barely see I have a cheekbone. I pull down my bottom lip and see a straight cut where my tooth went through. Bill is right; I look a mess.

I strip off my soiled uniform and wet a wad of paper towel under the cold faucet before scrubbing any remnants of the patient's blood off my skin. Then I put on the clean scrubs, splash some cold water on my face to try and numb the throbbing, wash my hands, and take a deep breath before I step outside.

Linda is chatting with Dr. Kevin Bogosh by the nurses' station, wincing when she sees me.

"You okay?"

"I should be fine."

"Go home."

"I can't, I have an hour left in my shift and I don't want to give you-know-who an excuse."

"Who? An excuse for what?" Kevin asks.

"It doesn't matter," I wave him off, pinching the bridge of my nose, but Linda speaks over me.

"Nurse Ratchet; Karla. You know she hates Hillary."

Kevin shrugs like he doesn't, but then looks at me with narrowed eyes.

"You can't be on the floor looking like that. Besides, you may have a concussion," he adds with a wink. "Go home. Doctor's orders."

"But—"

"This is not a negotiation. Go. It's not busy and I'll deal with Karla," he insists.

I look at Linda, who is bulging her eyes at me.

"Scram, girl. Get rid of that shiner, it won't look good with your cowgirl outfit for Saturday night."

Shit. Forgot about that.

I promised Linda a while ago I'd go line dancing with her and Maggie at a new western bar that opened up last November. She'd been bugging me for a while. I'm not exactly one for country music or line dancing, but I get few opportunities to bust a move and beggars can't be choosers.

"I'll come, but you better not expect me to get dressed in chaps and a leather vest, because that ain't gonna happen," I respond, poking a finger at her before I round the desk and open the drawer to grab my purse and my sweater.

"Where do you think you're going?" sounds behind me, just as I start walking to the exit. I swing around and see Karla standing behind Linda, her hands on her hips.

"I'm sending her home," Kevin states firmly. "She needs some ice on that swelling and rest."

Karla looks like she's going to protest but he stares her down.

"Fine," she grinds out, marching past Linda and Kevin before she disappears into her office.

I give Kevin a salute before I turn and head for the door, where I shrug on my sweater against the chilly night.

I'm surprised to see Radar walking toward me as I pull the car into my parking slot. His dog is pulling on the leash, trying to get to me when she sees me get out.

"Hey, pretty girl," I coo, crouching down to give her a good rub before I straighten and look a smiling Radar in the eye.

That smile turns into an angry scowl a moment later.

"Who the fuck did that to you?"

My hand comes up to my face. "It's nothing. An agitated patient."

"Like hell that's nothing."

For the second time tonight my arm is grabbed and I'm propelled toward the stairway up to my apartment.

"Radar, hold on," I protest, trying to twist from his hold to no avail. "Would you let go? You're hurting me."

The instant those words are out of my mouth, his hand falls away, and I turn to face him. His expression is full of shocked regret and even before he mumbles, "Jesus, I'm sorry," I've already forgiven him.

"I'm fine," I assure him. "We had a patient who was struggling and I was accidentally elbowed in the face. I've already been looked over by one of the residents."

"We need to get some ice on that."

I try to smile but it hurts.

"Which is what I intend to do the moment I get inside. Right before I roll into bed because I have to be at the shelter for seven thirty, I'm beat. Butter chicken tomorrow?"

He nods. "Yeah."

I rise up on my toes and kiss his stubbled jaw before heading up the stairs. About halfway up, I hear his footsteps following me.

"What are you doing?" I glance over my shoulder and recognize determination in the firm set of his mouth.

"Seeing you safely inside."

Too tired to argue with him, I step up to the door, unlock it, and walk inside flicking the lights on. He doesn't follow me in, but braces an arm against the doorway, his eyes burning in mine.

"Kiss me goodnight, Lady."

CHAPTER 10

RADAR

"HOLY SHIT."

Bree flips through the pages of profiles I spent half the night putting together. Sixteen kids—two girls, the rest boys—ranging from fourteen to seventeen and spread out over the US.

"There are more with mentions of that particular game, but these also have the hashtag in common," I clarify.

"What is the significance?" Jake asks.

"Don't know. All I know is that Jeremy Loman tweeted, *Score! Won top marks. #H10:30*, the day after the murder of Sandra Elliot. All other references to it appear to be from gamers as well, most of whom at some point or other also mention *Lock&Load*."

"What about the second attack? The waitress… Gina Castillo?" Yanis pipes up.

"What was the date on that?" Bree asks, already flipping through the pages.

"April seventeenth."

When she gets to the last one, she starts over again and finally looks up.

"There's nothing. You're sure this is all of them?"

"On Facebook, Twitter, and Instagram, yeah."

"What about the other ones; TikTok, Snapchat?"

I glare at Yanis, and already sleep deprived, I snap, "I didn't say I was done. I still have that game to dig into. It's not mainstream or publicly available, so I'll have to dive deeper."

He looks at me with a raised eyebrow before turning his attention to Dimas. "You tackle the hashtag and also make a list of friends any of these kids might have in common who live around here." Then he switches to Bree. "And I want you to contact the police departments in each of those locations." He points at the stack of profiles. "Find out if they've had any random attacks close to the date those hashtags were posted."

"On what authority?" Bree wants to know.

"Tell them to call Chief Underwood. I'll give him a heads-up in a minute."

"And me?" Jake asks.

"Find out what the fuck H10:30 means. Let's get to work."

Yanis grabs his phone off the table and already has it up to his ear when he leaves the conference room. The rest of us file out after him.

It's so easy to lose track, sifting through layers of encryptions as I try to find any information on the game. By the time the hunger pangs in my stomach alert me to the fact I skipped right over lunch, I'm no wiser on its origin, but I did find an encoded link containing the name. I've only gotten as far as a login page asking for a reference code and haven't managed to get much farther.

Looking into the office I notice only Bree is still there, talking on the phone. Another angry growl from my stomach has me dart a quick glance at the clock on my computer screen shows a quarter past five.

Fuck. Butter chicken at Hillary's, but I still have to get home to feed Phil.

THE STATE OF her face isn't much better in the light of day and a renewed anger at the bastard who caused it surges to the surface. The silky brown of her skin has turned a dark almost purple on her left cheekbone and around her eye.

"Hey."

Instead of responding in kind, I step over her threshold, slide my hands on either side of her neck, and claim her mouth with mine. Her hands come up to rest on my chest, her fingers curling in the fabric of my shirt, as her tongue boldly tangles with mine.

Oh yeah. I didn't imagine the matching hunger the first time I kissed her a few days back. Nothing tentative about the way her mouth moves against mine. She claims me right back and fuck if that isn't an even bigger turn-on.

"Hey back," I mutter against her lips, opening my eyes to find one of hers still swollen shut. It works like a bucket of ice water and I jerk my head back, letting my hands slide to her shoulders. "Shit, did I hurt you?"

"Not even a little," she assures me with a smirk, before reaching around me to close the door.

"It smells fantastic."

I only now notice the scent of dinner; rich with spices I can't quite place.

"Hope it tastes that way too," she says, moving ahead of me into the kitchen. "Have a seat. Beer?"

"Sure." I sit down at the kitchen table, which is already set with placemats and cutlery. "Anything I can help with?"

She walks up with a bottle from the fridge and hands it to me.

"I just have to fry up the chapati. Everything else is ready."

"Chapati?" I call after her when she makes her way to the stove.

"It's a little like naan, but much thinner and made with roasted cumin seed."

I can smell the cumin a minute later when she slides the first flat disk into a cast-iron pan and my mouth waters. Shortly after, I have a steaming plate in front of me and I barely manage to mumble my appreciation before shoving the first bite in my mouth.

Goddamn, the woman can cook. The flavor is deceptively smooth until the heat hits my taste buds.

She didn't mess around and I feel small beads of sweat forming on my forehead. When I try to surreptitiously wipe at my face, she chuckles softly.

"I should've warned you I'm pretty liberal with the heat."

"I'm finding that out," I admit, my double meaning not escaping her as she draws in a sharp breath between those lush lips.

My body is at war between a persistent need for nourishment and an undeniable craving for her. I'll deal with one first, so I have energy for the other later. There's no mistaking the promise in the way she absentmindedly bites the swell of her bottom lip.

Without breaking eye contact, I lift another forkful to my mouth.

Hillary

Have mercy.

I can feel the hair on my arms stand on end. Even from across the table I feel the heat of his gaze.

"Another beer?" I blurt out, never mind his bottle is still mostly full. From the slow grin stretching that wicked mouth, he's well aware of the effect he has on me. "Well, I need one."

I shove my chair back and head for the fridge, where I linger a little too long in the cold air before turning back. Thankfully his eyes are on his plate as he continues to eat as if he didn't just set me on fire with that look.

"So what happened yesterday?" he prompts me,

motioning to my face when I sit down across from him.

Grateful for the distraction, I tell him about the patient stumbling into the ER. Within minutes I relax and find myself sharing some of the more memorable moments in the life of an ER nurse. By the time we finish dinner, we've fallen into a relaxed conversation about our respective jobs. What Radar does falls well above my pay grade and I only understand about a third of what he talks about, but I could listen to the passion that shines through in his voice all day long. I always considered that kind of technical job tedious, but there's nothing boring about the enthusiasm with which he describes his work.

He's still talking when I stack our dishes and stand up to bring them to the kitchen.

"I'm sorry. Didn't mean to ramble on." He chuckles, mostly to himself. "I tend to get carried away and it wouldn't be the first time I bored someone to sleep."

This sheepish, self-deprecating man is quite the change from the confident, almost predatory one from earlier. The duality is captivating.

"I like listening to you talk," I admit, setting the dishes in the sink so my back is turned to him. "You clearly love what you do."

He doesn't respond right away and I turn on the faucet to fill the sink.

"I do."

His voice is much closer than I expected and when I look up, I see his reflection right behind mine in the kitchen window. I hold my breath when I feel his warm hand land on my hip and his head dip lower.

"Move over," he whispers, his lips brushing the shell of my ear. "My mom taught me cooks don't do dishes." With slight pressure from his hand, he moves me aside and takes my place. "Go drink your beer. I've got this."

My whole body feels charged as I go sit down at the table.

"Your mother is a wise woman," I comment.

"Was," he corrects me, glancing over his shoulder.

"I'm so sorry."

"Thanks. She died from cancer when I was twenty-seven."

"That must've been hard."

He shrugs. "It was. Mostly on my dad. He never quite recovered."

"Was it long ago?"

He turns around again with amused eyes and a smile playing on his lips.

"Is that your roundabout way to find out how old I am?" he teases and I smile back.

"Maybe."

He turns back to the dishes before answering.

"Thirteen years. I just turned the big four-oh. How old are you?"

"Thirty-six."

"Family?"

Fair is fair, I guess. Not my favorite topic, but it's the risk I took when I broached the subject myself.

May as well lay it all out and be done with it.

I busy myself peeling the label off the beer bottle when I start talking.

"I was raised by my grandparents, but they both passed on a while ago. My mother was fourteen when she had me and I never knew my father."

The sound of hands moving in water abruptly stops and when I look up his eyes are on me.

"That sounds tough."

"Not really. My grandparents were great people. Simple but decent, you know? We didn't have a whole lot, but they made a happy home for me."

"And your mom?"

"She's alive."

At least I assume she is. She left home at eighteen and had been a vague presence in the background while I was growing up. Drifting in and out of our lives until she married an investment broker from New York, she was quick to leave the reminders of her meager background and youthful poor judgments far behind. She didn't even bother to show when her parents passed away, one after the other. As far as I know, she still lives in the Big Apple with her perfect family.

"Here in Grand Junction?"

I can't stop the snort. "Hardly. She went on to bigger and better things and never looked back."

He's silent as he turns back to the dishes and I'm feeling a little exposed. I don't talk about my background a lot. People are quick to judge, and I'd rather be taken for who I am than where I'm from. I decided long ago I wasn't going to make myself a victim of my mother's rejection. That's her cross to bear—not mine.

"Her loss," he says suddenly, putting the last dish in the rack before draining the sink.

His comment's relevance to my thoughts makes me wonder if maybe I spoke out loud.

"Yes, it is," I confirm, smiling when he turns to face me, but the smile slides from my face when he wipes his hands on a towel and slowly stalks my way.

I have to tilt my head way back to look up at him as he bends over me.

"Thank you for an amazing dinner," he mumbles, right before his mouth brushes mine.

I feel a rush of disappointment when the kiss is brief and light.

"Leaving already?"

He straightens and takes my hand in his, pulling me to my feet.

"Who said anything about leaving?"

"Oh, it sounded like you were."

He grins and shakes his head slowly, as he tugs me to the living room.

"Didn't want to forget later. My mind might be on other things."

"What other…"

I don't get a chance to finish before he drops back on the couch, pulling me on top of him. Putting my hands on his chest I push up a little, looking down in his face.

"I see," I mutter, reaching to pluck his glasses off his nose and setting them down on the table.

He squeezes my ass with one hand and slides the other up my spine, cupping the back of my neck.

"Good."

His eyes crinkle and his lips curve when I lower my mouth to his.

Dear God, the man can kiss, making me forget where I am. Not rough but firm, sure, naturally confident in what he's doing. I tend to overthink, but he doesn't give me a chance to do anything but allow instincts to take over.

With my hands in his soft hair and my mouth thoroughly engaged, I let him tug my legs between the couch and his hip, lining my aching core up with the impressively hard ridge in his jeans.

Oh, yes.

Ever so slightly he tilts his hips in concert with the rhythm of his kiss, barely brushing the building need between my legs. Teasing and coaxing, until I'm rocking against him, looking for maximum friction.

I break my mouth from his, gasping for air, when I feel his hand slide down the back of my pants and trace down the seam of my ass. He groans when his fingers find me slick and I throw my head back when he searches for my clit, pressing his face in my neck.

All I hear is the blood rushing in my ears as he builds me up, strumming me like an instrument. I push up on his chest and gyrate my hips, aching for the climax that seems just out of reach. I gasp when his long digits enter me, pumping deep as I feel the heat of his mouth closing over a fabric-covered nipple. The sting of his bite has my body go into free fall and I cry out my release.

RADAR

I WELCOME HILLARY'S weight draped on me, and the tickle of her hair brushing my face.

My heart is pounding and my cock painfully hard, but I keep my arms wrapped tightly around her soft form while I allow both to subside.

"Am I getting too heavy for you?" she whispers, trying to lift up.

"No. Don't move, I like you right where you are."

"Okay."

She relaxes and snuggles her face in my neck. I sigh when her scent settles around me, the spice of her sex and a hint of coconut from her hair.

"You didn't…" She slides a hand down to my waistband and I quickly stop her.

"Next time," I tell her, but she's already lifting her head again. Languid brown eyes look into mine.

"You sure?"

I lift my mouth to hers in a brief kiss before I lie through my teeth.

"Positive."

She seems unconvinced and climbs off me, staring hard at my crotch.

"Really?"

"You're not helping," I grumble, swinging my legs around and sitting up.

"Any particular reason?"

I should've known she'd be direct. Something else that sets her apart from any other woman I've been with. No games, not with Hillary.

"Yes," I answer her as I get to my feet and face her, placing a hand at the base of her neck. "Doesn't exactly make me proud to admit, and I hope it doesn't offend you, but quick and easy has been my MO for the most part. It's not what I'm after with you."

"No muss, no fuss kinda guy?"

I know she's teasing when the corner of her mouth twitches and I lean my forehead against hers.

"I was. Now I'm not. I wanna do this right."

"Okay."

I kiss her lightly. Her arms snake around my waist, hands fisting in my shirt as she pulls me closer. I kiss her again, this time a little deeper and she rolls her hips against mine.

"All right, you minx," I scold her, as I pull away and see the sparkle in her eyes. "I should get going before you corrupt me." She snorts and follows me to the door. "What are you doing Saturday?"

"Going out with friends."

"Friends?"

The surge of jealousy is unfamiliar to me but seems to amuse Hillary.

"Yes," she confirms with a grin. "Linda and Maggie, my very lesbian, and very married friends."

"Good," I can't stop myself from saying.

"Thursday?" she suggests, an eyebrow raised.

"I can make that work. This time I'll take care of dinner."

"You're cooking?"

She seems rightfully surprised.

"I didn't say that. I do a mean takeout, though. My place same time?"

"Sounds good. Anything I can bring?"

I lean down and give her a hard kiss.

"Just you."

I force myself out the door before I throw my own rules out the window and take her up on her offer. I can wait a couple of days.

"Just to say," she says behind me when I get to the top of the stairs. "Wouldn't have thought any less of you if you'd fucked me quick and easy on the couch."

Fuck me, the woman's out for my blood.

"You're evil," I tell her, without turning my head as I start down; her rich chuckle following me.

Thursday is a fucking century away.

CHAPTER 11

RADAR

"ANY NIBBLES?"

Yanis walks into my office and sits down on the other side of my desk.

"Not yet."

Yesterday Dimi and I set up a couple of fake Facebook accounts, posing as teenage gamers.

We worked on filling the timelines with posts you'd expect to see and joined as many gaming groups as we could get into, taken from the profiles on the list we put together. Then we started interacting with any of the hashtag users each time we spotted one of them posting or commenting in the groups. We'd send them a friend request and tried to engage them in gamer talk.

The fake profiles were Bree's idea after she discovered at least two other bold, apparently random but lethal attacks in different cities. Both had similar witness accounts: two attackers wearing dark hoodies jumping their victims in the street. The victim in San

Luis Obispo was stabbed. He was the owner of a small landscaping company, a family man leaving behind a wife and three children. In Saginaw the victim—this one a seventeen-year-old girl—was doused with acid and managed to crawl under her car when a passerby scared off her assailants. She died from her devastating injuries the next morning.

"What did Underwood have to say?" I ask him.

"He's up to his eyeballs. He was almost relieved to hear there may be similar cases elsewhere so he can call in the Bureau. There's a lot of rumbling in the department as a result of the first few dismissals he issued. Can't find people to pick up extra shifts to cover the holes in the schedule and union lawyers are permanently staking out his office."

"Not like that wasn't expected," I offer.

"True, although I'm starting to wonder if Underwood was prepared for this kind of backlash. Apparently, City Hall is breathing down his neck as well. He's been putting out fires everywhere."

"City Hall? Didn't he have to get council's approval for us to investigate the department in the first place?"

"He did, in a behind-closed-doors session, but with most of the department in an uproar they're suddenly worried about votes in the upcoming elections."

Of course. Bloody politics. One of the reasons I'm glad to be working for a relatively small independent company. No back-office dealings, self-serving manipulations, or ass-kissing in this work environment.

Jake sticks his head in the door, a big grin on his face.

"Found something."

"The hashtag?" Yanis wants to know as he gets out of his chair.

"Yup. Come have a look."

I rush to follow the guys into the big office where Jake points triumphantly at his computer screen where a quote is visible.

For we know him who said, "Vengeance is mine; I will repay." And again, "The Lord will judge his people."

(Hebrews 10:30)

"Vengeance is mine? A Bible verse?"

I'll be the first to admit the Bible would not have been at the front of my mind to explore.

"Not just one," Bree, sitting at her desk, contributes. "There are a lot of references to revenge in the Bible; that exact line appears in two other verses."

My mind starts spinning. "Which ones?" I bump Jake out of the way and sit down at his computer. "Maybe there are other hashtags."

"Way ahead of you." Jake grins over my shoulder. "Romans 12:19, and Deuteronomy 32:35."

"Here…" Bree hands over a printout a few pages long. "Used the same hashtag format as the original to run both these. We got over thirty hits but were able to whittle the references down to sixteen and cross-referenced those to our original list of names."

I scan the copies she handed me. Nine, nine more names and dates to add to the shortlist for investigation. This is ballooning into something that sends chills down my spine.

"Are we going to assume each of these is connected to an attack?"

"We're gonna work from that premise," Yanis decides. "Same thing we did before to start. I think it's time for Underwood to call in the big guns."

Meaning the feds will be crawling all over this in no time. Wouldn't be the first time we had to hand over a case to the Bureau, but that doesn't mean it sits well with me. The past twelve or so years have done little to dull my animosity toward them.

Yanis places his hand on my shoulder and squeezes. He knows how I feel. Hell, he's the one who saved me from doing some serious time in federal prison. Not a period in my life I'm particularly proud of. I'd been a hobby hacker, mostly to prove I could get into anything, but I'd made a bit of a stir in that world when I managed to get into the University of Colorado's mainframe.

It was not that long after my mom died, and I'd been struggling. I was down, didn't see my life going anywhere, and let myself get sucked in with a criminal element. Not my smartest move, deciding my hobby could make me a nice income without breaking a sweat.

That's how the FBI got me; I'd taken on a job breaking into the server of a small pharmaceutical company to steal information on a new drug they were developing. It just so happened PASS was providing security for that company. With Yanis' intervention, I ended up assisting the FBI in bringing down the group that was brokering that information to competitors and was offered a job with PASS, instead of a lengthy stay in jail.

"But for now, it's late," he says, lifting his hand from my shoulder. "Let's get some rest, get at it again tomorrow when we're fresh. Good work, guys."

I open my mouth to object when I remember Hillary is supposed to be over in less than half an hour. As much as I'd like to start digging into this new information, the last thing I want is to stand her up. My tendency to get absorbed in my work was one of the main reasons I failed any earlier attempts at a relationship. Or so I've been told. I guess if I'm serious about pursuing anything with her I'll have to find a better balance.

I walk into my office and Phil lifts her head from the dog bed under my desk.

"Yes, we're heading home shortly," I mumble, and start to shut down my laptop.

I shove it, and a couple of files into my backpack and am about to slip the leash on Phil when an alert sounds from one of my desktop computers. A window popped up, displaying a message from a connection we made with one of our fake profiles, with an invitation to join a secret society of gamers.

"Guys!" I call out. "I think we've got a bite!"

Plopping down in my seat, I quickly respond while the others file into my office and crowd behind me to see the large computer screen. Fifteen minutes later we wait with bated breath to see if the code sequence I finally wrangled from my new friend, Billy Pope, will get us access to a *'rad new game.'* His words, not mine.

After what feels like an hour, but is in reality probably no more than a couple of minutes, a window pops up.

Welcome to Lock&Load - Revenge

Hillary

"Where are you?"

That's how I answer the phone when I see who's calling.

I'm pissed. I stood at his door, knocking, for five minutes before I called his number and got no answer. Thinking maybe I got the time wrong, I went back home, waited until seven and walked over again. Same result, no one home, and no answer when I tried calling.

It's now eight forty-five and having worked up a good head of steam, I'm well beyond niceties.

"At the office. Look, I'm sorry, we had a major development and—"

"And you promptly forgot about dinner, and apparently how to use your phone?" I cringe at how much like a nagging wife I sound, when I'm not even sure where I stand. "You know what? Never mind.

I've gotta go."

Before he has a chance to say anything else, I hang up, grab my purse and car keys, and head out the door.

I'd been looking forward to tonight and I'm not about to sit home and wallow. I need a friend to vent to. As it turns out, I get three for the price of one.

The moment Rosie opens the door I hear familiar boisterous laughter from inside the house.

"Hey…" she starts with a smile, which fades when she takes a good look at me. "What's wrong? Come in."

I don't even need to explain, she's already pulling me inside where two smiling faces turn my way.

"Well, I'll be damned! Rosebud didn't mention you'd be coming." Grant Peabody, a good friend of Rosie's, rises to his full height and opens his arms wide. "You gonna stand there or come give me some sugar? Been too long, girl."

Grinning widely—what else can you do when that man turns his charm on you—I let him wrap me up in a big hug.

"Good to see you, Grant," I mumble against his solid chest. I turn my head slightly to Willa, who returns my smile. "Hey. I didn't mean to interrupt."

"Pffft, interrupting my foot," Grant declares, finally letting me go. "Gives us an excuse to start a second pitcher of margaritas."

I notice the spread on the coffee table: nachos, salsa, guacamole, and a pitcher with the remains of the slushy cocktail.

"Rosie was getting cabin fever," Willa explains. "I brought food and some support, and Grant here showed up with the contents of his liquor cabinet."

"Where's Tessa?" I ask, looking around the room.

"Willa got her down," Rosie explains, sinking down on the couch with a sigh. "Finally."

"Sit, girl, you look like you need a drink. I'll hook you up."

I sit down in one of the La-Z-Boy chairs as he grabs the pitcher and heads for the kitchen. When I turn my eyes to Willa and Rosie, I find both of them staring at me.

"What?"

"Spill," Rosie prompts me. "There's a reason you're here and not on that dinner date you said you had."

"Ooo, new beau?" Willa sits up straight.

Yesterday I'd talked to Rosie and mentioned I had plans tonight. What I didn't tell her was with whom, since she seemed way too pleased when she caught Radar at my place and me in the shower when I looked after Tessa. That morning, after Radar left, she tried to milk me for details but there weren't any to share, and I firmly disavowed her of any romantic notions she might have about us.

Heck, I'm still not sure it's wise to pursue anything with the man since our lives are entwined in more than one way. Things would get decidedly uncomfortable if things went sour with everyone looking on. Turns out that was a good call or venting in present company would not have been an option.

"Guy from work," I lie. "A pharmaceutical rep. He stood me up and didn't have the decency to call to let me know."

"Oh, girl…" Grant walks in with an oversized margarita. "It's clear the man didn't have two brain cells to rub together, or he'd never have passed up on a chance to bask in your presence. His loss, darlin'. Good thing I poured you a double. You need to catch up."

"Grant, honey, I'm driving," I protest, but still accept the large glass when he hands it over.

"We Ubered it here," Willa volunteers. "The boys are hung up at the office and Dimas said he'd swing by to pick us up on his way home. He can drop you off too."

At least that part of it was true. I have to admit, it makes me feel a little better, but the fact both his teammates were able to call home, but he didn't give me the same courtesy is telling. Disappointment battles out the anger I felt earlier. I promised myself a long time ago, I wouldn't invest time and energy in someone who wasn't willing to do the same.

Better I find out now than when my heart is too involved.

"Jake'd be happy to drive you too," Rosie offers.

"Perfect." Grant claps his hands and takes a seat. "That's taken care of then."

"So was this your first date?"

I turn to Willa and force a smile. "Technically, yes,

so I haven't really lost anything," I lie.

"I'll drink to that!" Grant announces, lifting his glass.

"Hey, where is your husband?" I ask him.

"Left for a conference in LA this morning."

"And you didn't want to go?"

"Oh, hell no." He jerks his head with a look of disgust on his face. "Hanging out with a bunch of dusty old farts all weekend? I'm sure I can think of better things to do."

"I'm going dancing with some friends Saturday night. We're checking out that new place on Main. Hot Spurs? You should come."

"Oowee! I love me some cowboys. I'm game." He grins widely. "Serves Richard right for leaving me to fend for myself."

"I wanna come," Rosie whines, a dramatic pout on her face.

"Then come."

"I have a child, Grant," she snips at him. "Not like I can drop everything and go, like some people I know. Jake already said he'd be working most of the weekend so I can't count on him."

"You should go," Willa urges her. "I can look after Tessa. Dimas told me the same thing and I am allergic to anything country. Besides, I love that baby."

I've been here fifteen minutes, already I feel a bunch better and now I'm actually looking forward to Saturday night.

CHAPTER 12

RADAR

I CHECK MY phone again with the same result.

I fucked up and I know it.

Since our brief phone call Thursday night, after realizing I stood her up, Hillary hasn't responded to my calls or messages. Of course I've been holed up in the office most of the time since then, pretending to be a disgruntled teenager pissed at every adult in his life. That seemed to be what got the tongues wagging in the chat room my alternate persona landed in.

It took twelve hours to convince whoever the moderator of the group was to deem me fit and grant me entrance to the actual game. Most of yesterday Dimas and I spent taking turns getting familiar with *Lock&Load - Revenge*. The graphics were rudimentary at best, comparable to a cross between the first editions of *Grand Theft Auto* and *Quake*. The game is rife with random violence. The more violent the act, the more points rewarded. Sickening at first, but after just hours of playing, even Dimas and I became desensitized to the gruesome displays. Something Yanis pointed out might well be by design.

We discovered parallels between the virtual and the real-life attacks. In both cases, the attacks were carried out by a team of two. One serving mostly as lookout while the other assaulted the victim. The weapon of choice was often one of convenience. Anything the perps could get their hands on.

I'm just explaining that in the game, if the attack is successful, the primary character is granted access to the next level, while the lookout is assigned a target of their own. Then begins a period of recon, following and stalking the target, discovering their habits and movements, and deciding on a time when they are at their most vulnerable. Then a proposed scene has to be submitted and when approved, the green light is given for the attack.

"I think it's safe to assume the same protocol was followed for the actual killings," I suggest.

We're at the police station in the briefing room, meeting with Underwood, Detectives Garcia and Bissette, and a couple of federal bureau investigators who joined us this morning. Purpose of the meeting is getting the agents up to speed on our progress, which is quite a bit since breaking through last Thursday.

We've been able to compile gamer handles, found some names and locations associated with those, the relevance of the hashtags, and access to the game. Unfortunately, what we don't have is information on who is behind the game, or what the motivation is.

The feds have profilers for stuff like that.

"Possible," SAC Sanders says with a hard look in my direction, "but we prefer dealing in hard concrete facts than making assumptions."

Asshole. I'm sure he's had a look at my file and dismissed me before he even stepped into the meeting; never mind what I can contribute to the case.

"Not an assumption if everything we've uncovered is pointing exactly in that direction," Underwood comes to my defense, but I can tell Sanders is one of those guys who won't easily be swayed from his views.

"Be that as it may, we can't go off a civilian's opinion. Agent Sarah Dunn is our computer specialist." He waves at the other agent, who has so far been a quiet presence in the room. "She will be taking over your online identity."

"Like hell she is." The woman, along with the others in the room, turn their eyes on my outburst. "No offense, Agent Dunn," I add for her benefit. "But if you think I'm handing over my computer, my contacts, my files, or my online reputation, you are mistaken."

"None taken," she mumbles with a shrug. Out of everyone, I'm sure she is the one who would understand how invasive that would be.

Sanders doesn't give a fuck. "If you want to make this difficult, it'll take me less than an hour to get a warrant for you to hand over all you have."

I bet it will, he's probably right, but I'm not about

to hand over access to all of my online history to someone I don't trust. And I definitely don't trust Sanders any more than he trusts me.

"Actually," the soft-spoken Dunn surprises by addressing her boss. "It would probably be far more beneficial if Mr. Jansen and I were able to collaborate. Time-saving as well. I'm sure I could catch up—" The tiny smirk twitching the corner of her mouth underscores her cocky claim. It may not be clear to everyone else, but Agent Dunn just tossed down the gauntlet, a challenge from one hacker to another. "But why waste time? We'd be able to work much faster together."

"You're welcome in our office," Bree jumps in, sending me a warning look not to object.

Not that I was going to. Not after Agent Dunn provoked me. I want a chance to see how good she really is.

"We need to get familiarized with the case and conduct some interviews first," Sanders announces.

"The door will be wide open Monday morning," Yanis offers. "We can offer you the use of our conference room and facilities whenever you need."

Sanders hesitates and looks in Agent Dunn's direction, who raises an eyebrow at him.

"Fine," he agrees less than graciously.

"Pleasant guy," Bree comments when the three of us walk out of the police station a few moments later.

"Sanders has eleven years with the Bureau," Yanis explains. "This is his first case as Special Agent in

Charge. He's flexing his newly discovered muscles."

"You sound almost sympathetic," Bree observes, eyeing our boss curiously.

Yanis shrugs. "Being the boss isn't always easy. Comes with a lot of strings and restrictions."

The look he throws Bree is one of regret, I'm sure of it. Something has been brewing between these two as long as I can remember. I used to think it was because Bree had a chip on her shoulder, being the only female operative in a male dominated industry, but it's more than that.

Bree stares back at him and I suddenly feel like the proverbial third wheel. I'm about to head for my truck when Yanis suddenly turns to me.

"I've got some shit to do. Drop Bree off at the office and you guys go home. I don't want to see either of you until Monday."

Without giving Bree another glance, he stalks to his vehicle and we watch as he peels out of the parking lot.

"Let's go," she says, and starts walking toward my truck.

"What was that all about?" I ask when I get behind the wheel.

"Who knows?" She clips her belt with jerky movements and faces forward. "And who cares?"

I turn the truck toward the office and intend to give her some space when she suddenly turns in her seat.

"Wanna go dancing?"

"Dancing?"

"Yeah. Jake mentioned Rosie was going to Hot Spurs for some line dancing with a few friends. It's a new bar on Main, we should go."

"I don't dance."

"Oh, come on, live a little," she coaxes.

The truth is, I have no sense of rhythm whatsoever. I don't dance, I can't sing either, and the only music I enjoy is classic rock. Line dancing means country, which tends to give me a headache.

"Sure," I answer anyway, because Hillary said she had plans. Logic dictates if Rosie is out dancing, one of those friends she's with will be her.

The only person I'd subject myself to country music for is Hillary. Hell, I'll even hit the dance floor if it'll get her to listen.

HILLARY

"YOOHOO! OVER HERE!"

I do a double take when I spot Grant. Not that hard to do, since he's done up like a rhinestone cowboy, complete with fringed, sparkly vest over a black western shirt and a huge gaudy belt buckle holding up black jeans. But it's the large white hat that takes the cake; the colored lights around the dance floor reflect in the pattern of shiny studs, making him look like a beacon in the sea of moving bodies.

"What on earth?" Maggie mumbles behind me.

"That's Grant, and the little redhead he's dancing with is Rosie," I explain.

I'd shared with Linda we'd probably be joined by

some friends and her easy response had been, "the more the merrier." Of course I had not warned her about Grant's bigger than life presence, but one look at him would tell her enough. I figured the two would probably hit it off since Linda herself has a louder personality, in contrast to her wife who is more of an observer.

Linda's arms are already over her head, hips swinging, as she makes her way through the bodies on the dance floor to where Grant is still waving.

"I think Linda just found her soul mate," Maggie mutters.

I hook my arm through hers and we follow her into the throng. By the time we join them by the edge of the dance floor, Grant is already spinning Rosie with one large hand and Linda with the other.

"I'm gonna need a drink first," I tell him, when he tries to engage me as well.

"Me too," Maggie agrees.

"We've got a table over there." He points at two massive cowboy boots in the middle of a table a few feet away.

"Yours?" I ask with my eyebrows raised, as I check out his sock-covered feet.

"Works to keep poachers away."

"Order me a Mai Tai?" Linda calls out.

Rosie and Grant add to the order and I manage to snag a waitress on our way to the table. By the time the three of them file off the dance floor and take a seat at the table, a collection of cocktails are lined up.

Linda does the honors, introducing Grant and Rosie to her wife as if she's known them forever. That's the way she rolls, making friends is as easy as breathing to her. Maggie is a bit more reserved, but that doesn't last long with Grant cranking up the charm. In no time flat he has everyone roaring with laughter, and our table is drawing some attention despite the loud music.

This is just what the doctor ordered, a fun night out with friends who can make me laugh. I've been a bit down in the dumps the past few days, struggling to resist the temptation to respond to Radar. I know I'll eventually have to answer, but I need time to build up my resolve. It sucks because I really like him, but I don't know if I can handle being an afterthought instead of a priority. That's a bar I set for myself many years ago but have failed to meet, resulting in a sequence of short-lived affairs that inevitably ended with me disappointed. I'm afraid if I started something with Radar, I wouldn't be left simply disappointed. I'd be devastated.

Hope can be a brutal bitch and I've been letting her toy with me too long.

"*The Git Up!*"

Linda jumps up at the first notes of the popular song and grabs Maggie's hand, dragging her to the dance floor. Grant is not far behind her with Rosie in tow.

"Come on, Hillary," he calls over his shoulder, but I wave him off.

I'm good right where I am, sipping my Long Island ice tea and watching the four of them dip and twirl, giggling like crazy on the packed dance floor.

"Oh no, you can't be sitting this one out."

The voice so close to my ear startles me. It belongs to a nice-looking guy who seems out of place, with wire-rimmed glasses and thinning hair, wearing chinos and a golf shirt. Not exactly the kind of patron you'd expect in a bar like this, but his smile and the sparkle in his eyes seem genuine.

"I guess I can't," I agree, taking the hand he offers me as he leads me to the dance floor and finds a spot for us on the opposite side from my friends.

"You must be Hillary," he says, ignoring the crowd following the dance instructions the song provides them with and holding on to my hand while his free arm slips around my waist.

I feel a brief moment of panic, but he quickly introduces himself, putting my mind at ease. Then he starts to move, and boy, he may not look the part, but the man can dance. He expertly leads me into an elaborate two-step, dirty dancing style, and moves us slowly closer to where my friends are dancing.

Rosie spots us first and a smile spreads over her face. Then Grant catches sight of us, and his mouth drops open.

"What? Honey, what are you doing here?"

Before Richard—Grant's husband who decided to surprise him by coming home early—has a chance to explain I feel an arm circle my waist, pulling me back against a warm body.

"You're gonna want to let go," Radar's familiar voice snarls over my head.

Richard immediately releases me, and I'm dragged off the dance floor toward the exit.

The last thing I catch before the chilly outside air hits me is the shit-eating grin on Rosie's face.

CHAPTER 13

Radar

"WHAT THE HELL do you think you're doing?"

She struggles against my hold and I reluctantly let go. The moment I do, she swings around. She looks pissed. Good, I'm angry too. If I'd known going out with some friends included letting some guy with slick moves grind on her, I wouldn't have tried so hard to chase her down these past few days.

"Saving you from making a spectacle of yourself," I snap, almost instantly regretting my words when I see her face pale, but my temper overrides my brain. "The guy was nearly fucking you right on the dance floor."

She inhales sharply before she gives it to me, both barrels.

"You're an idiot, Radar Jansen—or whatever the hell your name is—you know that? You're behaving like a goddamn caveman, and for what? I wasn't that important to you a few days ago, what changed?"

Fuck. That's a lot of questions and I decide the best

course of action is to focus on one at a time.

"Murray." At the blank look on her face I feel compelled to clarify. "Murray Jansen is the name on my driver's license. My dad started calling me Radar when I developed an interest for technology."

She shakes her head in disbelief.

"That's all you come back with? Your name?"

I open my mouth to tell her I was getting to the rest when we're interrupted.

"Everything okay here?"

Shit. Bree—who I left inside—and she's not alone. Jake is glowering at me over her head.

He'd been sitting in a corner of the bar when we walked in earlier, nursing a beer while watching his wife have a blast with her friends from a distance. One of whom, I was relieved to find, was Hillary. He seemed surprised to see us here, but Bree explained she'd arm-wrestled me into checking the new place out. I only had to make an occasional sound to pretend I was listening to their conversation about this afternoon's meeting with the feds, but my eyes never left Hillary.

I caught the older guy closing in on her, watched as he whispered something before she let him take her hand and lead her to the dance floor. It took half a second for me to jump to my feet when I watched them start bumping and grinding.

"It's fine," I tell Bree, but my eyes are on Jake's hard ones.

"What the fuck is going on? What do you want

with Hillary?"

"Nothing," she answers herself. "Absolutely nothing."

Then she turns toward the parking lot and starts walking. After a few steps she stops in her tracks and curses softly, probably realizing she caught a ride. I didn't see her car when I got here.

I ignore Jake's question and catch up with her, putting my hand on her arm.

"I'll take you home." I keep my voice low so only she can hear.

"You haven't answered my question," Jake insists loudly.

"That's because it's none of your business," I return.

Hillary turns her head, her eyes suddenly without fire and the look on her face almost pleading.

"Like hell it's not," Jake barks, when I hear the front door of the bar slam shut.

"He's right," Rosie's soft voice interrupts her husband. "It isn't your business."

"Are you kidding me? Someone has to look out for her. He's—"

I'm not sure what it is he's about to say, but it's safe to assume it won't be complimentary, so I cut him off. Keeping a firm hand on Hillary's arm, I turn to face him.

"I'm taking Hillary home. If you want to discuss something with me, you can do it on Monday. On office hours," I can't stop myself from adding with a bitter taste in my mouth.

I considered Jake a friend, but I guess that friendship only goes so deep. It's not like I'm known as a man whore, someone who goes through women like tissues. I've never given my team any reason to doubt me, so his distrust is cutting deep.

"I'll call you," I hear Rosie yell out to her friend, as I steer Hillary toward my truck.

Once inside she turns on me.

"You were afraid I'd make a spectacle of myself? There was no chance of that until this little stunt of yours. That man is Richard, who is not only gay, but also married to Rosie's friend, Grant. You're the one who turned this into a circus."

Oh hell. I pinch the bridge of my nose, squeezing my eyes shut. I just wanted a chance to talk to her, how the fuck did this get so out of hand?

She stays silent, brooding the entire way home, while I attempt to analyze what went wrong in the first place. But by the time I pull into my parking spot, she doesn't wait to jump out of my truck, my focus is sharp and completely on her.

"Lady, wait," I call out when she takes off toward her apartment. "Hold on." I rush around her to block her path. "You know I've been trying to apologize to you for days. I didn't think I'd have to do it again so soon."

I'm surprised to see a watery smile tug at her lips when she looks at me, shaking her head.

"It doesn't matter," she says, despite the smile, a

sad tone to her voice.

"Like hell it doesn't," I counter, putting my hands on her shoulders. "I fucked up. Again. I wasn't thinking…I just reacted. You mess with my head."

She snorts at that. "I mess with *your* head? You scramble mine, but like I said, it doesn't matter. This…thing between us, it's not going to work."

I take a step closer and slide my hands along her shoulders and up her neck, tilting her chin with my thumbs so she's looking up at me, instead of down at my feet.

"It could." She tries to shake her head, but my hold restricts the movement. "Yes, it could. I'm gonna fuck up, that's almost guaranteed, but I promise I'll work hard to keep that at a minimum. And you…" Her eyes flare with fire, but I continue anyway, "You're gonna have to relax those defenses you have up, because, Lady, you're giving up before we even get started."

"You know nothing about me."

"Not yet," I counter, "but I plan to. One thing I do know, though, is that you're not a quitter. So why start now?"

HILLARY

I WAS SO sure I was doing the right thing.

Heck, I was actually enjoying myself tonight without thinking of him every second. Then he shows up and rattles my conviction with that unexpected alpha display. I didn't see that coming, both literally and figuratively speaking. It's a side of him that is as infuriating as it is attractive. Either way, it stirred my blood.

Now he challenges me, calls me out from behind my wall, and damned if I'm not tempted to take that leap.

Jesus, I'm a mess. My whole life I've set my course using my head, but for some damn reason this time my heart is louder.

What am I supposed to do now?

"You're thinking so hard I can almost hear you," he says before brushing my lips with his. "I need to take Phil for a walk before she springs a leak. Walk with me?"

He takes my hand, slides his fingers between mine, and waits for me to take the first step, which I do almost without thinking.

The dog is clearly happy to see us, and Radar needs both hands to properly greet her, but when he has her on the leash and we step back outside, he takes my hand again.

I don't think I've ever appreciated a hand holding mine more. We don't talk while we walk Phil through the dark, quiet streets, but that simple connection—the small patch of skin touching skin—communicates enough.

It seems natural to follow him back to his apartment, where he heads for the kitchen to grab us a drink and leaves me to check out his living room. It's a surprisingly uncluttered and comfortable space, with a large sectional, a rustic coffee table, and a solid wall unit housing a TV and a sizable collection of books that immediately draw my attention.

My grandma taught me you can learn a lot about a person by their choice of reading material. I run my fingers along the spines, taking stock of what is there. Most of it doesn't surprise me—textbooks about programming, an occasional spy novel from Forsyth or Ludlum—but a few obviously well-read books are unexpected. Harper Lee's *To Kill a Mockingbird, Beloved,* by Toni Morrison, and finally *The Art of Happiness,* by Dalai Lama.

I'm just flipping through the pages of the latter, reacquainting myself with some of the words I read many years ago, when Radar walks in. His eyes go instantly to the book in my hands before lifting to mine.

"My copy looks at least as well-used as yours, but I haven't looked at it in quite a while," I confess, slipping the book back on the shelf.

"How come?" he asks, handing me a beer before sitting down on the couch.

I grab a seat beside him and take a sip, buying myself some time to answer.

"I don't know. Maybe I thought I had it all figured out."

A light shiver ripples down my spine when he stretches an arm along the back of the couch, his fingers lightly brushing the base of my neck.

"Mmm. Not sure we're supposed to figure it all out. I'm thinking it may be more about appreciating the journey than rushing to a destination."

I twist in my seat and scrutinize him.

"There's a great deal more to you than meets the eye, isn't there?"

He winks at me, one side of his mouth pulling up in a lopsided grin, while he tugs at a strand of my hair. Then he takes the beer from my hand and sets both bottles on the table before turning back to me.

"You bet. So much more for you to uncover," he teases warmly, and I find myself leaning in.

For a moment our faces hover a few inches apart, eyes locked and searching. The next my mouth is opening under his, welcoming the confidence of his probing tongue. I slide a hand in his hair, holding him close as I swallow his satisfied groan.

I realize I don't have all the answers—not yet—but what I do know is this man makes me feel a way I haven't allowed myself before. His mouth as he explores mine, hands stroking the outline of my body as he stretches out, pulling me on top of him. The response of his hard body under mine clears the last lingering doubt from my mind, and I let myself get lost in the discovery.

I tug at his shirt, slipping a hand underneath to find his skin almost hot to the touch. My fingers find ridges and firm planes to a smooth, sculpted chest. I brush the pad of my thumb over a tight nipple and feel his hand flex; digging fingers into the swell of my ass.

"Lady…" he groans against my mouth. "If you don't want—"

I kiss him hard, cutting him off.

"I want. I'm done thinking."

"Thank fuck," he mutters under his breath; scissoring up and taking me with him.

My eyes are focused on his back as he leads me down the short hallway toward his bedroom. He pulls me inside, shuts the door, and before I know it I'm on my back on the bed, his body looming over mine.

"Last chance…"

Instead of answering, I grab the hem of my shirt and pull it up and off. I can feel the heat of his eyes as he lets them drift down to where my moderate breasts are straining against the flimsy lace of my bra. At best a handful, but that doesn't seem to bother Radar, who takes my wordless response at face value and reverently tugs down a cup.

"So damn pretty," he mumbles, as his lips cover my nipple.

I can feel the sweet tug of his hot, wet mouth straight down to my core, and I moan softly as he transfers attention to the other side.

He builds me torturously slowly, until I impatiently pull on the back of his shirt, wanting it off. I need to feel his skin against mine. He releases my nipple with a pop and lifts his head, his eyes searching.

"Yes," I plead, my fingers already fumbling with the buttons on my jeans.

He reaches behind him and grabs a fistful of shirt, yanking it over his head, and tossing it aside. Immediately my attention goes to the chest my fingers mapped out earlier. I push up on my elbows and with my tongue circle the small brown disk. He responds by cursing sharply under his breath and then his hands get busy.

My jeans are pulled down—panties and all—and when they get stuck around my ankles, he slides off the bed to remove my shoes and strips me down to my skin. There's no chance for me to feel self-conscious because while his eyes devour me, he rushes to get himself as naked as I am.

Good Lord.

Long, well-defined legs that seem to go on forever; lean hips that flare out to strong, wide shoulders. He's beautiful. All that pale, golden skin covered in a fine dusting of hair, except for the dense strip that leads from his stomach down to arguably the most impressive part of him.

He rips the wrapper of a condom he fished from his jeans pocket and rolls it on, palming his length and stroking lazily. He's playing with me. I feel no shame and spread my legs, watching his nostrils flare as his eyes drift down to my wet center. The next moment his weight is on top of me, the blunt head of his cock slicking along my folds.

"Was gonna eat you," he growls, pushing in slowly. "Take my time." I feel myself stretching around him. "But I couldn't wait…to get…" He suddenly drives deeper and my mouth falls open at the feeling of being filled so completely. "…inside you."

Then he starts moving. Slow and deep.

Oh, yes. Oh God, yes.

My hands find his firm glutes and I tilt my hips to take even more of him.

"No mercy," I mumble, my eyes closed as I'm lost to sensation.

He stills and I groan my displeasure.

"Lady?"

My eyes pop open and see concern on his face.

"I can feel you holding back. You call me Lady, but I'm not fragile." My fingers curve around his ass, teasing the top of his crack. "I can take all of you." I lift my head and graze my teeth along the tendon in his neck. I can feel a shudder running through his body. "Show me no mercy, baby."

He hesitates for only a second, before he pulls my arms from around him and stretches them above my head,

"Hold on," he grunts, and my fingers curve around the slats in the headboard.

Then he hooks me behind the knees, spreading me wide as he looks down at where we're joined—his light skin in stark contrast between my dark thighs—and slowly pulls out.

"Perfection," he whispers, right before he lets go.

He's strong, his pace is furious, and as he wrecks my body in the most delicious way, I realize I almost walked away from him.

From this.

CHAPTER 14

Radar

I BURY MY face in her hair and inhale deeply. She smells of coconut and sex, her body boneless and heavy on mine.

I don't ever want to move.

In fact, I'm not so sure I could right now. My stamina is clearly no match for my hunger for her, because even as I'm gasping for breath after round three, I already crave her again. Unfortunately, I have a condom to deal with and a dog who's been scratching at the bedroom door for the past five minutes.

"Where'you going?" she mumbles when I try to move.

"Clean up, and Phil needs a pee."

I ease her off me and slip out of bed. She's on her stomach, one arm curved over her head and the hand of the other tucked under her chin, face completely relaxed. I run a hand down the curve of her back and the swell of her ass, enjoying the sight of all that silky skin in my bed. Bending down I kiss her between the shoulder blades.

"Mmmm."

"Be right back."

I catch the time on my alarm clock, a little after midnight, and pad into the bathroom where I quickly clean up. When I walk back into the bedroom moments later with a washcloth for Hillary, she's sitting at the foot end of the bed, bent over, digging through the pile of clothes that ended up on the floor.

"What are you doing?"

Her head pivots around and she smiles a little guiltily.

"It's late. I should head home."

Oh hell no.

She finds her shirt but before she can pull it over her head, I pluck it from her hands.

"Stay."

"But I…"

I lean down and cup her face.

"Stay," I repeat. "Makes no sense for you to trek across the parking lot to roll back into bed there. We're both off tomorrow. Not gonna be long and I want to fall asleep with you in my arms."

Her dark brown eyes turn warm as a smile tugs at the corner of her mouth.

"Can I use your bathroom to clean up?"

I hand her the washcloth.

"Brought you this, but knock yourself out. Spare toothbrush in one of the drawers, clean towels in the linen closet."

I snag my jeans and tug them on, grab a hoodie from the hook on the back of the door, and give her mouth a hard kiss. Then I open the door to find an almost desperate Phil turning circles.

A quick walk around the block is usually enough for Phil's bedtime routine. The streets are quiet until I walk up the driveway to the back of the building. I hear glass breaking and the subsequent blare of a car alarm. I notice movement on the far end where the damn manager still hasn't replaced the broken lights edging the parking lot.

"Hey!" I yell, as I start jogging in that direction, Phil hobbling along on her short legs.

I see the flash of a white face against the dark hoodie, as the asshole looks in my direction before he hoofs it the other way. My instinct is to go after him but I stop in my tracks when I see the vandalized car is Hillary's silver Honda. I curse under my breath when I see the windshield bashed in, but my body locks tight when I make out 'BITCH' crudely written on the hood of her car.

The piercing alarm abruptly stops and I can hear the sound of running footsteps approaching, just as I spot a crumpled shape on the ground by the driver side door.

"What the hell?"

I turn and just manage to catch Hillary with an arm around her waist, blocking most of her view.

"Take Phil inside and call 9-1-1."

She glares at me and tries to struggle free, managing

to peek around me. Her sharp inhale tells me she saw what I tried to spare her from.

"Lady, please," I plead softly and her eyes snap to me. "Take the dog? I left my phone on the nightstand so you'll have to call. Tell them young white male, five foot ten or eleven, no facial hair, and I couldn't make out hair color. Go. I'm gonna stay here until the cops show."

She nods sharply, her lips pressed together as she takes the leash from my hands. With one last look at her damaged car, she turns and heads back to my building.

As soon as she disappears inside, I crouch down by the dead animal. It's a raccoon and it looks like it's been dead a while.

"Everything all right here?"

Earl, the building manager, comes sauntering up and my anger flares.

"How about fixing those lights I've been telling you about for weeks? Goddammit."

He raises his hands, holding them up defensively.

"Whoa, easy there, my friend. Heard the alarm and came to check it out."

Earl is one of those good-natured, golly-gee-whiz type characters. Lazy as fuck, but friendly about it. Hard to stay mad at someone who's always smiling.

I take a deep breath in and force myself to calm down. It's wasted energy anyway.

"Someone vandalized Hillary Glenwood's car."

I step aside so he can see. He *tsks* and shakes his

head.

"Now, that's not nice. Did'ya call the police?"

I look over his shoulder at my apartment.

"Hillary is."

No sooner are the words out of my mouth when I see her coming down the stairs. Judging from the rushed clip she's moving at and the dirty look she's throwing Earl, she may have a choice word or two for him as well.

"Didn't I tell you?" She walks right up to him and jabs a finger in his chest. "It's been almost a month, Earl. You know I get home late from my shifts and don't feel safe crossing a dark parking lot. Now look at my car."

"Tomorrow," he promises, apparently more impressed with Hillary's anger than he was with mine. "I'll make a call first thing tomorrow. They'll be fixed by sundown."

"Too late for my car." She glances at the damage before her eyes drift to the mangled animal. "Is that…"

"Raccoon. Dead for a while, I'm guessing roadkill."

Her face scrunches up.

"Eww."

"Why aren't you inside?"

"Oh." She shoves her hand in her pocket and comes out with my phone, handing it over. "They said it might be a while, but I mentioned who I was and asked for Detective Garcia. He called right back, he's on his way."

I bet he is.

I give up on trying to get Hillary to go inside and when a police cruiser pulls into the parking lot; I throw my arm around her shoulders and pull her close.

"Obvious much?" she mumbles, as Garcia gets out of the vehicle.

He glances over and his eyes stare hard at me for a moment before he turns to Hillary with a tight smile.

That's right, sucker.

Hillary

"So you didn't see anything?"

It's the third time Detective Garcia asks the same question.

"No," I tell him again, holding on to my last thread of patience as I watch the tow truck take off with my car. It's late and I'm tired. Besides, it's chilly now the sun is down and all I'm wearing are my jeans and Radar's shirt I grabbed off the floor. "I heard the alarm, recognized it as mine, and ran outside."

"Maybe I should come and check your apartment," he offers.

"She came from mine."

Garcia shifts his attention to Radar, who tucks me closer to his side.

"I see. Well then, I think that's all I need for now. If you're sure you can't think of anyone who could've done this…"

"You mean aside from the kid I identified at the police station? Or his father?"

"Right," he acknowledges, tapping his notebook.

Those were the only two people who might have a beef with me I can think of. Unless…

I turn to Radar.

"Could it have been…" I stop myself and shake my head. That's too farfetched. "Never mind."

"What?" he prompts.

"The person you saw running away, could it have been a woman?"

"Didn't give me that impression."

"Anyone in particular?" the detective wants to know, but I'm already regretting mentioning anything.

What if he goes to question her? It'll give her even more reason to make my life hell. Besides, I doubt she'd get her hands dirty.

"No, no one. Just wondering."

Both men scrutinize me, but Garcia is the first one to break the tension.

"I'll get this written up and drop off a copy. Are you going to be around?" He asks me but Radar answers.

"We will be."

Then Garcia turns to Earl, who's been listening closely.

"Do you have something to clean that up with?" He points at the dead raccoon. The car was already towed

"Sure. I'll toss it in the dumpster."

"Thanks, and get those lights fixed, a dark parking lot is an invitation for vandals and thieves."

"Tomorrow," Earl confirms, throwing a furtive

glance our way. We watch as the detective climbs into his vehicle and drives off. “You folks head inside where it’s warm. I’ll take care of this.”

We leave him to deal with the mess, something I don’t feel even the slightest bit guilty about. Inside the apartment, Radar points in the direction of the bedroom.

“Get under the covers, you’re shivering. I’m just going to lock up. Want me to make you something warm to drink? I don’t have tea, but I have decaf coffee.”

“I’m fine, thanks. I should probably get my stuff and head—”

He tags me behind the neck and drops his forehead to mine.

“We’ve had this conversation. Nothing’s changed.”

He gives me a hard kiss before turning me toward the bedroom. I’m too tired to argue. My clothes are stripped off and I’m rolled up in his comforter like a cocoon, when he walks in moments later. From under heavy eyelids I observe as he tugs off his hoodie, kicks off his shoes, and sheds his jeans.

“Quit looking at me like that,” he growls, crawling into bed beside me. “You were dead on your feet out there.”

He rolls toward me, tugging one side of the bedding loose to cover himself. Then he curves his arm around me, pulls me close, and tucks my head under his chin. He’s like a furnace. I moan, rubbing my cold feet against his warm ones.

"Hillary? Who's the woman?"

Shit.

"Someone from work. I shouldn't have said anything. I can't see her doing something like this."

"What's her problem?"

His long fingers stroke lightly down my spine and I feel the tension drain from me.

"She hates me," I mumble, half asleep.

"Yeah?"

"Mmm. She has a thing for Dr. Sugarlips and I dated him." His fingers still for a beat before they resume their path over my skin. "Radar?"

"Right here, Lady."

"Can we talk tomorrow?"

I feel his lips kiss my forehead.

"Sure. Go to sleep."

I burrow my face in his neck and sigh deeply, warm and content.

"Radar?"

I can feel him chuckle.

"Haven't moved."

"You smell good."

A BEAM OF early morning sun sneaks from between the curtains, playing across his sleeping face. Surprisingly long lashes throw a shadow on his cheekbones and his slow, deep breaths escape his slightly parted lips.

Gorgeous.

The man hides a lot behind his outdated glasses, the almost ever-present beanie, and the slightly baggie clothes he seems to prefer. All strong angles and lean muscle. He must work out, there's no way a desk jockey can be in this type of physical condition by good genes alone.

I'm surprised at how well I slept. I'm not in the habit of sharing a bed. I mean, I may go to bed with someone, but don't stay there. And I can count the times I've invited someone to mine. Either way, it always resulted with me waking up alone at home.

I let my fingers trail down his chest and over his abs.

Maybe I missed out.

I carefully lift my head from his shoulder and look down, getting an eyeful of his long erect cock, awake before he is. The sheets slid down during the night, only covering our legs, leaving most of our bodies exposed. It's an invitation to explore I can't resist.

He is both hard and soft as I slip my hand around his length, feeling the bristle of his pubic hair against my knuckles. It almost feels illicit to get turned on by someone who is unaware. I hesitate for a moment before I slide down his body and tentatively trace the thick vein running the length of his cock with my tongue.

I sense the moment he wakes, a slight hesitation in his breathing and a tightening of his leg muscles. When my eyes track up, I find his open just a crack.

"Morning," he croaks in a voice thick with sleep.

"Morning," I return a little sheepishly. "I'm sorry if I—"

"Don't be. I like that you take what you want."

Well then.

Keeping my eyes locked on his slitted ones, I open my mouth and slide the tip between my lips. The groan rumbling deep in his chest vibrates all the way down between my legs. He hisses when I swallow him down as far as I can take him, and I can feel his body tense with restraint.

His nostrils flare and his jaw tightens as I let him almost slip from my mouth before taking him deep again. I use my hand to cup his balls, gently massaging them, and he groans again, biting his plump bottom lip.

"Fuck, Lady…"

I always thought giving head was about giving someone else control, which is why it's never been a favorite. I was so fucking wrong. I have him at my mercy and it's a huge turn-on.

Yup, definitely missed out.

CHAPTER 15

RADAR

WORKING WITH AGENT Sarah Dunn wasn't half as bad as I anticipated it to be.

For one thing, she turned out to be as much of a computer geek as I am, complete with little regard for outward appearances. That much was obvious when she showed up dressed in a pair of yoga pants and an old men's flannel shirt, her hair up in a messy bun, and a pair of tortoiseshell glasses perched on the tip of her nose. A far cry from the prim and proper woman I met two days ago, dressed in a pinstripe suit, her collar buttoned to the top, and hair sleeked back in a ponytail.

This Agent Dunn I could at least identify with.

To top it off, she'd walked in this morning, barely managing to hold on to a box of donuts and a double tray of coffees that were quickly disbursed through the office.

"Oh what a relief," she blurted out, looking around. "I contemplated wearing my bureau suit, but I gambled maybe you guys weren't that firm on appropriate attire. Besides, I don't function well unless I'm comfortable."

Dimas was the first to reassure her with one of his disarming smiles, telling her we don't stand on protocol in this office. It's true. We have a locker room for a reason and each of us has at least a jacket and dress shirt to change into, in case we need to look 'professional.' The rest of the time it's come as you are.

Sarah also surprised me when she seemed completely at ease navigating the dark web. Almost with the comfort of a dyed-in-the-wool hacker.

I spent the morning getting her familiarized with the chat room and the game. Rather than piggybacking on to my alter ego, she set up an online profile for herself in no time and managed to con her way into *Lock&Load's* chat room with lightning speed. Her reasoning had been that as two identities we can spread the net a little wider. The tricky part with this investigation is you set yourself apart from the rest if you ask too many questions, so you have to tread carefully while at the same time rushing to get a decent lead.

Bree heard through her contacts another attack had taken place earlier, this one in Montrose, and the pressure is on. The victim in this case was the coach of a high school football team. The single man in his late thirties was found dead in the school's locker room shower, strangled and with his face bashed into the tile floor. The ligature had been a jock strap.

Local police reviewed the school's security footage from the outside cameras and saw two figures, identities obscured by the dark hoodies pulled low to cover their faces. Since word of the chain of attacks has been doing the rounds in law enforcement, they immediately contacted the FBI. Sanders is on his way there now.

Montrose makes me think of my dad and I make a mental note to call him tonight to check in and firm up our fishing weekend in two weeks. Maybe I'll see if Hillary has any vacation time due and would like to come. I'd love to introduce her to my family.

She and I spent a long leisurely morning in bed yesterday, after which I dropped her off at a car rental place. Her insurance would send out an adjuster to the repair shop, where it was towed, to inspect the damage in the next few days, but she was covered for a temporary rental.

She went home after that, insisting she had stuff to do before her double shift today. I would've liked her to hang around with Phil and me but got the sense she needed a little space. I may not be an expert on women or relationships, but I'm not stupid. There are times you can push but this wasn't one of them.

Ironically Hillary isn't that different from me. We're both independent, used to being by ourselves, and as far as I know she hasn't really been in any kind of serious long-term relationship either. Maybe neither of us is cut out for one, but it's something I definitely would like to explore with her.

So I backed off, and let her get on with the rest of her Sunday by herself.

Today I know she's both at the shelter and the hospital and won't be home until after midnight, but I'll be sure to at least keep a watchful eye out to make sure she gets inside okay. Luckily Earl pulled some strings and had a cherry picker out in the parking lot yesterday fixing the lights.

"Who is >*Fury#1*?" I look up and meet Sarah's eyes over my screen. "A private chat just opened up. He wants to know my location."

I scoot my chair back and round the desk, leaning over her shoulder.

"You bouncing your IP?"

She gives me an eye roll.

"Obviously. He can dig deep but he won't get further than a Denver address."

"No way for him to trace it to the Bureau?"

"None," she confirms.

"Tell him and see what he wants. Keep him busy."

I head back for my own computer and do a little digging of my own into the handle while she has him occupied.

>*Fury#1* is busy. I'm not about to pump the name into the chat room search engine but he—or she—seems active on just about every topic thread I open. What stands out is his general tone. He sounds almost parental: praising, mediating, correcting, and… moderating.

"Is he still on?"

"Yup. I tried to avoid answering, but he pushed so I gave him Denver."

"Where is it gonna lead him?"

"Imperial Coffee. An internet coffee shop in Larimer Square."

"You may want to get some eyes on the place," I suggest. "I have a feeling this guy is our chat moderator."

I listen with half an ear as she passes on instructions to someone on the phone while I probe a little deeper, running a few searches to see if I can come up with any information for this *Fury*.

"Huh," Sarah mumbles. "Just like that he's gone."

Right at that moment my screen starts filling with code, auto-scrolling through pages and pages of encrypted computer language and then it goes black.

"Fuck!"

On my screen a single large icon appears of a wagging finger.

"What've you got?"

"I've been made," I grind out, as I duck under my desk to pull the power on my computer.

"What now?" Yanis asks, ducking his head in the office at my outburst.

I've already hooked my office backup server to my laptop. The server is programmed to automatically record every keystroke as well as a continuous screen video from when I log in until I sign off. Then it stores the information on a secure web server. Even with my computer compromised, I'm able to retrace every step I made.

"Now I'm going to find out how the bastard locked onto me." I turn to Sarah. "Printing off two hundred thirty-six pages of code, make sure the printer has paper?"

I'm pissed as hell. It's been a long time since someone caught me snooping around and it burns to have been bested. Not only that but trying to decipher that many pages of encrypted language is going to take fucking ages.

"There's good news," Sarah announces, as she feeds a full ream of paper into the printer.

"Oh yeah?" I bite off sarcastically.

She doesn't seem to care and throws me a wide grin.

"You bet. *Fury* just took the bait and confirmed himself to be a major stakeholder in *Lock&Load*. We have a lead, we have a name, and with a bit of luck…" She points at the sheets of code the printer starts spewing out. "…we'll have an address."

"Need anything from me?" Yanis asks, pushing away from the doorframe.

"Yeah. Something to eat," I jump on the offer. "Looks like we'll be here for a while."

HILLARY

"DID YOU TELL them?"

I startle when Jeff grabs my arm and pulls me into the meeting room down the hall from my office, closing the door.

"Tell who what?"

I just finished a quick early lunch and was heading back to write up reports for the two new residents I interviewed this morning, before I head over to the hospital.

"The cops. I thought I told you I don't want nothing to do with them," he hisses.

So far I've never felt unsafe at the shelter, but the hand holding onto my arm is squeezing really tight, and we're alone in here.

"I don't understand." I try to wrangle my arm from his hold, but he only digs his fingers in deeper. "About the attack on you? I didn't tell the police. Why would you think that?"

He leans close enough for me to smell the alcohol fumes coming from his pores. Doesn't seem like a good time to bring up the shelter rules of no booze.

"There's a cop waiting in your office. Willa just showed him in. Wanna tell me he's here for a social visit?"

I flinch at the spittle hitting my face. Spreading my feet, I twist my body while at the same time bringing my forearm up and out, breaking his hold on my bicep. Struggling with his balance, he teeters on his feet, giving me a chance to pull the door open and step into the hallway where I'm no longer hidden from view.

Suddenly I wonder if perhaps Jeff had something to do with the damage on my car.

"They're probably here to talk to me. My car was vandalized early Sunday morning." I watch him closely for any sign of guilt. There's none. He looks confused.

"Your car?"

"Yeah. In the parking lot outside my place. The detective was supposed to come by with the report."

"Oh." His face displays remorse as his eyes drop down to the floor. "I thought…"

"I know what you thought, Jeff, but it's been three weeks. Do you honestly think if I was gonna break my word to you I wouldn't have done so right away? Doesn't mean I don't still think you should talk to them yourself, but I can't make you."

I rub my arm where I can still feel his hand and his watery, bloodshot eyes follow the movement before he lifts to mine.

"I…I'm sorry. Didn't mean to hurt you. I just…if I talk, he's gonna find me."

"Who, Jeff? Who's gonna find you?"

He shakes his head and ducks past me into the hallway, mumbling under his breath, "You don't wanna know."

I watch as he stumbles through the lobby and out the front door. I should talk to Willa about him. I'm worried about his state of mind.

"Hillary."

Detective Garcia gets to his feet when I walk into my office. It's the first time he's used my first name.

"Detective," I respond, rounding my desk.

"Manuel, please."

"What can I do for you?" I ask, sitting down in my chair and he follows suit.

"Have you had any luck with your insurance company?"

Not what I asked, but okay.

"I'm waiting for the adjuster to call with a time. What brings you here?" I try again.

"I just wanted to make sure you were being looked after." He slides a card across the table with the name of a local body shop. "My buddy owns the place. I talked to him this morning. He'll do a good job for you. Reasonable. I told him to give you my discount."

Either the detective is on the take—which I highly doubt, I don't get the sense auto-body repair is a big money business—or he is trying to win my favors. Probably the last, which pisses me off since Radar couldn't have been more clear in that parking lot, conveying I am with him.

"Appreciate the thought," I tell him as diplomatically as I know how. "But at this point I'm not even sure it's worth getting it fixed. I may be looking around for a new vehicle."

"I can help you with that."

Okay, first of all, why is it that men immediately think because something has an engine a woman is useless? And secondly, is he dense?

Fuck diplomatic.

"Actually, I think I'd prefer Radar to help me with that. I'm sure he has an opinion on the kind of car he'd like his girlfriend to drive."

It's a bit of a stretch, but I figure after spending a night and part of a day in his bed, I'm allowed to represent myself as such.

"Ah, I see," he says and gets to his feet.

I have to keep from rolling my eyes. Finally.

He starts digging inside his jacket and comes up with a folded document.

"It's the report," he clarifies. "I mentioned I would drop it off? You'll probably need it for insurance."

"Yes." I stand as well and take the paper he hands over. "I appreciate it."

With a sharp nod he turns and starts walking out of my office.

"Oh, Detective? Have there been any developments?"

He stops and looks over his shoulder.

"Nothing yet. Like I mentioned Sunday morning, all we have is a single, vague description of the perp. Very little to work with. If there is any movement, we'll be sure to let you know."

"And the murder of Sandra Elliot?"

His eyes narrow.

"You'll have to talk to the FBI; they've taken over the investigation." Then he leaves me with his parting shot. "Of course, you could also ask your boyfriend since I understand he's working with the feds."

Oh yeah. He got the message this time and he's not liking it.

I spend my remaining time working on those

reports and manage to get them done with five minutes to spare. I duck my head into Rosie's office to give her a quick goodbye and have to promise I'll tell her what happened Saturday night next time I'm in.

My phone starts ringing on my way to the small SUV I rented.

"Hey."

"Lady," Radar rumbles. "I need a favor."

I slide behind the wheel and look at the dashboard clock.

"I'll do my best."

"This case just went hot and I'm gonna be tied down here for however long." He sounds tired and rushed so I hold off on asking what happened. "It's Phil. I left her home this morning, thinking I'd be back to let her out tonight. Looks like that's not gonna happen."

"Oh shit, Radar. I could walk her now real quick, but then I have a shift at the hospital until midnight and I don't know if you'll be home before me. Can she last that long?"

"She has before. Normally Bree looks after her in cases like this, but she's up to her eyeballs in this case as well. I'm sorry to put you on the spot. I hope to get out of here at some point, but more likely I won't be coming home tonight."

"Sure. It's not a problem. But…uhh…how do I get in? I don't have a key."

"Earl has a spare. I'll get him to meet you there and I'll text you the alarm code."

"Okay. I'm on my way now."

I start the car and set the phone to hands-free.

"Oh, and Hillary? Why don't you sleep at my place?"

"When you may not even be there?"

I hear rustling and then a door close before he comes back on the line, his voice low.

"But I'll know you're in my bed, where I can picture you."

A warm balloon expands my chest and butterflies dance in my stomach.

"I can do that," I whisper.

CHAPTER 16

HILLARY

"COME ON PHIL, you're gonna make me late."

I swear the dog has sniffed every single blade of grass since we left the apartment ten minutes ago.

I was already running late after waking up about half an hour after I should've. I'm blaming Radar, not that I've seen him—he never made it home—but his bed is comfortable and smells of him, so when the alarm on my phone rang this morning, I turned it off just so I could linger a little longer. I promptly fell back asleep.

Then I discovered I forgot my shampoo and relaxing conditioner when I packed a quick overnight bag before my shift yesterday afternoon. Apparently real guys use some three-in-one crap that comes in a convenient single bottle, but does nothing for my hair, which is air-drying into frizzy little curls. But at least I smell good, just like Radar.

"Come on, girl. Wanna go home? I'll give you a treat. You wanna treat?"

Apparently, the promise of food works and Phil picks up the pace, or as much as she's able to on those short legs.

Unfortunately, we bump into Earl who's hanging off the side of one of the dumpsters, pouring out what looks like a gallon of bleach.

"Morning!"

I open my mouth to respond when the smell hits me and I slap a hand over my face.

"My God, what is that?"

"Ah, yes. I'm afraid that's from the other day. Roadkill? Gettin' a little ripe," he explains.

Not sure the bleach is doing much other than turning it into a cocktail of noxious fumes that stubbornly clings to the inside of my nose as I give him a wave and hurry past.

Inside I give Phil her promised treat, grab my purse and rush back out, locking the door behind me.

When I run into the shelter almost ten minutes late, a gray-bearded homeless man is sitting in the lobby. Probably waiting for me.

Technically I offer some basic medical care for our residents, but word gets out and these days I'm not surprised to see a random homeless person walk in with some kind of medical problem. The policy is not to turn anyone away, but there's only so much I'm able to do.

"I'm sorry, I'm running a little late," I apologize. "I'll be with you in a few minutes."

He doesn't say anything, just looks at me from

age-drooped eyes and grunts. I give him a quick smile I know won't be returned, as I start walking and promptly bump into Brad.

He grabs onto my upper arms to steady me and I sharply suck air through my teeth. Shit, I'd almost forgotten about the deep bruises Jeff left on my arm, which reminds me; I should have a word with Rosie.

"Tell me you have some coffee."

"Are you hurt?" Brad ignores my question when he catches me rubbing a hand over my sore arm.

"Bumped it. Coffee?"

He cocks a thumb in the direction of the cafeteria. "Banana nut muffins too."

"You're a lifesaver." I smile at him brightly and dart around him to get myself some much-needed sustenance.

Rosie's door is open when I walk past carrying my breakfast, but no one's inside. I'll have to catch her later.

I groan at the first sip of my coffee and some more when I'm chewing Brad's awesome muffin. Five minutes later, when I go to fetch the homeless man from the lobby, I feel a ton better.

Talking to Eddie—the bearded guy's name—is like pulling teeth, of which he has few left. Like a lot of longtime street people, he doesn't trust easily, and despite admitting he's here for medical attention, it takes me a while to talk him into letting me examine him.

Diabetic neglect would be my guess when I see the

necrotic ulcers on his ankles and toes. Probably Type 2 because it's not likely he'd still be alive without treatment for Type 1.

"Eddie, are you diabetic?"

A grunt is my answer and I take it as confirmation.

"Take any meds?"

"Nah. Used to."

I look at the darkening tissues around the sores. At best they need debriding, but part of me worries there may already be too much damage done and he may need to have at least that big toe amputated. It's a miracle he can still walk.

"I'm not sure I can help you here, Eddie. This looks pretty bad. That dead skin has to be cut back, but I worry that might not even be enough."

"So cut it off."

An hour later Eddie hobbles out of my office, his wounds taken care as best I could. Of course, he refused to go to the hospital, and I winced as he pulled his grimy-looking sock and running shoe over the clean bandages I wrapped his feet with.

I tried to get him to stay here at the shelter so we could monitor his diet and maybe get him on Metformin, but he wouldn't have any of it. At least he promised to come back in a few weeks so I can check on him

"Who was that? New customer?"

I'm wiping down the treatment table with disinfectant when Willa walks in.

"That was Eddie." I crumple up the paper towel

and toss it in the garbage. "Untreated diabetic with major foot problems."

She winces. "Let me guess; won't take a trip to the hospital?"

"Eddie has trust issues."

"Don't they all," she sighs, letting herself fall back in a visitor's chair.

"Tough day?" I feel compelled to ask, sitting down across from her.

"More like frustrating. Have you seen Jeff? He skipped out on the group yesterday and was a no-show this morning for his counseling session. I checked and he wasn't here last night."

My inner alarm goes off and I sit forward in my chair.

"He didn't come back?"

Something in my tone must've alerted Willa too, because suddenly she sits up straight.

"You saw him leave?"

"Yesterday around lunchtime. Watched him walk out the front door. He was…upset."

"About what?"

Now it's my turn to sigh. As much as I don't want to betray his confidence—again, I guess, since I already told Radar—I'm concerned about his safety.

"Remember last month when he had a black eye and stitches? I gave him those." At Willa's shocked expression I quickly clarify, "I mean the stitches. He insisted he wouldn't go to the hospital."

I relay the story he'd given me about the attack

on him but leave out the part about the kid with the broken arm. That was just conjecture on my part, and I already got in trouble for sticking my neck out. Besides, Radar was going to look into him and I'm sure if he'd found any connection he would've told me by now. In any event, he's dealing with more important things.

I continue to tell Willa how Jeff pulled me into the group room yesterday morning.

"He was drunk?"

"Had alcohol seeping from his pores."

"Shit. And I thought he was doing so well."

"Not so much. He hurt me. He was so out of it, he actually scared me."

"Hurt you?" Now she looks alarmed. "What did he do?"

I pull up my sleeve and show her the dark bruising on my arm.

"I had to struggle to get free," I admit.

"You should've mentioned that right away," she admonishes me gently.

I know I should've, but with the shelter's no-tolerance policy it would've meant him getting booted and I didn't want to be responsible for that.

"Yeah. I'm aware. I guess I was hoping maybe—"

She leans forward and puts a sympathetic hand on my knee.

"You could fix him? Don't we all. The hardest part about working with these people is coming to terms with the fact you can only help them as far as they will allow you. You can lead a horse to water…"

"But you can't make it drink," I finish. "I know."

"He can't come back, Hillary. The no-tolerance policy is there for our safety." She pats my knee and gets to her feet. "Come on, let's go talk to the boss-lady."

Rosie looks up from behind her desk when we walk in. A big grin appears on her face.

"Are we finally gonna talk about that thing between you and Radar Saturday night?" She sounds hopeful.

"Actually, we need to talk about something else," Willa announces, and Rosie's smile drops at her serious tone.

"Close the door."

RADAR

"HIS FACE WAS caved in. The coroner actually thinks they used the removable showerhead to beat him with it. But strangulation was the cause of death."

SAC Sanders just got back from Montrose and is updating us on the latest attack. Pretty gruesome photographs from the scene are tacked up beside the pictures of the other crimes in our conference room.

"They all have that in common," Bree points out. "Even the victims in San Luis Obispo and Saginaw were unrecognizable. Five victims we know of and in each case great care was taken to obliterate their faces. What does that tell you?"

"They know their victims," Kai, who drove back from Colorado Springs this past weekend, suggests.

"Exactly," Bree agrees before turning to Sanders. "Each attack conducted by a different team, but at least one of them would've had a personal connection to the victim."

"Teams? You make it sound like some organized group of killers," the agent reacts.

"I think in a way they are," Sarah confirms, sliding a piece of paper across the table. "We're pretty sure each time one of these hashtags is used it links to a crime that was committed. There's one to correspond with the dates of four out of the five murders. Unfortunately, we only have the name for one possible suspect and that was only because we lucked out with a partial license plate. We haven't been able to get further than online identities with the other three."

"I can't bloody well do much without an actual name or an address," Sanders grumbles.

"We're working on it," she says with an edge, and her boss seems surprised at her tone.

This time I hand him a sheet.

"Those are IP addresses. They will tell you the location of a computer or network a certain signal originated from," I explain.

"I know what an IP address is," Sanders snaps.

"Good. Saves me time," I respond dryly. "If you look at the list, it shows the IP address, the date of the signal that included the hashtag, and the corresponding location. It also shows the online identity used. Aside from Jeremy Loman, we've been able to cross-reference two other identities with social media accounts, and you'll see the names and geographical location on there as well. Neither of those are local and only one corresponds with an attack we know of."

It's up to Sanders to follow up on those. I tune out when Sarah takes over again, explaining yesterday's system crash. I mentally go over what we've discovered since then.

First of all, this *Fury*-guy is slick. Before I managed to pull the plug on the system, he already managed to syphon off most, if not all, of the information from my computer. I spent most of last night and this morning in damage control. I ran checks on my online server—the nerve center of our network—to make sure no one and nothing had accessed it, and built an additional layer of protection on top of the tight security already on there. Then I checked every other computer in the office connected to our network, ran a deep clean to make sure no spyware was hiding, and instructed everyone to change all their passwords.

While I've been busy with that, Sarah divided her attention between *Lock&Load* and the piles of printouts, scanning for any information that could lead us to whomever is behind *>Fury#1*.

I rub the heels of my hands in my gritty eyes. What I wouldn't give for a few hours of sleep, preferably with Hillary in my arms, but I'll probably have to contend with a measly hour or so on the cot in the locker room. We need to stay on top of this and can't afford to lose traction, or we'll never catch up with him.

"Radar? Got a minute?"

Jake is standing beside me and I notice everyone else is already filing out of the conference room.

"What's up?"

If I sound testy it's because I am. I'm still pissed about what transpired Saturday night and I avoided him yesterday.

"You and Hillary."

I bite my tongue and wait to see if he's going to elaborate, but apparently not.

"Still not sure what business it is of yours what happens between Hillary and me. I don't know where you get the idea she needs to be protected from me, Hutch. Who do you take me for?"

"That's not what…" He seems flustered. "Look, Hillary is special."

"You don't think I know that?"

He throws up his hands. "Hear me out. Hillary has no family other than Rosie and now me. She's like a sister to me. You can't blame me for worrying what'll happen if this thing between you and her blows up."

I surge to my feet and get in his face. Not something I'd normally do—he may be shorter by a couple of inches but could wipe the floor with me ten different ways—but no sleep, frustration, and yes, hurt at his lack of trust has me lose my temper.

"Blow up? You're a hypocrite; you know that? Wasn't that long ago you put the company at risk when you fucked around with a witness, now was it?"

"She's my fucking wife."

"Exactly my point. And what about Dimi? Did you give him a hard time when he started sniffing around Willa? Rosie's employee? I didn't think so. Guess I know where I stand with you. Fuck you, Hutchinson."

I turn on my heels and almost run into Yanis.

"The fuck is going on here?"

He glares at me, so I cock my thumb over my shoulder.

"Ask that asshole. I'm outta here."

Bree starts to say something, but I cut her off with a raised hand. I'm still vibrating with anger. I need to get a handle on myself before I say something else I may regret.

I can feel eyes following me to my office, where I stuff my laptop and a stack of printouts in my backpack with Dunn quietly looking on.

"I'll be in touch," I mumble on my way out the door.

By the time I pull into my parking spot the anger is gone and I'm left with an unhealthy mix of hurt and regret. So much for well over a decade of building a rational, level-headed, and reliable reputation on the team.

Shot to shit in one go.

I open the door to my apartment where Phil is already waiting to greet me.

"What happened?"

I look up at the sound of Hillary's voice.

Fuck.

CHAPTER 17

HILLARY

I SHOULD GO.

In the past two hours the door I've been keeping an eye on down the hall has stayed firmly closed. Radar disappeared in what I assume is his home office about two seconds after he unexpectedly walked in the door.

I'm not blind. I could tell something was up when he walked in, but I didn't expect him to breeze right past me without a word and slam that door shut behind him. I thought I'd give him a little space and took Phil for an extended walk—something I'd been about to do when Radar showed up—but that lasted only half an hour when the pooch started pulling me back toward home.

Since then I've been sitting on the couch, flipping through his copy of *The Art of Happiness*, waiting for him to make an appearance.

I'm not sure if I'm more pissed or hurt. I mean, he's the one who insisted I stay here, that he wanted to think of me in his bed.

Whatever.

Either way I'm an idiot for sitting around waiting for him to pay attention to me. I've done enough of that in my lifetime and promised myself I wouldn't go that route ever again.

My mind made up, I go to put the book back on the shelf, take my water glass to the kitchen, and tiptoe past the closed door to the bedroom to pack up my stuff. I'm on my knees next to the bed, pulling my phone charger from the outlet I found behind the nightstand last night when I hear a door open and footsteps head into the bathroom next door. Angry tears blur my vision and I turn, sitting my ass on the floor and my back to the wall, hoping to stay out of sight.

Definitely more hurt.

I sit and listen to water run in the sink and moments later turned off again. I hear him walk down the hall and wait for the sound of the door closing. It doesn't come. I'm ridiculous, a grown woman hiding behind the bed. Using the hem of my shirt, I wipe my face and get to my feet. It takes me two seconds to throw everything in my bag before I walk out of the bedroom.

I force myself not to peek at the open door, but I can't escape his voice as I walk past.

"Hey, Sarah. Sorry I took off. Yeah, things got a little heated, didn't they?"

I can taste bile as I listen to him chuckle with whoever the woman is on the other end.

Sarah.

No one by that name works for PASS, I know that much.

I tiptoe through the living room giving Phil—who is curled up in her bed—a scratch between the ears in passing, grab my purse, and as quietly as I can slip out the door. I manage to hold it together until I close my own door behind me, and then I let the sob I've been holding escape. It's followed by another one, and then another, but that's all I'll allow myself.

I'm such an idiot.

Taking a deep breath in, I swallow the rest and angrily swipe at my eyes. No more. It doesn't even matter who this Sarah is, but he was clearly able to talk to her. Hell, he even apologized to her when he didn't even bother with a simple hello for me. I listened to his excuse before, claiming communication is not his strong suit. Well, he communicated just fine with this other woman.

That's what hurts. Especially after convincing me to let down my guard this weekend.

Damn him.

I toss my bag in the bedroom and duck into the bathroom, splashing my face with cold water. Then I quickly change into jeans and running shoes, toss a bottle of water, my wallet, and phone into a small backpack, and head back out.

I need some nature, a bit of exercise, and some fresh air to clear my head. It's been a while since I've hiked Devil's Kitchen Trail. It's about a mile and a half—a couple of hours at most—and perfect this time of year when it's not that hot yet.

The drive is only fifteen minutes or so from town. All this beauty within easy reach and most of the time I forget it's even there. There is only one other car with Kansas plates in the parking lot at the trailhead. Come summer this place will be busy, but for now I'm glad for the peace and quiet.

I bump into them halfway up the trail, an older couple I spend a few minutes chatting with before they head back to the parking lot. I've gone only a few steps when my phone rings in my backpack.

Radar. Now he wants to talk? Screw that.

I turn off my ringer and return it to my pack—I'm not going to be available at his whim—and resume the trail.

Right before the path switches back I find a large rock to sit down on and for a while I simply take in the view and let my mind quiet down.

By the time I turn back, the sun is already low in the sky and the temperature has dropped dramatically. It looks like I spent more time out there than I thought; it must be getting close to eight. The display on my phone confirms it and I ignore the numerous messages that were left. I'll deal with those later. I turn the sound back on and slip it in my pocket.

My rental is where I left it and I quickly turn on the heat before heading home. I feel better, back in control of my own destiny.

I am hungry, though. Haven't had a thing since that early lunch at the shelter, so I stop at the Wendy's drive-thru and order a bacon jalapeño cheeseburger. I deserve it after today.

My phone rings while I'm waiting for my food. At first I'm afraid it's Radar again but am relieved to see the number for my insurance company pop up. It's the adjuster to set up an appointment to come look at the car. I agree to meet with him tomorrow morning at the auto repair shop.

That'll be one less thing to worry about.

I'm barely inside my apartment, enjoying the first bite of my guilty pleasure, when someone starts banging on my door. I'm not entirely surprised to see Radar standing on my doorstep through the peephole, looking none too pleased. I take a deep breath, mentally steel myself to be unaffected by anything he has to say and open the door, which is promptly ripped from my hold as he barges inside.

"Where the hell were you?" are his first words as he slams the door shut behind him.

"Excuse me?"

The thin veneer I managed to coat my emotions with quickly melts away as anger takes over.

"I've been worried sick. One minute you're there and the next you're gone. For hours," he adds accusatorily.

Trying not to notice he looks hot with his hair mussed like he just rolled out of bed, I shore myself up to my full height, which is still probably a foot short of target.

I go for what I hope is an unflappable tone when I

respond.

"I wasn't under the impression you'd notice."

RADAR

STALKING INTO HER living room I let myself sink down on her couch, my hands immediately going into my hair. Much like they've done for what may well have been the longest couple of hours of my life.

I'd probably been an ass, yes, but I'd still been working on a short fuse when I got home earlier. Rather than risk alienating Hillary, along with everyone else, I chose to hide out in my office. In hindsight I could've said something before shutting her out, but I already felt raw and wanted some time to sort my shit.

When I finally did, I made a quick call of apology to Agent Dunn and a much longer one to my boss. I wanted to get that out of the way and make sure I still had a job, so I wouldn't have that hanging over my head the rest of the day. After that I went in search of Hillary.

I look up to find her standing in front of me, hands on her hips and an eyebrow raised high. I lower my eyes, unsure of where to start.

"I got into it with Jake at the office," I finally say, registering her surprised gasp, but I keep talking. "I haven't slept since Sunday night, this fucking case has put everyone in a pressure cooker, and Jake said something that tripped my trigger." I lift a quick hand. "I'm not excusing anything, I'm just trying to explain what happened before I was an ass to you."

I can feel her stare at me before she sits down beside me.

"Okay. Explain."

"Things got heated. Yanis had to intervene and I stormed out of the office." I snort derisively. Not my most glorious moment and definitely not fun admitting.

"Did it get physical?" she asks.

I finally look at her and it warms me to see concern on her face.

"No, thank God. I can hold my own, but probably not against Jake. Anyway," I continue, "I was good and fired up, came home, and found you there. Felt I needed to get my head sorted first—I'm not particularly proud of my temper—so I hid out in my office. I should probably have communicated that first."

This time it's Hillary who snorts. When I look over she's wearing a sardonic smile, but then she turns serious.

"What exactly did Jake say that set you off?"

Fuck. This part I'd hoped to avoid, because I know it'll piss her off, and I have no doubt she'll make that known to Jake and/or Rosie, which may make things even more uncomfortable than they already are. Exactly what Jake was afraid of.

"The fact you hesitate to tell me suggests it had something to do with me. Did it?" she prompts.

I'm officially stuck in damned-if-you-do and

damned-if-you-don't territory.

"He's just looking out for you." I can't believe I end up defending him, but it won't do any of us any good if this stirs up more trouble.

"Oh, I can guess," she mutters, clearly not pleased. She gets up to pace, understandably agitated, and then she lets loose, her hands flying. "You know what boggles my mind? Every guy I know seems to think by merit of having a dick, they're responsible to protect those of us who are apparently nothing but a set of walking tits and therefore unable to look after ourselves."

"Lady…" I start carefully, but opt to leave it at that when she shoots a fiery glare my way.

"Don't even start," she growls, pulling at her hair in frustration, and starts pacing again. "If men learned to communicate properly, let go of their misplaced superiority complex, and maybe began to value women as equals, I bet you the world wouldn't be such a fucked-up place."

I open my mouth, but I've got nothing.

She makes valid points.

"What?" She stops in front of me with narrowed eyes. "No argument?"

"Nope." I can see I surprise her. "No argument, but a defense."

"Can't wait to hear this." The sarcasm is thick, but I don't let it stop me.

"What we've got going on here is new. I like it. Hell, I like you, but I'm in uncharted territory, have already fucked up once or twice, and didn't think it was a good idea to give you a front-row seat to my temper and risk strike three." Her expression softens as she sits back down beside me. I take her hand and am encouraged when she doesn't immediately pull away. "I'm trying not to mess things up."

She lifts her hand to my face and strokes along my jaw, but the faint smile on her face is sad.

"You know…that's what relationships are supposed to be; messy. You take the good, the bad, the ups, and the downs. It's not gonna work if you can't give all of you, and it definitely won't work if you don't trust the other."

"I trust you," I blurt out, sensing despite the gentle hand on my face, this conversation is not heading in a direction I like. The sweet smile is not helping.

"No, you don't," she says softly, almost apologetically. "Not really, or you would've walked in this afternoon and shared your miserable day with me like I invited you to."

I'm looking for words, trying to find the right response, the one that will avoid what I know is coming, but before I have a chance to say anything she leans in and brushes her lips against mine.

"Here's the thing, Radar; I'm not sure I trust you either."

CHAPTER 18

Hillary

I CATCH MYSELF glancing out the kitchen window again. So much for self-control.

It's been two days since I watched Radar walk out of my apartment, convinced I was doing the right thing by letting him go. Every minute since I've questioned that decision and I'm pissed at myself for it.

I'm also irrationally disappointed that he didn't fight to change my mind, even when I just finished telling him I don't want or need a man to hold dominion over me. How fucked up is that?

To boot, Rosie's been calling all morning and I've ignored her calls. I'd just admitted on Tuesday in her office I was trying things on with Radar, and I'm not ready to hear her tell me what an idiot I was for breaking things off almost immediately. Because I know that's what she'll say. She'll probably call me a coward; tell me I'm just looking for excuses because I'm too much of a chickenshit to take a chance on a good man.

She'd be right on all accounts.

Still I can't bring myself to message or call him, tell him perhaps I'm having second thoughts. What if he changed his mind too and decided I'm more trouble than I'm worth?

Round and round I go.

Maybe it's better like this; keep my heart safe. Hope hurts. Never mind I already feel like I'm bleeding.

I dry the last of my grandmother's china. Not that I used it but it was getting dusty and besides, I needed something to do with my hands. It's my day off and it's been steadily raining since early this morning. I've already scrubbed the apartment, washed and folded my laundry, paid bills, looked at *Consumer Reports* comparisons for a new car, and reorganized my linen closet.

I met with the guy from the insurance company yesterday morning and he signed off on the quote Chris, my mechanic, gave him for the repairs on the spot. Of course, after he left Chris quoted me half the price using an aftermarket windshield and suggested I trade in the Honda for something a little newer. I was going to shop around some of the dealerships, but the rain isn't exactly conducive to that.

With the china clean and put away, I'm about to make myself some tea when there's a rap at the door. I almost drop the teapot I'm holding and curse my heart for almost leaping from my chest.

I push down the hope that feels like a bubble of air in my chest and force myself to walk at a normal pace to the front door. I succeed but can't help holding my breath as I peek through the peephole. My chest deflates like a popped balloon when I recognize the red mop of hair.

"You!" Rosie pokes a finger in my chest as she forces herself inside my apartment. "Can you not pick up your damn phone? I've been trying to get a hold of you all day."

Since she's already pissed, I feel it safe to assume she already found out I sent Radar packing.

"Look, I'm sorry I didn't answer your calls, but I wasn't ready to hear what kind of monumental fool you think I am."

It takes me a moment to realize Rosie looks confused.

"What are you talking about?"

"You're here because of the thing with Radar, right?"

Now her eyes turn to slits. "What did he do?" she growls in a low voice.

As sweet and innocent as my friend looks, she can be fierce. If I don't set her straight on her obvious misinterpretation, I wouldn't be surprised if she went after Radar and wouldn't bother asking for explanations. That's Rosie; jumping in for those she cares about without so much as a thought. Fiercely protective, much like her husband is.

Or…Radar?

It takes a minute for the significance of that last thought to register and in that time, Rosie's already aiming for the door.

"It's more what I did," I quickly clarify, and she spins around. "I…may have made a mistake."

"One that involves Radar?"

I scrunch my face up. "Possibly."

"Oh shit. You chickened out, didn't you?"

I'm fortunate to have a friend who knows me so well, but right now I wish I wasn't such an open book to her.

"I kind of did," I confess.

She rolls her eyes and sighs dramatically.

"I'm sure it's nothing that can't be fixed. You can tell me all about it but later; right now, we have bigger problems."

"We do?"

She walks up to me and takes me by the arm, leading me to the couch.

"You may wanna sit down for this."

She sits and so do I, turning my body toward her.

"What's going on?"

"It's Jeff." She shakes her head and I brace myself for what I'm afraid is not going to be good news. "I heard it from Jake, who heard it from Bree, who happened to be at the police station when the call came in. A body wearing a green Boston Celtics windbreaker was found floating in the Colorado River, underneath the railroad bridge just south of the shelter."

I can see it clearly; the dirty green jacket Jeff wouldn't even take off long enough for us to wash at the shelter. He loved that jacket, the only thing in his life he was attached to. Tears burn in my throat, realizing I'm glad at least he had that when he died.

"How?"

She shakes her head. "Don't know yet. Could be he fell or slipped trying to get out of the way of a train while crossing the bridge. Maybe he jumped. I don't know. Jake says he'll try to find out more, but it may depend on an autopsy and who knows when they will get around to that."

"I can't believe it. I just saw him two days ago."

Rosie grabs my hand and gives it a squeeze.

"I know, which is why I was trying to get a hold of you. The police will inevitably come knocking at the shelter and find out you were the last one there to speak to him or see him alive."

No doubt about that. After meeting with Willa and Rosie on Tuesday, word went out that Jeff was not allowed back at the shelter. Everyone would've heard.

It could've been suicide. He was pretty distraught the last time I saw him.

Or maybe, whoever Jeff was so afraid of caught up with him.

Radar

"Heads-up."

I look up to find Jake standing in the doorway to my office.

I succeeded in avoiding him after Yanis called us into his office first thing yesterday morning when

I showed up. He didn't mince words and made it perfectly clear he didn't give the first fuck about what set our heated exchange on Tuesday in motion, but expected us to behave like the professionals we are paid to be. Especially when the feds, who were footing that bill, were sitting in the next office listening to every word.

Needless to say, both of us walked out of the office duly scolded and with the proverbial tail between the legs—at least mine was—and managed to stay out of each other's way since then.

Which makes me curious, and a tad uneasy, why suddenly Jake is in my office talking to me.

"What?"

Granted, my response could perhaps have been a little less hostile, but I blame him in part for the clusterfuck my life seems to have turned into since then.

The situation with Hillary aside, I discovered coming out of Yanis' office yesterday morning, SAC Sanders felt it necessary to move Sarah into the conference room with him. She caught my confused look and followed me into the small kitchen to apologize and tell me it hadn't been her idea. That made me feel moderately better until her boss came to let me know since I had been compromised by whomever is responsible for *Lock&Load*, his people would investigate online while I'd be working on deciphering the pages of code.

That was a kick in the ass.

Let's face it; I'm still butt-hurt.

"Look," Jake says, keeping his voice down and stepping farther into my office, "we'll deal with that shit later, so save me the attitude. This is about your girlfriend."

I snort. "You can rest easy, that was over Tuesday night. And before you start pointing fingers, it wasn't by my doing."

"Hillary ended it?" he asks, disbelief all over his face.

"Before we even got properly started. Told me it was done so I walked." I can hear the bitter tone of my own voice.

"So, you walked?" he echoes back.

"Yeah, I walked."

Then he closes the door, plants his clenched fists on my desk, and leans in my face.

"Are you insane? You don't walk out on a woman like Hillary. You stay and you fucking fight for her."

I look at him incredulously.

"Am *I* insane?" I hiss, trying not to lose my cool again or I might be out of a job. "Weren't you the one who warned me away from her in the first place?"

"Yeah, about that. Rosie had a few choice words for me when I mentioned something about it last night." He straightens up and looks a bit sheepish. "I may have been out of line. According to Rosie, Hillary is into you in a big way and she threatened to castrate me in my sleep if I didn't make things right."

"So that's what you came in here for? An apology?"

I shake my head. "You could've just said I'm sorry I was an ass and left it at that."

"Didn't I just say that? But that's not the reason I came in. One of the shelter's residents was fished out of the Colorado River this morning. I was talking to Rosie and she thinks Hillary may be the last person who talked to the guy. The cops will be all over that."

I'm out of my chair and shove my laptop in my bag.

"Why didn't you fucking say so right away?"

Before he has a chance to answer, I already have the door open and dart out.

"You're fucking welcome!" he calls after me.

My phone is ringing by the time I get to my truck and I answer without looking as I climb behind the wheel.

"In a hurry, Radar?"

It's Yanis.

"Yeah, something came up. I'll—"

"Jake just told me," he interrupts. "Keep us in the loop."

Not what I expected but I'll take it.

"Yeah, okay."

In typical Yanis form, he hangs up without wasting another word.

Her front door is just opening when I come up the stairs. Rosie steps out and spots me, her face splitting open in a wide grin.

Then she leans her head and yells inside, "Told you it could be fixed," before adding for my benefit,

"She's all yours. Don't let her scare you off."

"Who are you talking to?"

Hillary pokes her head out the door and freezes when she spots me. Rosie pats me on the shoulder as she slips by me, and heads down the stairs.

"What are you doing here?" she asks, as I put my hands on her shoulders and carefully back her up into the apartment.

"Cops been by yet?"

She shakes her head. "How did you know?"

"Jake."

"Oh. So that's why you're here."

She turns and heads for the kitchen and I catch her by the arm to stop her, when she pulls away with a sharp hiss. She immediately covers the area I touched with her hand. I notice it doesn't quite cover the bruise on her arm.

"What is that?"

I peel her hand away and I can almost make out the shape of a fucking hand against her dark skin.

"Nothing," she mumbles, trying to pull her short sleeve to cover the bruise.

"That's not nothing, Hillary," I snap.

"Fine. I had a run-in with one of the shelter residents on Monday morning. It's not an issue."

She resumes her trek to the kitchen, and I follow behind as I process what she said.

"Monday morning? And you didn't tell me?"

The air in the kitchen goes electric as she swings around and pins me with angry eyes.

"Tell you? When would I have told you, Radar? When you blew right by me and locked yourself in your room for hours? Or maybe when…"

As suddenly as the anger appeared, I see it drain from her features.

"You know what, it doesn't matter." Her beautiful brown eyes are dull, and she looks tired when she looks up at me. "Go home, Radar."

"It matters." I take a step closer and cup her face in my hands. "And no, I'm not leaving. You can keep throwing Tuesday's clusterfuck in my face to keep me at a distance, but it's not gonna work. I'm staying, Hillary. I'm gonna be here when the cops come to question you and after that, I'm still gonna be here."

I bend down and run my nose along hers, ending with a light brush of my lips on hers. I half expect her to push me away when she covers my wrists with her hands, but she surprises me by pulling me closer.

CHAPTER 19

HILLARY

I CLOSE THE door behind Detectives Bissette and Garcia, leaning my forehead against it.

They showed up half an hour ago, interrupting my capitulation to the power of Radar's charms. The man can kiss. I'm well aware he's quite capable in other areas as well, which I'd kind of hoped to explore when the doorbell brought our lip-lock to a screeching halt.

Garcia barged right in, pointedly ignoring Radar who wouldn't budge from my side. He wanted to know if I knew a Jeffrey Cain, how I knew him, and then zeroed in on my last interaction with him.

I explained about the beating he'd received last month and how he refused to file a police report. I relayed how he'd been drunk and paranoid when Garcia himself showed up at the shelter three days ago, and Jeff had manhandled me when he thought I'd called the cops on him. That led to Detective Bissette producing her phone to take some pictures of the bruises on my arm, while I could feel Radar seething at my back.

What tipped Radar over the edge was when Garcia asked my whereabouts since that altercation. I told him, but Garcia seemed particularly interested in the hours I spent on the Devil's Kitchen Trail on Tuesday. He wanted to know how come an hour-and-a-half trail took me almost four to complete, and seemed suspicious when I explained I lost track of time while sitting on a rock enjoying the view. Then he asked if anyone could verify any of it.

I never got a chance to tell him about the couple with the Kansas plates because that's when Radar jumped in. He told Garcia he was done, and I was not answering any more questions unless my lawyer was present. The detective pointed out what a coincidence it was my name was connected to two violent deaths.

I thought for sure Radar was going to deck him when Bissette intervened and hustled her partner to the door.

That was a minute ago.

I slowly turn around and see Radar in my kitchen on his phone.

"Your guy is barking up the wrong goddamn tree," I hear him say. "The woman is a hundred and forty—maybe fifty—pounds soaking wet…" More like one seventy but I'm not about to correct him on that. "…and he's acting like she single-handedly lifted a grown man over her head and tossed him off a railroad bridge." He runs an agitated hand through his hair as he listens to whomever he has on the line.

"Yes, you do that. And just so we're clear; for any further questioning of Ms. Glenwood contact Hank Fredericks. That's right."

He ends the call, tosses his phone and his glasses on the counter, and turns on the faucet over the kitchen sink to splash water on his face. He braces his hands on the edges of the sink and leans his head down, letting the water drip off.

I softly approach, taking a kitchen towel off the hook, and put a hand in the middle of his back.

"Here. Dry yourself."

He snaps his head around but the moment his eyes hit me they soften. I wait until he's wiped his face and put his glasses back on.

"Who was that?"

"Brian Underwood, the chief of police."

My mouth falls open. "You called the police chief?"

"Yeah, I did. Not going to stand by and have you badgered by that idiot when he should be out chasing real criminals. Underwood is a decent guy. He's the one who initially asked us to assist with the murder of Sandra Elliot, before the feds were called in. Garcia is on a wild-goose chase and I don't know why he decided to focus on you, but I do know it's a load of bullshit. And now his boss knows as well."

"I see," I respond testily. "And this Hank guy? Maybe I should know who that is? Since apparently he'll be speaking for me as well?"

"Fredericks is a lawyer. Our lawyer, actually. PASS

has him on retainer."

"I don't work for PASS," I point out, and notice Radar flaring his nostrils as he puffs out a sharp breath. It would appear I'm testing his patience.

"You don't but I do, and you're with me."

"It's that easy?"

He shrugs and picks his phone off the counter.

"Pretty much. I just need to give him a heads-up. Put him on standby in case that asswipe Garcia wants another go at you."

He puts in a call and I let my thoughts drift, while I start on the chicken curry I had planned for dinner tonight.

I have a feeling Garcia's sudden animosity against me may have something to do with the fact I made it clear I have no personal interest in him when he stopped by on Monday. I glance over at Radar, who is still talking on the phone but is tracking my movements with his eyes. Not so sure this is a good time to tell him about that little incident in my office at this moment.

Instead, I get busy trying to figure out whether I should be upset about Radar jumping to my defense without asking. My auto-response is I should be, but if I put aside that particular chip on my shoulder for a minute, I have to admit it feels good to have someone stand up for me without even a second thought.

Scratch that. Not someone; *Radar.*

"He's on board," he says behind me. "Got a piece of paper so I can write down his cell number? You can reach him anytime."

I turn and point.

"Should be a notepad up there somewhere."

While he rummages through the junk on top of my fridge, I pull out my cast-iron pot, toss in a decent amount of butter, and set it on the hot burner.

"What are you cooking?"

His arms slip around me from behind and he rests his chin on my shoulder, as I slide a couple of chicken breasts in the pan.

"Chicken curry."

"That sounds good. Looks like there might be enough for two," he mumbles, his breath brushing my ear.

"There might be."

My voice sounds breathy as I try to concentrate on cooking. Not an easy feat when every one of my senses is fully aware of the fine man wrapped around me.

Guess I can always grab a salad at the hospital cafeteria for dinner tomorrow, instead of the leftovers I had planned.

I tilt my head to give him more room when I feel his lips brush the sensitive skin where my neck meets my shoulder.

"Mmmm," I mumble, promptly feeling the chill as his touch disappears.

"You make sounds like that and I'm at risk of forgetting I have a dog who's likely to start making puddles on my floor if I don't take her for a quick walk," he says from a fair distance. When I turn my head, I see he's on the other side of the kitchen, staring at me with heavy-lidded eyes that make a flush crawl up my chest.

"We can't have that," I offer in a less than steady voice.

"No," he agrees. "And I'd hate to see that dinner go to waste, but all bets are off for after." A delicious shudder runs down my body and doesn't go unnoticed by Radar, who sucks in a harsh breath. "Right. Dog first. Mind if I bring her with after?"

"I'll save her some chicken."

He nods, seems to forcibly pull his gaze from me, and eats up the distance to the front door with those long legs.

Radar

I give Yanis a quick call while Phil is doing her standard, meticulous grass inspection.

"Everything okay?" he asks right off the bat. "Hillary good?"

"She's okay. Garcia and Bissette showed up. Garcia grilled her on her whereabouts for Tuesday night pretty hard. I called Fredericks just in case."

"Good. Tuesday night, that when they figure he died?"

"Probably. Did Bree hear anything from her contact?"

Phil is done with the clump of grass that held her interest and moves on to the next.

"Yeah, one of the uniforms told her when they fished the guy out of the water, they discovered he'd been worked over and his eyes were gone."

"*Jesus…*" A chill runs down my back. "Why would someone do that?"

"You're asking me? Agent Dunn suggested it could be symbolic."

I let that process for a minute while Phil finds a new spot and goes through her haunches to pee for the twelfth time. Weird dog always lifts one leg a little, like she can't decide whether she's a girl or a boy.

"The vic mentioned something to Hillary about someone looking for him. She said he couldn't talk about the assault for fear someone was gonna find him."

Yanis is quiet for a while, but I can hear him shuffling through some papers.

"When was that again? The date when he was attacked?" he asks suddenly, just as Phil starts moving again, but this time I firmly lead her away from the grass. She's dawdled long enough.

"Let me see. She told me after I came back from visiting Dad in Montrose. It must've happened that weekend, she works at the shelter on Saturday mornings."

"Same weekend Gina Castillo was killed right outside the diner downtown," Yanis reminds me. "Do you know where he was attacked?"

"No, but Hillary mentioned he'd refused treatment and ended up being dropped off at the shelter. She actually stitched him up herself."

"Who dropped him off?"

Phil pulls on the leash wanting to head for my apartment and seems confused when I lead her up the stairs to Hillary's place.

"I assume a uniform? I can ask, I'm almost at her place."

"I'll get Bree to check. There should be a record of it."

I stop outside her door.

"You're thinking this is connected?"

"I think it's worth looking into. What if this victim saw something? What if that's the reason he got beaten and was warned not to talk? Maybe that's why they removed his eyes."

"And he was freaking out when he thought Hillary had spilled to the cops." I start fitting pieces into the possible scenario, but it leaves me with a chilling realization. "Fuck, if whoever did this was keeping an eye on the guy, they may know…"

I let my voice drift off but Yanis finishes my thought.

"The last person he spoke to was Hillary. I'm gonna put someone on her," he adds immediately.

"Yeah, *me*," I snap. "I'm already here."

I silently dare him to tell me otherwise. Sure, it's been a few years since I've seen action beyond what's on my computer screen, but I've made sure I've stayed sharp physically, and I'm plenty proficient with a gun. But more than that, there is no way in hell

I'd let anyone near her.

Apparently Yanis comes to the same conclusion.

"Fine. Lock her down and stick like glue. We'll be in touch."

I tuck the phone in my pocket and put a hand on the knob when the door swings open. Hillary sticks her head out and looks down the gallery.

"I thought I heard you talking to someone," she says, as she crouches down to greet Phil.

"I was on the phone with Yanis."

She looks up at me.

"Everything okay?"

I hesitate a moment. Neither of us is going anywhere soon so there's no rush telling her she might be in danger. No reason we can't share a quiet meal first.

"He was just checking in." I reach down and pull her to her feet, before guiding her inside. "Smells amazing. When's dinner? I'm starving."

I let Phil off her leash and she immediately starts sniffing down the apartment. Hillary stares at me for a beat before she takes off toward the kitchen, saying over her shoulder, "I'll let you off the hook until we've eaten, but after that you fill me in."

She reads me like a goddamn book, but I'll be damned if that doesn't make me feel good. As do the scents wafting from the kitchen. My stomach rumbles in response.

"Beer in the fridge," she says, as she drizzles dressing on a salad she managed to put together while I was gone. "Dinner is ready."

"Anything I can do?"

"Get me a beer too."

The meal tastes even better than it smelled. The cold beer is a perfect companion for the curry, which has a bit of a bite to it. After polishing off my second helping, I shove my chair back and resist the temptation to undo my jeans.

"Do you always cook like this for yourself?"

She shrugs and smiles.

"I like cooking. Granted, it's more fun when it's not just for me, but that doesn't usually stop me."

"More than happy to volunteer to be your extra at the table."

She tilts her head and raises an eyebrow.

"You would, would you?"

"Not only that, I'd volunteer cleaning up afterward."

She chuckles, shaking her head as she gets up and starts gathering the dishes.

"An offer like that is hard to resist."

I catch her hand when she reaches for my plate and pull her around the table and on my lap.

"I'm sure you meant to say a man like that, right?" I tease, glad to see warmth in those brown eyes she fixes on me.

"You have your moments."

She never quite told me I would have the second chance I asked for, because I was interrupted in the middle of my attempts to sway her when the cops knocked on the door. Every signal she's given me since has been encouraging, but I don't want to assume and be wrong.

"Does that mean we're good?" I slide a hand under her hair and curve my fingers around the back her neck. "You and me?"

Her nod is slight but enough for me to confidently take her mouth. Beer, curry, and the best taste of all: Hillary. My relief is complete when her arms wind around my neck and her fingers find my hair.

"Lady…" I mumble against her lips, as my body responds to her soft ass shifting on my lap.

Unfortunately, she pulls back and gets to her feet.

"Now that that's cleared up, why don't you share what had you looking so serious earlier?"

Fuck.

CHAPTER 20

HILLARY

"SICK?"

I flinch at the blatant disbelief in Karla's voice and glare at the top of Radar's head. He's bent over the laptop he has open on my kitchen table.

This was his idea.

Don't get me wrong, I don't particularly relish the idea of making myself an easy target, but the last thing I need is to give Karla more ammo against me. Already with the prospect of getting a new vehicle, my plan to be debt free in five more months is in jeopardy. Maybe I should just get the Honda patched up with the insurance money and cross my fingers nothing else happens.

"Hillary!"

Karla's sharp voice in my ear snaps me to attention.

"Yes, I'm here, sorry," I mumble.

Radar's head comes up and he shoots me a quizzical look. I turn my back.

"I was asking what exactly is the matter with you?"

she prompts.

"Flu. Fever, shakes, stomach issues, achy all over." I really suck at lying.

"I see," she reacts disapprovingly.

"Yeah, I don't think I should expose our patients to this."

"Have you seen a doctor?"

"Not yet."

If I'm not mistaken, she just huffed in response.

"Well, I suggest you do because I expect a doctor's note when you return."

I don't get a chance to respond—probably for the better—because she's already hung up.

"How did it go?" Radar asks behind me and I swing around.

"Just great. The woman already hates me, and this doesn't help."

I walk into the kitchen, toss my phone on the counter, and start pulling ingredients from the pantry for cookies. My hands need something to do and I want to nurse the mood I've been in since he explained last night, I might not be safe. The fact he and Yanis decided, without my input, Radar would stay with me had not gone down well.

I mix my ingredients into a bowl and let the events of last night play out in my mind.

When he mentioned I'd have to take some time off work I got pissed and disappeared to my bedroom, where I promptly fell asleep. When I got up this morning, Radar had been stretched out on my couch, his feet hanging over the armrest.

In all truth, I'm concerned—if not plain scared—wondering if the message left on my vandalized car was only a warning. I feel cornered and out of control, which almost scares me more, and I'm taking it out on Radar.

My hands are working the chocolate chips into the dough when I glance over and see his focus is back on his laptop.

"I'm sorry." I wait for him to look up before I add, "I'm not taking this as well as I probably should. I feel unsettled, and I'm taking it out on you."

Whatever I expected from him, it isn't the wide grin he aims my way.

"My mother always said she wouldn't be yelling at me if she didn't care."

Guess that's one way of looking at it. It's not exactly a lie. I do care, more than might be healthy for me.

"Be that as it may, I was a bear."

I watch as he gets to his feet and moves toward me. Dough is stuck to my fingers; so I lift my hands out of the way when he turns me to face him and pulls me flush to his body. Then he proceeds to kiss me soundly. It isn't until my knees start to wobble that he lets me go.

"That kiss and those cookies you're baking me is more than enough apology," he says, smirking as he takes a peek in the bowl.

"Who says I'm baking these for you?" I tease, still

a little breathless.

A gleam settles in his eyes as he grabs my hand and with great care licks my fingers clean, sucking each of my digits between his lips.

I'm this close to making up for all the time I wasted and strip naked right here in my kitchen, when Radar's phone on the kitchen table starts to ring.

I turn to the sink to wash my hands and give myself a minute to cool off, while he goes to grab his phone.

"Hey, Sarah."

Every muscle in my body tenses up hearing that name and I tune into the conversation.

Radar

"Couldn't believe she just spilled it. This kid was still on a high."

I'm keeping an eye on Hillary, who seems to be doing her best not to look at me as she putters around the kitchen, while listening closely to Sarah.

"Apparently our Saginaw victim, who was on the cheerleading squad and dating the school football team's quarterback, was a relentless bully. Jenny was her favorite target."

"Jenny?"

"Yeah…" She scoffs, "Stupid kid gave up her legal name ten minutes into the chat. I had Dimas run that name and it comes back to the same location as the IP address. It's her."

"And she admits she exacted revenge?"

"She says she did. Was positively giddy with it."

"Jesus."

"Yeah. I had to be careful not to ask too many questions, which wasn't easy, I don't want to blow my cover. I'm pretty sure my online activities are being monitored. Have been since that *Fury* character messaged me. I have to be careful."

She's right. I look at the stack of printouts I'm still digging through to find some kind of thread to link to whoever is behind *Lock&Load*. She makes one wrong move and she stands to lose all the hard work she's put in so far. It took her days to draw out any possible suspects. She'd gone down the list of online profiles, who used either of the hashtags on or around the dates of the attacks we know of, and tried to engage them in the *Lock&Load* chat room. It had been a long shot but one that apparently paid off.

"No alerts for spyware?"

"No, but you know as well as I do just because it can't be detected doesn't mean it isn't there. I have a strong hunch about it but don't want to go digging around and alert whoever is watching."

"I agree. What can I do?"

"Local law enforcement is picking her up and Sanders is on his way to Saginaw to interview her himself. In the meantime, I want to dig up anything that might connect Jenny Churchill to Jeremy Loman, other than the game. Any information we find he can use in his interview. It would help if you could check social media accounts, friends they have in common, other groups, anything that might connect those two kids."

I'm happy to be doing anything that doesn't involve the sheets of tightly printed code that have my eyes crossed.

"I'm on it."

"Thanks. I'll email you what I have on the girl."

She ends the call and I immediately log in to the various social media platforms while I wait for Sarah's email.

Jenny Churchill isn't that hard to find but apparently the girl uses social media as her diary, because she posts between fifteen or twenty times a day. Geeky memes and pictures of her cat alternated with what I'd consider typical angsty teenage girl posts. I'm suddenly not so sure if this is preferable to what I was doing; five minutes in and already I have the beginnings of a headache.

It's not until a plate of freshly baked cookies is slid in front of me, I remember I'm at Hillary's.

"You weren't kidding," she says with a little smile when I look up at her. "You really do get lost in your work."

"I'm sorry," I mumble around a giant bite of the still-warm cookie I already managed to shove in my mouth. "Just got a new lead."

"Is that what the phone call was?" she asks, again avoiding my eyes as she starts putting things away in the kitchen.

"Yes, that was Sarah Dunn, one of the FBI agents we've been working with," I explain, observing her closely.

"Ah."

Her voice is casual but she's trying to hide a little smile as she starts to run water on the dirty dishes in the sink. She pretends not to notice when I get up and move in behind her. I put my hands on her hips and slide them to her belly.

"Who did you think I was talking to?"

She shrugs her shoulders, meticulously scrubbing the mixing bowl.

"No idea."

"Lady, you know you're a shit liar, right?"

I nuzzle her neck and notice to my satisfaction she seems to lean into my touch, but only for a moment before she refocuses on the dishes.

"What's the new lead?"

I recognize the distraction for what it is but decide not to call her on it. Instead I step away and lean my hip against the counter so I can watch her profile. I normally wouldn't be talking about the case, but Hillary is up to her eyeballs in this one. I figure she deserves to know.

"They may have found the perp in the case in Saginaw and want me to pull some background info."

Her eyes flit my way before returning to the sink.

"Is that normal? For you guys to be working with the FBI?"

"We rarely do, our work is more focused on security than investigation, but in this case, we were already involved when the feds came on board." I head back to the table and sit down behind my laptop.

"Anything I can do?" she asks, wiping her hands on a towel as she sits down across from me. "If I have to stick around, I may as well make myself useful."

"I don't know. Are you familiar with any social media platforms?"

"I have Facebook and Twitter accounts I rarely check. I'm not a complete dud on a computer. I can get my laptop."

Ten minutes later she's bent over her screen, scrolling back through Jenny Churchill's tweets. I had her open a dummy account, just in case, cautioning her not to interact with any of the posts. Last thing we need is to draw more attention to her.

Earlier this morning, Yanis called to let me know the initial attack on the guy they pulled from the river had taken place in the alley behind a convenience store downtown. Only a block from where Gina Castillo was killed.

He also warned Bree was on her way over to pick up Phil, said he didn't want me to leave Hillary alone in the apartment.

Want to bet the guy saw something? Of course there's no way to know for sure—the man is dead—but it did reinforce the danger Hillary could well be in. Anyone with eyes on Jeff could know he saw her the morning after he was attacked, and again before he met his end.

If Jeff thought Garcia was at the shelter because Hillary called him, it wouldn't be too far-fetched to think the perp thought the same thing.

With Hillary engrossed in her task, I quickly shoot off a message to Yanis, letting him know she's helping me. Last thing I need is for him to find out via Rosie or something and get called on it afterward. I think I may have already earned a few strikes against me with the boss, don't need any more on my record.

Yanis: Whatever it takes to keep her close.

"What the hell is a UniCon?" Hillary asks sometime later.

I look up from my screen.

"A convention, like Comic-Con or something. Why?"

"Just curious, apparently she went to one last June. A birthday gift from her parents. She clearly had a blast because she talks about it the rest of the summer. Have you ever been to one?"

"I may have, once or twice, many years ago," I admit.

She grins at me, lightly shaking her head. "Why doesn't that surprise me?"

"Every self-respecting techie, or hacker, or gamer does. It's where you get the dirt on all the new stuff on the market."

My own words echo in my head and I realize Hillary may have stumbled on another lead.

"Does she say where it was?" I ask, as I put UniCon and the year in my search bar.

"Dallas," she says at the same time it appears on my screen.

UniCon, Dallas, June 26 through 28. I'm already scanning back through Jeremy's tweets until I get to last summer's.

"Son of a bitch," I mumble under my breath.

"What?"

I smile at her over my screen.

"You may have just blown the top off this case."

CHAPTER 21

HILLARY

HIS ARM IS heavy across my middle as I try to check the time on my alarm clock.

Only half an hour has passed since I looked last. Five o'clock and I've barely slept, while Radar has been softly snoring since his head hit the pillow a few hours ago.

Yesterday was intense after I found the reference to that convention in Dallas. I have a completely new appreciation of how much of a time suck that kind of work can be. Radar asked me to keep looking through this girl's posts for usable information and without realizing it, hours had gone by.

There were phone calls back and forth between Radar and the office—apparently none of these people eat or sleep much—as they pieced together a disturbing picture. My mind had trouble keeping up with them, or maybe I just had trouble wrapping my head around that kind of evil.

I was exhausted by eleven, crawled into bed, but

ended up unable to do more than doze. My mind still trying to process it all.

Radar barely noticed; he'd been so wrapped up in what he was doing. This time I didn't feel slighted in the least, though. After seeing him in action most of the day—his singular focus on catching whomever is manipulating these kids into committing horrific crimes—I discovered a whole new way to appreciate the man.

I don't want to wake him, but my bladder needs relief, so I carefully try to slip out of bed.

"Come back…"

His sleepy mumble trails off and I freeze, until I hear his soft snore resume before I head to the bathroom. There I quickly take care of business and have a good look at my sleep-deprived face as I wash my hands. I doubt I'm going to get any sleep so may as well get up and make some coffee. I tiptoe back into the bedroom to grab some clothes—it's chilly this morning—when I hear stirring from the bed.

"Come here, Lady."

Radar is propped up on an elbow watching me. He looks a rumpled mess with his hair sticking out in every direction and sleep creases lining his face, but his eyes are perfectly focused.

"I didn't mean for you to wake up. I was just gonna make some coffee."

"Did you sleep?"

"A bit."

Even in the semi-dark room I can see his eyebrow

pull up.

"You need to sleep. Come back to bed."

Normally I'd bristle at getting ordered around but his tone is one of caring and not control. I walk over and slip under the covers he holds up for me, letting him spoon me, surrounding me with his warmth.

"Close your eyes," he mumbles, snuggling in my neck.

"How do you know they're open?"

I can feel the deep rumble of his chuckle at my back.

"Lucky guess. Close them and relax."

Easier said than done when his hands are smoothing down my stomach and his knee is pressing up between my legs. The light brush of his fingertips as he slips his hand into my panties has me draw in a sharp breath.

"Mmm," he hums, finding me warm and slick. "Open up for me."

He lifts his knee—spreading my legs—and rubs his long cock along my folds as his fingers work my clit. Teasing, building, and retreating until even my mind is ruled by sensation. When his other hand finds my breast and starts tugging on my nipple, I'm all out of patience.

"Fuck me already," I growl, getting that same deep chuckle as a response.

"Thought you'd never ask," he whispers, pulling

my panties aside as he fills me all at once.

"More coffee?"

Radar startles. "Oh, yeah, sure."

When I finally got up a little after ten, he was already busy on the computer and the phone. From what I can piece together, FBI and local law enforcement are gearing up to knock on a bunch of doors throughout the country.

There seem to be quite a few kids they'd like to talk to. All the kids had three things in common; they're part of the *Lock&Load* group, they've used one of the numbered hashtags in the past twelve months, and all of them attended the convention in Dallas last year.

He places a hand on my arm when I top up his coffee.

"Sorry."

I bend down and brush my lips over his.

"Don't apologize for doing your job. I just feel so damn useless."

"You kidding me?" he calls after me when I return the coffeepot to the kitchen. "Because of you all those pieces we were juggling are starting to fit together."

"I mean now. I'm restless." I grab the dishrag and start wiping down the kitchen counter, again. "There's only so much I can do around the apartment before I start climbing the walls."

He looks at me with a half-smile.

"Is that why you work two jobs? To stay busy?"

I can't hold back the bark of laughter. I wish it were that simple.

"Not exactly. I told you I was raised by my grandparents?" I wait for his confirming nod before I continue. "I probably mentioned they were simple people of limited means. They died close together when I was just in my second year of college. They had a decent health plan, thank God, but had never made arrangements for their funeral. I ended up dropping out halfway through the year and worked for a year and a half to pay off their funerals."

"Where the hell was your mother? Their daughter?"

I shrug. I've long ago given up the anger that weighed me down for far too long, around about the same time I gave up on the woman who gave birth to me.

"In the wind. Anyway, already long story short; I eventually went back to get my nursing degree but had to take out student loans. Five more months and I'll be free of those. Then I can relax, maybe get a life."

I aim a self-deprecating grin at Radar but he's not smiling back.

RADAR

I CAN'T SAY I've felt ashamed very often, but I feel it now.

For years I used my less than stellar childhood as an excuse for my questionable choices and behavior when I was younger. My mother died but I never had reason to doubt she loved me, whereas Hillary's mom rejected and abandoned her, leaving her to take on responsibilities she was too young to shoulder.

My life was a fucking cakewalk in comparison.

"What's wrong?"

She looks confused. I shake my head, get up, and walk over to her, taking her face in my hands.

"Nothing. You amaze me, that's all."

Her lips part under mine as her hands grab on to my shirt. There's no hesitation in the way she gives herself over to me. Lord knows I don't deserve it, but I'm falling hard for this woman. Her taste, her scent, the feel of her soft body against me is all I know in this moment.

The shrill sound of ringing penetrates, and Hillary pulls from my arms. I reluctantly let her go as she reaches for her phone.

"Hey, Chris," she answers, after a cursory glance at her screen.

Who the fuck is Chris? I send her a questioning look to which she mouths, *mechanic*.

"I'm so sorry, I totally forgot. Yeah, things have been a little crazy."

I lean against the counter and observe as she paces through the kitchen.

"I know, but I'm not sure this is the right time to look for a replacement. Maybe toward the end of the year. Thanks for keeping an eye out, though." She nods at something the guy says, but her eyes flit my way. "I'll try to pick it up today, otherwise maybe Monday? I appreciate it."

"Your car?" I ask when she hangs up.

"Yeah. I was supposed to pick it up yesterday and turn in my rental. I forgot."

"We'll go now," I tell her, closing my laptop and tucking my phone in my pocket.

"What about your work?"

"It can wait," I state firmly.

Chances are, if she was supposed to drop off the rental yesterday, she's paying out of pocket for any extra days. What I'd really like to do is buy her a new vehicle, but I have a feeling that wouldn't go over well. Making sure she's not out more money than necessary is the best I can do. For now.

I stick to her bumper the entire way to the rental place and follow her inside. As I suspected, insurance covered only up to yesterday. My hand automatically goes for my wallet but when she catches me, she gives a sharp shake of her head as she hands the clerk her own credit card.

I'm in pretty good shape financially. I'd like to help her out, but she's looked after herself most of her life and has made it clear she doesn't feel comfortable accepting any. I'll have to be patient.

When I get behind the wheel, I check my phone I'd left in the truck, noticing two missed calls from the office.

"Gimme one second," I tell Hillary, who buckles in beside me.

"Where are you?" Bree asks when she picks up.

"Picking up Hillary's car. Why? What's going on?"

"Sarah Dunn is missing."

"What?"

I look over at Hillary, who is looking at me with big eyes.

"She didn't show up this morning and we couldn't raise her on her phone, so Sanders went to check her apartment. She wasn't there but her car was in the parking lot with the keys dangling from the lock."

"Jesus."

"Sanders has a tech specialist flying in from Denver but that may take a few hours. He's requested you be here."

"On my way," I tell her, starting the truck. "I'm bringing Hillary with me."

"That's probably best."

I end the call and start driving, my eyes on the road as I fill Hillary in on what Bree told me. She doesn't ask any questions, just gives me a subdued, "Okay," when I tell her she's coming with me, even though we're stopping at her place to pick up my laptop. There's no way in hell I'm leaving her on her own.

I should've asked Bree if they found her laptop, it may hold helpful information. Otherwise the only thing I can do is sign in to her fake profile and see what I can pull from there.

Hillary is quiet the entire drive to her place and then to the office. When I pull into my assigned parking spot, I turn off the engine and turn to face her.

"Things will likely get crazy in there and I apologize in advance if it looks like I'm ignoring you, but this is the safest place for you to be."

"Of course," she responds immediately. "Do what you need to do."

I hook her behind the neck and lay a hard kiss on her before getting out of the truck. There are more vehicles than normal in our parking lot, so I'm not surprised to find the office crowded and chaotic.

I put a hand on Hillary's lower back and guide her to the front desk where I introduce her to Lena, whom I ask to organize a place she can be comfortable. Then I wade into a small crowd gathered in the conference room.

Sanders, another two guys who look like feds, our crew, and Detectives Garcia and Bissette.

"About fucking time," Sanders barks when he sees me. If not for the worry I see etched on his face I would've given him a piece of my mind, but given the circumstances he gets a pass.

"Had to pick up my laptop." I hold it up. "Any chance you found Sarah's?"

The agent shakes his head. "Nothing. Figure she had it on her. A neighbor says she looked out her window a little before seven and says she saw her walking toward her car, but she got distracted by her kids. One security camera on the parking lot, but whatever took place is out of range."

"Fucking great," I mumble.

"If she has it with her, would you be able to track

it?"

"I doubt it, her security is pretty tight, but I can try. It may be easier to track her phone, though."

"Start on that," he instructs me. "We need a place to start."

I nod and head to my office, leaving the rest of them to figure out what to do next.

Tracing a phone just with a number isn't too hard. These days they have apps you can download to check on family members without their knowledge. But clearly Sarah hadn't left herself vulnerable like that and it takes me a while to track it down.

"Bingo," I mutter to myself when I see a red dot on the map appear on my large screen. "I've got a hit!" I call out.

Within seconds Sanders storms in, Yanis close on his heels.

"Where?"

I point at the screen. "Near the Exxon truck stop outside Palisade."

"Is it moving?" Yanis asks.

"Doesn't look to be."

Sanders is already stepping outside, barking instructions.

"Keep an eye on it and let us know if it moves," Yanis orders before he too walks out of my office.

I leave the map on my large screen while I open my laptop and log in to Sarah's undercover profile. I can see the last time she was online was from around eight last night to one in the morning. I haven't gotten very far when Bree shows the Denver agent, Matt Dunlop, into my office and I spend the next hour or so getting him up to speed.

"They found the phone," Bree says, popping her head around the door. "Garbage bin beside the truck stop. They also found bits and pieces of what looks to have been a laptop."

"Hard drive?"

"Not sure. Sanders is having whatever they can find packed up and brought in."

Shit. Not exactly unexpected—the dot hadn't moved all this time—but it means things don't look too good for Sarah.

Matt curses under his breath before renewing his focus on the equipment he hauled into my office. I log out of the tracking software, we don't need that anymore, and decide to check in on Hillary.

I find her in the small kitchen, sitting at the table with her head resting on her folded arms. She startles when I slide a hand down her back.

"Were you sleeping?"

"Nodding off," she admits. Then she abruptly sits up. "Did you find her?"

I shake my head and her face falls.

"Found some of her belongings outside of Palisade, but no sign of her. Not yet."

"Oh, no. That's not good, right?" She reaches up and strokes her fingers along my jaw. "I'm sorry. I hope you find her."

Fuck, so do I, but I'm afraid we may be too late.

I close my eyes and lean into her touch. I may not have known Sarah long, but I recognize in her a kindred spirit, and the thought something may have happened to her messes with my head.

"Me too."

My phone starts ringing in my pocket and I pull it out, noting an unknown number on the screen.

"Hello?"

"Is this Murray Jansen?" I'm immediately on alert when I hear the woman use my legal name.

"It is. Who's this?"

"I'm calling from the emergency department at Montrose Memorial Hospital."

"My dad?" I interrupt her, fear making my voice hoarse.

"I'm afraid so. The doctors are in with him now."

"What happened?"

I barely notice Hillary getting up and wrapping an arm around me in silent support.

"He was found unresponsive by a neighbor. Unfortunately, I can't tell you much more at this time."

"I'll get there as soon as I can."

CHAPTER 22

HILLARY

"I HAVE TO go."

I listened to his side of the conversation, felt the distress come off him in waves, and don't have a good feeling about this. When he tries to dodge past me to the door, I wrap both arms around him and hold on.

"Tell me what happened?"

His eyes, which were unfocused before now, find their focus on mine.

"It's my dad. A neighbor found him and he's been taken to the hospital. I don't know what's going on but I have to get to Montrose."

"Oh, honey. I'm so sorry," I mumble, pressing myself against his body until I feel his arms close around me.

"Lena said you were in here." Yanis walks in the kitchen carrying a box. "I've got the—"

Radar abruptly lets me go and faces his boss.

"My dad's in the hospital. I have to leave. Give it to Agent Dunlop."

"Of course. You good to drive?" he says immediately, sliding the box on the kitchen table. "I can get—"

"I'm good."

"I can drive," I offer.

Both men look at me and then at each other. Some unspoken communication takes place I'm not privy to, but it's Yanis who speaks first.

"You're safer here. We have this hornet's nest riled up and who knows where they're going to strike next? It'll be tough for Radar to keep an eye out for you."

The truth of it stings. I want to help, want to be there for him, but I hate the idea of being a burden.

"What about him?" I ask Yanis in return. "Who's going to look out for him?"

"He's a trained operative, Hillary. He can look after himself."

"Is there nothing I can do?"

Radar suddenly pulls me against him and buries his face in my neck.

"This helps," he mumbles in my hair. "Knowing you're safe helps. Knowing you'll be here when I come back helps." He takes in an audible breath and blows it out. "I'll call you as soon as I know more."

When he lifts his head, I notice Yanis has slipped from the room. Radar's kiss is gentle, but too brief. Then he seems to shore himself up, taps me on the nose, and starts walking to the door.

"Wait," I call after him. "Can I call anyone for you?"

He turns with a sad smile on his face.

"My brother. I'll message you his number when I get to the truck."

I follow him into the hall and watch him walk to the front door.

"Be safe."

I don't know if he heard me, but moments later my phone alerts me with an incoming message.

Radar: 907-635-1455 Hugh, his wife's name is Leslie

Me: Got it. Be careful please.

Radar: TY. Will be in touch.

It's tempting to keep engaging with him—to stay connected—but I don't want him to drive distracted. It'll be hard enough as it is. Besides, I should notify his brother in Alaska.

I make myself a coffee in the small kitchen for some reinforcement and sit down at the table, my phone to my ear.

"Jansen."

His voice is very similar to his brother's and I swallow my nerves.

"Hugh? This is Hillary Glenwood. I'm…uh…a friend of Radar."

"Friend, huh?" He chuckles. "Better let my brother down easy then. Last time I talked to him he seemed under the impression he was more than that."

I feel my cheeks flush at the thought Radar spoke to his brother about me, but then I remember the reason for my call.

"Hugh, Radar asked me to call you. He's on his way to Montrose."

He doesn't interrupt once while I tell him what I know, which sadly isn't much, and stays silent for a moment after I'm done.

"Hugh?" I prompt.

"Right. Give me ten minutes to find a flight. I'll call you back with the details."

I don't get a chance to respond before the line goes dead. All I can hear is the hum of low voices from the offices outside, but despite that the kitchen feels oppressively silent.

I flip through the magazine Lena left me with a few hours ago. It's no more engaging this time around. My mind is churning, and I find myself staring at an ad for fake eyelashes when my phone rings.

"Hey, stranger," Linda teases when I answer. "Where were you yesterday? Everything all right?"

I haven't spoken to her since my shift last Wednesday and should probably have called her. With Radar's brother calling back any minute I don't want to get into lengthy explanations, but I don't feel right perpetuating the lie I told Karla either. Not with Linda.

"I'm okay," is the only thing I can think of to say.

"Hmm," she hums after a long silence. "Methinks something is up with you. Is this shit with Karla getting to you? It's not like you to be a no-show."

Wait. A no-show?

"I talked to Karla, told her I wouldn't be in, that I wasn't feeling well. Didn't she tell you?" When she doesn't respond right away, I get uneasy. "Linda?"

"Are you serious? Any chance you recorded that conversation? Because that bitch is saying she tried calling but you weren't answering."

That uneasy feeling becomes a hot fist in my stomach. Just last month the director of nursing reprimanded me for the way I handled that CPS case, a failure to report for work could cost me my job.

"She's setting me up."

Even as I say it I know down to my bones that's exactly what she's doing. Lord only knows what else she's been whispering in the director's ear.

"That jealous piece of trash," Linda snarls. "I'm gonna—"

I miss what she says next when another call comes in. That must be Hugh.

"Linda, I have another call. Don't do or say anything that'll get you in trouble. I'll fill you in later. Gotta go."

I don't give her a chance to answer and switch to the other line.

"Hugh?"

"I can't get to Montrose any sooner than tomorrow morning. Flying United Airlines and I'll land at a little after eleven, coming from Denver."

"I'll let Radar know."

"Tell him I'll rent a car so he doesn't have to worry about picking me up. Any news?"

"No, but he left not that long ago. I'm sure once he gets to the hospital he'll know more."

"I'm not flying out until later tonight, so if there's anything to report…"

"One of us will let you know," I assure him.

"Right. Well, despite the circumstances I look forward to meeting you in person."

"Likewise."

The moment I end the call I type out a quick message to Radar, giving him the details. I stare at my screen, hoping for some kind of response but none is forthcoming. He's probably still driving; it wouldn't be safe to answer.

I'm sure he'll get in touch soon enough.

Radar

Fuck.

That's what you get for speeding.

The flashing blue lights in my rearview mirror have me slam the heel of my hand on the steering wheel. Of all the times to be pulled over for speeding. Reluctantly I brake and pull over to the side of the road, keeping an eye on the rearview mirror.

I'm about thirty miles south of Grand Junction and am surprised when I recognize a police department cruiser. I can't quite make out the person behind the wheel. What the hell are they doing out here on US 50, this far south? I would've expected a state trooper but this doesn't look like a CSP vehicle.

For a moment I consider calling Yanis, but I shouldn't bother them with a simple roadside stop. They'll already have their hands full with Sarah's disappearance and the rapid developments in this case.

Since the discovery of the Dallas UniCon as the apparent common link in this case twenty-four hours ago, the feds haven't let any grass grow on bringing in as many names as we've been able to connect. The wheels are coming off for whoever the mastermind is behind *Lock&Load - Revenge*. I imagine interviews are taking place all over that will hopefully start shedding some more light on who is behind this.

My phone pings, alerting me to an incoming message, and I grab it from the cupholder.

Hillary: Hugh flying out tonight. Arriving Montrose around 11 am with UA. Thinking of you.

A smile pulls at my mouth at that last line. Fuck, I wish she were sitting beside me right now.

I'm about to send her a message back when I catch movement in my side mirror. Immediately alarm bells start going off. The driver's side door of the cruiser is open, but I don't see anyone and there's nobody behind the wheel. Can't see anything in my rearview mirror either. What the fuck?

The moment I open my door to look, I'm hit with a spray that instantly blinds me and my hands fly to my face. *It fucking burns*. I gasp for breath as I feel myself pulled from the truck. My knees land hard when something hits me on the side of my head, sending me face-first into the gravel.

CHAPTER 23

HILLARY

"ANY WORD?"

I startle and look up in the mirror over the sink to find Bree behind me.

I've been drinking so much coffee these past few hours, this is my third visit to the bathroom. Time has crawled and I'm almost grateful for the change of scenery from the small kitchen where I've been confined.

Hugh called once, right before he was scheduled to board his flight, and Jake has checked on me a few times. Lena was kind enough to turn on the small TV mounted on the wall in the kitchen, so I had something to watch. I tried to distract myself with reruns of *Criminal Minds*, but not even the byplay between Derek Morgan and Penelope Garcia could hold my attention for long.

Every time I'd heard a phone ring, or someone walked past in the hallway, my anxiety would crank up a notch. I can't help worry about the welfare of the

FBI agent everyone is looking for, and my concern for Radar only amplifies my apprehension. I finally tried calling him a few times, getting his voicemail, and the message I sent him is still unanswered.

"Nothing yet," I repeat what I've told Jake a few times. "Maybe he turned his phone off," I offer, mostly trying to convince myself.

It's been about three and a half hours since Radar left and I'm getting really concerned about his lack of communication. Of course there are a lot of scenarios I can think of that would have him out of reach, but what if his father died and he's alone dealing with that?

Bree's face betrays her own concern.

"Have you tried the hospital?"

"No, they don't usually give out information about patients. Besides, I don't even know Radar's dad's name."

"Give me a second and I can dig that up. Maybe they can get word to Radar to contact us."

I wait for her outside the bathroom and she invites me to follow her into the large office space. There are far fewer people here than there were earlier, and Bree explains most of the federal agents left to run down leads, leaving only PASS staff in the offices.

Jake is on the phone and looks up, throwing me a distracted smile. Dimas is sitting at the desk beside him and seems engrossed in whatever he's doing on his computer. Bree indicates a chair at an empty desk beside hers and I sit down. She flips open her laptop and starts typing.

"Harold Eugene Jansen," she says, picking up the phone on her desk. "Let's see what we can find out."

Dimas looks up, his attention now firmly on Bree. Jake seems to follow suit, mumbling a quick, "I've gotta go," before ending his call.

"Yes, hi. This is Bree Graves from PASS Protection and Security Services. It is imperative I connect with one of our operatives who is visiting his father, but it's possible his phone is turned off. Is there any chance you could get word to him to call his office?" She looks at me and nods encouragingly. "Of course, the patient's name is Harold Eugene Jansen. He would've been brought in by ambulance earlier today. Yes, I'll wait."

"I may have something here!"

The voice is coming from one of the smaller spaces on the far side of this room and everyone turns in that direction. Yanis appears in a doorway and ducks into the office next door. Dimas is up from his chair and heads in the same direction. Jake is not far behind.

I look at Bree who shrugs and turns her attention back to the phone in her hand.

"Yes." Her eyebrows pull together and her eyes flit my way. "Are you sure?" The hair on my neck stands up and I find myself leaning forward in my chair. "I see. Thank you."

I open my mouth to ask what is going on when she holds up a finger and then makes another call. Her eyes pop open in surprise.

"Mr. Jansen, hello. Uh. I work with your son at PASS in Grand Junction; my name is Bree. By any chance have you seen or heard from him today?" A large fist squeezes my chest as the implication of what she's saying registers. "No, he's probably forgot to charge his phone again. Yes, of course, I'll have him call you as soon as I track him down."

"What?" I blurt out the moment she ends the call. "What's going on?"

Instead of answering me she yells for Yanis, who comes charging out of the office, but she has her eyes on me when she starts talking.

"Radar's father was never at the hospital. He's perfectly fine, I just talked to him."

"Dimi, Jake…we've got a situation!" Yanis calls out.

I BARELY NOTICE Lena draping a sweater over my shoulders until she gives my arm a little squeeze.

I've been shivering since the realization Radar has gone missing hit home. The office is a blur of activity. Everyone seems to have something to do except me. I just sit here—staring around me numbly as law enforcement comes and goes—feeling utterly useless.

They found his truck, but no sign of Radar. His phone had been recovered from under the vehicle and there were signs of a struggle in the gravel.

Dimas and the FBI agent managed to track the

phone to a quiet stretch of the US 50 about thirty miles south of Grand Junction. Jake and Yanis went out as soon as the red dot showed on the map, while Bree alerted Colorado State Patrol.

I have no concept of how much time has passed since Jake called with the news, other than night has fallen outside. In here all the lights are on and everyone is doing their thing to try and find Radar. Everyone but me.

I straighten up in the chair I was slumped in for God knows how long.

"I need to do something," I tell no one in particular, but Bree hears me. "This is not me. I don't sit idle. Give me something to do. Anything."

She narrows her eyes at me before asking, "When did you last eat?"

"I'm not hungry."

Last thing I can think about is eating. Not sure I could get anything down right now.

"Not what I asked, but enough of an answer to know it was a while ago. I don't think any of us had anything substantial for a while." She leans forward and places a hand on my knee. "We all need fuel to keep us going, Hillary. Won't do Radar or Sarah any good if we start dropping like flies."

I was thinking more along the lines of checking lists—like I did for Radar—or maybe making phone calls or something, but I can't blame her for questioning me. Heck, at this point I'm not even sure myself I can be of any use.

But I'm pretty sure I can manage to organize some food if that's what they need.

"I can order something," I volunteer, and Bree manages a smile that doesn't quite cut through the stress on her face.

It's a reminder I'm not the only one affected by Radar's disappearance. These are people who love him too.

Jesus. I love him. For someone who guards her heart so carefully, I sure have fallen fast. I'm in love with him and I'm not sure if I'll ever have a chance to let him know.

I force a sob that wants to surface back down, making my chest feel tight. I can't think like that. Pulling the sweater around my shoulders, I get to my feet.

"Pizza is easy," Bree says, looking up at me. "We have a running tab at Pablo's Pizza downtown." She hands me a pen and a notepad. "I like their Santa Fe on a cauliflower crust."

I scribble down her order and go in search of Lena, who is on the phone. I mouth, "Pizza?" and she nods motioning for me to hand over the pad so she can write her order under Bree's. Next are Dimas and the FBI agent whose name I now know is Matt, and finally I check in the boardroom to see if anyone is still in there.

The room is empty, but my eyes are drawn to the whiteboard spanning almost the entire wall behind the large conference table. At the top of the board is written: *<Fury#1*. Below it is a maze of lines connecting groups of names, and at the center—in bold lettering—are what I assume are the victims' names. *Jeffrey Cain* is written at the bottom with a question mark beside it. No lines intersect with his name.

Curiosity has me take a step closer when I hear movement behind me. Matt walks by and up to the board. He picks up a red marker, uses it to circle the name at the top, and scribbles something beside it.

<Fury#1 = C. Philips

C. Philips. Curtis Philips?

"What does that mean?" I want to know.

Matt looks over his shoulder at me.

"Something Radar was working on before Agent Dunn went missing. I've been poking through his laptop to try and find anything that might help us. Looks like he was on to something and all I did was follow his trail. I don't know how much you know about the case, but we think this…" He points at the board. "…is the online identity of the mastermind behind this game connecting all these attacks. All we have to do is find him."

I shake my head in disbelief. It can't be.

"But he's just a kid…" I mumble.

Radar

The first thing I notice is water dripping and an offensively dank smell.

My head is pounding and despite the dim space,

forcing my eyes open only makes it worse. I try to breathe through my mouth against the stench as I take stock of my surroundings.

I lift my head from where it was resting on the cold, dirty porcelain bowl of a toilet, and gag when I imagine the kind of filth my face was pressed in. My glasses are gone, but I can tell I'm in a bathroom; a small window lets in just enough moonlight to recognize the space has seen better days. A huge chunk is missing from the edge of an old tub and about half the tiles are missing from the surround. The dripping sound is from what is left of the shower, now no more than a rusted pipe poking out of the wall.

My ass is on the floor, hands cuffed behind me to the drainpipe of a wall-mounted sink. The door is open a crack and I manage to make out debris on the floor, an old bed frame leaning haphazardly against the wall, and a partially collapsed ceiling, despite my blurry vision. I listen for signs of life, anything to indicate I may not be alone, but all I can hear is the occasional vehicle engine in the distance. I can't be too far from a road.

I never got a look at my attacker. Don't know if there was one or more. I just saw one person in the cruiser, but that doesn't mean another person wasn't ducking low to avoid being seen.

My rattled brain is starting to clear some. Last thing I remember is my face heading for the gravel on the shoulder of US 50. Not sure how I ended up here or where *here* even is. All I know is it was light when

I left and now it's night.

Jesus. Dad.

Pain shoots up my arms when I violently yank at my restraints. The resulting clanking is loud—too loud—and I freeze right away, listening. When I'm sure no one comes running, I try again with a little more care.

There is movement, and when I tilt my head back I see the actual sink slightly pulling away from the wall. Dust trickles down from where two bolts hold it anchored. Grabbing on to the pipe as best I can, I throw my weight forward and clench my jaw at the jolt of pain. Grinding my teeth I do it again and this time I feel it give a little.

I keep at it, every so often stopping to listen. Anyone close by would be able to hear the groaning of the pipes and since no one has come running, I assume I'm alone. For now anyway.

Whoever managed to get me from the side of the road to this bathroom must've been a big guy to haul me around, or there was more than one. There's no doubt in my mind this is related to the investigation. We were closing in, so they took Sarah first and now me, which means someone was able to keep track of the progress we were making.

It suddenly occurs to me that phone call about my father may well have been a way to get me out in the open. Fuck, I hope so.

With renewed determination I work to loosen the sink from the wall, ignoring the hot burning in my shoulders until it finally rips free, showering me in dust and drywall debris.

One of the benefits of being as tall as I am is that my limbs are long. Long enough to slip my arms around the sink as I struggle to my feet. I sway for a moment as the blood flows back to my extremities, leaving me light-headed. My hands are still bound behind my back, but at least I am free.

As soon as the floor feels solid under my feet again, I open my eyes and my heart lurches in my chest.

An old shower curtain is covering something in the cracked tub. I try to hold on to hope it's just some debris, but the strand of blonde hair peeking out from under an edge tells me it's futile.

I have to be sure.

I sit down on the edge of the tub, reach down behind me and pull at the curtain as I twist around to look. For once I'm glad for my lack of sharp vision, because the blank eyes and indistinguishable features underneath what I know is blood are enough to have bile burn the back of my throat. *Sarah.*

I'm still forcing down the contents of my stomach when I hear car doors slam close by.

I drop the curtain back over her face and surge to my feet. There's nothing I can do to help her now and I need to get the fuck out of here.

Slipping through the door, I step into what I now recognize is a motel room. At least, what once was a motel room. I immediately know where I am. I passed the place on my way out of town and am surprised

I'm this close to where the cruiser pulled me over. If I can get away, I should be able to walk to my car, provided it's still there.

"Fuck you!" I hear yelling from right outside the door and scan the room for a place to hide. There's a hole in the wall beside a ripped-up headboard, which is still partially bolted to the wall, revealing another room beyond. As I dart across the room, I hope it's large enough for me to get through.

"No, fuck you. This is all your fault, you might as well have pointed an arrow in my direction with that stupid picture you posted. You know the rules and still you needed to show off. You fucked us all over."

Both voices sound young and now I know one of them likely belongs to the councilman's stepson.

"Come on, Curt. It ain't my fault we can't find his computer."

My ears perk up at the name, but I don't have any time to waste.

I keep half an ear on the heated argument right outside and duck my head through the hole, but I get stuck on my shoulders. I shoot up a silent prayer I won't make too much noise before I force my way through, hearing a distinct pop as I launch the rest of my body through the hole. My shoulder feels like my arm was ripped right from its socket, but I don't have time to assess the damage. Every step is agony, with my arms still cuffed behind my back, but I have to get out of here.

The door to this room is closed as well, but I notice

someone knocked out part of the bathroom wall. I carefully traverse the rubble-littered floor, trying not to make a sound, when I hear the door open next door. I'm running out of time.

I have one foot outside when I hear yelling. *Fuck*. Launching the rest of my body through, I start running along the back of the motel, hoping I can make it to the road to wave someone down. I stop at the far end, peeking around the corner to make sure the front is clear before darting across the empty parking lot to US 50.

Running with your hands tied behind your back is harder than you think, and when I hear the crack of a gunshot behind me, I know I'm not going to make it.

CHAPTER 24

Hillary

"TELL US AGAIN."

I glare at Special Agent Sanders, who's been grilling me for the past half hour.

"Why? I've already gone over it twice."

I want to scream. They should be out there looking and instead they're wasting their time with me.

"Because I want to make sure we didn't miss anything."

"I've told you everything. I don't know what happened to him after Child Protective Services got involved, but that shouldn't be too hard for you to track down. Or contact his mother."

"We're already on that, Ms. Glenwood. I just want to understand how it is you seem to be connected to every aspect of this case."

My mouth falls open at that not quite veiled accusation and my eyes lock on Yanis, whose jaw has gone hard.

"A word, Sanders."

The two of them leave the boardroom.

I'm on the verge of throwing a hysterical tantrum when Jake steps in front of me, pulling me to his chest.

"We all wanna get out there and look, Hillary," he mumbles over my head, "but we can't do anything until we know in which direction. Sanders is desperate, he has people disappearing on his watch."

"I don't have any more information, though."

"You'd be surprised how often people unconsciously add in a small detail that didn't seem that important when they retell a story a few times."

"He thinks I have something to do with this," I complain, pushing back on Jake's chest, and he lets me go.

"Honey, he doesn't. He's just frustrated."

"Jake!" Bree yells urgently from the main office space.

"Be right back," he says, as he slips by me and out the door.

Instead of waiting, I follow him. He joins the group already crowded around Dimas' desk.

"Emily Philips was Emily Loman before she married her late husband," I hear Dimas explain. "Emily Loman, as in Ingrid Loman's sister and Jeremy Loman's aunt."

"So Jeremy and Curtis are cousins?" Jake asks.

"They are," Bree confirms. "And apparently Councilman Briscoe contacted the local CPS office last month, strongly discouraging them to pursue an investigation into his sister-in-law and her son."

"Where are those boys?" Sanders barks.

"Even if he knows, I doubt Briscoe would be forthcoming," Jake suggests. "Best bet is to get a hold of their mothers."

"Detectives Garcia and Bissette have been trying to find Emily Philips," Yanis says. "Without any luck so far."

"Where is Ingrid Loman?" Sanders wants to know.

Yanis turns to Bree. "Got a number?"

"Give me a second."

She flips through some paperwork, and a moment after she dials a number on the desk phone and hits the speaker so everyone can hear.

"Hello?"

You can barely hear the woman's voice above the din in the background. It sounds like she's in a bar or something.

"Yes, Ms. Loman, this is FBI Special Agent Sanders. I need your help. I need to know where your son is tonight?"

"Jeremy? He was home when we left."

"You're not home?"

"We're at a function at the Marriott downtown, my spouse is about to give his speech. We left Jeremy at home. His cousin is with him. Why? What is going on?"

Sanders looks around the table and catches sight of me. For a second it looks like he's going to call me out and I lift my chin in defiance, but then he turns back to the phone.

"Would that be Curtis? This cousin?"

"Yes, my sister's boy. Can you tell me what this is about?"

"Are they alone at your house?"

"My housekeeper is there, but—"

Sander doesn't give her a chance to finish; he thanks her and quickly hangs up.

"Dunlop," he says to Matt. "You're coming with me."

"Hold up," Yanis stops him. "I can guarantee Ingrid Loman is right now trying to contact her son. Let's call the home and get a hold of the housekeeper."

Bree is already dialing.

I listen to her introduce herself and immediately switch to Spanish. I speak maybe half a dozen words, so I understand little, but when Bree hangs up she turns to the group.

"The boys are not there. They left twenty minutes after the parents did."

"Shit," Sanders mumbles before Bree continues.

"Aracelli says she overheard them mention a new property Councilman Briscoe recently bought. Apparently they like to hang out there. It's an old motel."

"Where?"

Bree turns to Yanis who asked the question. "The old Lazy S."

"Jesus, we drove right by there," Dimas blurts out, shooting out of his chair.

The room erupts in chaos as everyone starts moving

for the lobby. I manage to grab Bree by the arm.

"Where are you going?"

"There's an old motel right up the road from where Radar's car was found." She shakes her head. "He may have been right under our noses. Maybe Sarah is there as well."

She starts moving toward the doors again but I keep in step. I can feel her looking at me.

"I'm coming," I announce.

This time it's her turn to stop me with a hand on my arm.

"You can't. Stay here with Lena. We'll call."

I shrug her arm off.

"I'm coming. What if one of them is hurt? I'm a nurse. I can help."

"Bree! Goddammit, let's go," Dimas yells, sticking his head in the door.

"I'm coming with you or I'll find my way on my own."

Bree looks at the door, then back at me.

"I'm going to get fired for this," she mumbles, as she grabs my hand and pulls me along.

"He's gonna kick your ass for this, you know that, right?" Dimas points out when she shoves me into the cab of his truck and climbs in after me.

"She can help."

He shakes his head at her and floors it out of the parking lot.

"No matter what, you stay in this truck. You hear me?" he addresses me without taking his eyes off the road. Good thing too, because we're flying.

"Yes, sir."

Luckily at this time of night there isn't a lot of traffic on the road, but I still have a hand braced on the dashboard in front of me as Dimas whips around what little there is to get to the south side of town. When we hit US 50 stretching out before us, he puts his foot to the floor. In no time we've caught up with the two black SUVs that tore out of the PASS parking lot before us.

"Coming up on the right," Dimas announces.

In the distance I see the derelict building, the large sign at the roadside lit up by the headlights from the vehicles in front of us.

Then I spot movement; a figure running awkwardly toward the road.

"There!" Just as I point in that direction I see a flash, and whoever is running pivots on his axis as he's falling to the ground. Oh no…

"Shots!" Bree yells.

Already the SUVs in front of us are turning into the motel's driveway, but my eyes are peeled on the prone figure. I suck in a sharp breath. It's pretty dark out and possibly my mind is playing tricks, but I thought I recognized a flash of blond hair as headlights bounced over him.

Tires squeal as we turn in after them but come to a sudden halt only a few feet from the body.

"Stay here!" Dimas yells. He slams the truck in park and jumps out, as does Bree on the other side.

My shaking hand struggles to release the seat belt as I watch them run up to the man. Then I slide over, my hand ready on the door when a car suddenly peels out from behind the other side of the motel, and barrels straight toward the rear of the truck. It's going to squeeze by and get away.

I don't think; I react.

Shoving the gear in reverse, I slam my foot on the gas and the truck surges back. The crash is deafening as the rear of the truck broadsides the car. I'm launched forward, my head hitting the steering wheel.

I barely have a chance to register a warm trickle running down my face when the door beside me is yanked open.

"Jesus, woman," Dimas' voice is soft by my side.

Lifting my head I turn to him, blinking the blur from my eyes.

"Is he…" I can't bring myself to finish the question.

"Breathing."

A sob threatens to rip from my chest as I push Dimas out of the way.

"Hey, you're hurt," he protests trying to stop me, but I slip from his hold and run toward Radar.

He landed on his side and is moaning when I kneel at his front, opposite from Bree.

"You're bleeding," she notes.

"I know." I brush her off. "So is he. Where is he hit?"

"Hard to see. I think he's lying on it. I'm trying to get the handcuffs off."

Suddenly a beam of light hits us as Dimas walks up, a large flashlight and what looks like a first aid kit in his hands.

"Need some light here, Dimi," Bree indicates, and a few seconds later she has the handcuffs off.

Time for me to take charge.

"Help me roll him over. Toward you. Slowly," I warn Bree.

Radar moans louder when we move him.

"Hang on, buddy," Dimas mumbles, aiming the light at Radar's bloodstained shirt. "Ambulance is on the way."

"Have scissors in that pack?" I ask, gently pulling away the shirt so I can see the damage.

His shoulder looks out of place and the bullet appears to have exited just below the clavicle where it connects to the shoulder joint.

"I've got it."

My head snaps up at Yanis' voice. If the narrowed eyes and tight lips are any indication, he's not happy with me. Too fucking bad. I pull my hand away as he takes Bree's place and deftly cuts through Radar's shirt.

Between us we have the wound loosely packed and his arm stabilized, as best we can, by the time sirens sound in the background.

"Fucking hurts…" His voice is hoarse and his eyes are barely cracked. Suddenly he opens them wide and in a much firmer voice adds, "Jesus, Lady, you're bleeding."

The sob I've been pushing down finally bursts free.

RADAR

I'M IN PAIN and I'm pissed.

Hillary was whisked away the moment the ambulance carrying us both arrived at the hospital. That was a good while ago, and the nursing staff won't tell me how she is.

Now they're wheeling me to the OR to repair my fucked-up shoulder and I still don't know anything. Nor have I seen any of my team so I can ask them.

They roll me past a nurse stepping out of a room. She looks vaguely familiar and throws me a sympathetic smile.

"Hey, wait up," I croak, lifting my head, despite my body already giving in to the sedative they administered just moments ago. "Hillary Glenwood," I slur her name, struggling to fight off the drug.

The bed stops and the nurse steps into my field of vision.

"You're Radar," she states, grabbing my good hand. "I'm Linda, Hillary's friend. She's just gone for a CT scan to look for signs of a concussion, but she should be fine."

I drop my head back and blow out a relieved breath, as my eyes get too heavy to keep open.

"Tell her…tell her…"

I growl, frustrated the words don't seem to come. The woman pats my hand.

"Don't worry. I'll let her know."

I wonder how she can possibly tell Hillary what I don't even know how to put in words. It's my last thought before the lights go out.

I SMELL COCONUT.

Part of me would prefer to linger in this semi-conscious state where everything is muffled. Pain, light, voices. The only thing that seems real is her scent. It gives me a sense of well-being.

My mind, on the other hand, is battling for clarity, and I will my eyes open only to squeeze them shut again when light blinds me.

"He's waking up."

I recognize the voice as Jake's.

"Trying to."

That one is softer, gentle, and accompanied by a soft touch on my face and a stronger whiff of coconut.

"Hillary…"

This time when I open my eyes her face is blocking out much of the light.

"Hey, tough guy."

It's only when she smiles that I notice the cut between her eyebrows and the swelling surrounding it. I lift my hand to touch her face, but I'm held back by an IV line.

"Your face."

"Yeah," she mutters, her own fingers going straight for her forehead. "Pretty, right?"

"What happened?"

"I…uh…had a come-to-Jesus moment with the wheel of Dimas' truck." She winces. "I may have wrecked it."

A deep chuckle sounds behind her and I look up to find Jake grinning over her shoulder.

"She definitely wrecked it," he says, looking amused. "Two FBI agents and most of our PASS team weren't able to stop the suspects from taking off, but Danica Patrick here reversed Dimas' truck into their getaway car."

She shrugs sheepishly when I look at her, wide-eyed.

"I was pissed," she confesses, as if that justifies her reckless behavior.

I open my mouth to tell her what I think when Jake interjects.

"I wouldn't if I were you," he says, still with that annoying grin on his face. "Yanis tried to read her and Bree the riot act earlier and your girlfriend verbally dissected him. It was both a thing of beauty and utterly terrifying."

"You told off my boss?"

This time she bites her lip, clearly trying not to grin.

"He deserved it. He was being mean to Bree."

CHAPTER 25

HILLARY

"HOW IS YOUR guy doing?"

I glance at Linda over the rim of my coffee cup.

She physically dragged me out of Radar's room fifteen minutes ago and marched me to our favorite coffee shop, a block from St. Mary's. Since Yanis and FBI Agent Sanders had just arrived to talk to Radar, I let her kidnap me.

"Physically better. He's got a long road of physical therapy ahead of him but he's healing well. He was lucky that bullet didn't hit him lower, the story might have had a different outcome then."

I keep seeing his body spin and hit the ground. If not for my emergency room experience to draw from, I would've lost it right there and then. Instead, I relied on muscle memory to take over and was able to hold it together.

He ended up with a concussion, a dislocation, and a gunshot wound that did some damage to the already injured shoulder. Nothing irreparable, though. He was very lucky, and so was I, because I feel like puking every time I think of how it easily could've ended.

Linda reaches across the table to put a hand on my arm.

"He'll get through just fine," she assures me, and I realize tears are running down my face.

"I know," I mumble from behind the napkin I'm quickly mopping my face with.

"He'll be back to normal in no time," she assures me.

Unfortunately, I'm not convinced of that. Physically, yes, but he's been different. Distant, almost detached. He's told me several times to go home, that I didn't need to be there. I ignored him, for the most part, thinking maybe it was pain or something, but each time he mentioned it the hurt burned a little deeper.

"I don't know," I confess. "He's been different. He hasn't even touched me."

Linda barks out a laugh. "No shit. I'd be different too if I'd been beaten, kidnapped, and shot. Look, this is a grown-ass man who got bested by a bunch of teenagers. Not only that, from what I hear through the grapevine, he also discovered the body of someone he was working with. You don't think that messes with a guy's head?"

I found out about Agent Sarah Dunn yesterday morning when her boss showed up at Radar's bedside. I could tell from the sound of his voice, answering the agent's questions affected him.

I tilt my head and observe my friend.

"You're an expert on men now?"

This time I get an eye roll.

"Hardly, but maybe I'm far enough removed to look at them more objectively," she offers. "Seems to me your own insecurities around the male species are shining through."

That shuts me up, because she's not wrong, though I'd rather bite my tongue than to admit that to her smug face.

Not only haven't I seen this brooding side of him before—and it throws me off—but I also haven't seen this emotional side of me, and I'm not sure what to do with it all.

"He unsettles me."

"Good. That means he snuck his way past your barricades."

"I don't have barricades, what are you talking about?"

"Oh, please…they're up so high most men won't even try with you. You're gorgeous, with those high cheekbones, curves in all the right places, and that flawless, bronze skin. And that's just the outside. By all rights, they should be falling over themselves to get a shot at all that you are with even the slightest hint of encouragement, but you don't give an inch."

"Bill Shearer asked me out," I counter defensively.

"Right, Dr. Sugarlips." She shakes her head. "Only because the man's ego is so big, he can't see what's obvious to everyone else. You're not available."

"Radar pursued me."

Her grin can only be called triumphant.

"Yes, he did." She leans over the table. "And don't tell me the man didn't work hard to get in there."

Since I don't have a valid argument to counter that point, I take a massive bite of my Danish, leaving Linda chuckling softly at my expense.

"Believe me, honey," she imparts. "There's no way to control what the heart wants. You have to trust it'll lead you somewhere beautiful…if you only let go of the rudder."

I'm not sure how we got from Radar's behavior to my lack of trust, but Linda's words settle deep.

The rest of lunch—if you can call coffee and a Danish that—was eaten in silence. Linda apparently said all she planned on sharing and I was left with a lot to think about as a result.

"It's five to two."

A voice that has the hair rise on my neck interrupts the silence. Linda's eyes point somewhere over my head and she arches an eyebrow.

"And?"

I shift my chair and turn around to find Karla hovering over me. The coffee shop is a favorite with hospital staff, but why did she have pick now to get her caffeine fix?

"Your shift starts at two," she directs at Linda before looking down on me. "I'd like to see you in my office."

"She's injured," Linda pipes up, coming to my

defense. "She's only here for lunch with me.

"If she's well enough to have lunch with a friend, she can work."

With that parting shot she walks out of the coffee shop, leaving me to stare after her. It takes me one point two seconds to come to a decision.

"Where are you going?" Linda asks when I shove my chair back and stand up.

"You heard the woman. She wants to see me."

When I start walking, I can hear the scrape of a chair and hurried footsteps behind me.

"You're insane," Linda hisses beside me. "She's gonna fire your ass."

I turn my head and grin at her.

"I'm not going to give her the satisfaction."

I hustle down the block but only catch up with Karla as she slips into her office. I follow her in and shut the door behind me. Surprised, she swings around. Then a sly smile appears on her face and she opens her mouth, but I'm way ahead of her.

"You're sad, you know that?" I start, and feel some satisfaction at the sudden shock on her face. "I can't for the life of me figure out how you can be so obsessed with a man who is only capable of loving himself. You've tried to make my life here miserable ever since I made the mistake of briefly dating him. Something I regretted almost instantly, but you've made me pay for all this time."

"You all but threw yourself at him! Typical of your kind."

I wasn't sure, but I had my suspicions jealousy may not have been the only reason why she felt the need to target me all this time. Now I know, and it makes me even angrier.

"My kind? Are you referring to the fact I'm a person of color?"

Her eyes narrow and she hisses, "He's too good for you."

"Word of warning, Karla, your prejudice is showing."

I can tell she hears it because her demeanor instantly changes to one of innocence.

"Oh, don't give me that wide-eyed look, you know it and I know it," I cut her off when she gets ready to defend herself, because I'm nowhere near done with my long-overdue blowup. "You know what the worst part is? You're so obvious about it—he knows it too. He doesn't give two cents about me, but he flirts and lays it on thick when you're around because he enjoys getting a rise out of you. That's what he likes, playing with people. It makes him feel powerful."

Her face colors a deep red and her mouth forms a straight line.

"You can't talk to me like that. You're—"

"I quit, Karla. I'm done. Life is too short for me to work in such a toxic environment. I can live with the consequences of my actions; I just hope you can."

When I walk out of her office I do so with a much lighter step.

Radar

I've HAD MY eye on the door since Hillary walked out.

"Radar," Yanis says sharply, and I drag my focus to him. "We can come back if you're not up to it."

I reach for the button that raises the top of the bed a little higher.

"No. This is fine."

"All right," Yanis says, sitting down in the chair Hillary vacated. "You mentioned you recognized the voices outside the motel room."

"Technically I didn't. One of them accused the other of screwing things up when he posted that picture. That *stupid picture* to be exact. It was a safe assumption he was referring to the social media post with the image of the bloody baseball bat, and therefore was talking to Jeremy Loman. He then called the other guy 'Curt,' and I'd just been looking into Curtis Philips, so that was a pretty easy conclusion as well."

"What made you look into him?"

I turn to Sanders. "Who, Philips? Hillary asked me to look into the kid."

"Yes, Ms. Glenwood already filled us in on what made her ask you to do that. I'd like to know why you waited so long."

I close my eyes. Fuck, if that isn't the question I asked myself many times over the past forty-eight hours. Sanders' implication is clear, his agent might still be alive had I moved on it faster.

"Trust me, I wish I hadn't. Hillary's request was based on a suspicion she had. Nothing tangible, but a gut feeling. Short of the kid having an injury Jeff—

the shelter resident—claimed to have inflicted on his attacker, there was nothing to tie Philips to this case. Not until Jeff was found dead. That's when we discovered he may well have been a witness to the murder of Gina Castillo, and then the name Curtis Philips became one of interest."

I reach for the cup of water on the nightstand and take a sip before I continue.

"But it wasn't until I was able to connect his name to the convention in Dallas, I started suspecting he might be a bigger player than we thought."

"Matt told me something about an award?" Sanders asks.

"The BAFTA Young Game Designers Award. The convention featured a panel of previous award winners. Curtis Philips' name was listed. I was trying to find evidence of his connection to *Lock&Load* when I got the call from the hospital."

"Yeah. Matt followed your trail and was able to make the connection," Yanis fills in. "Dimas started digging into the kid's background and discovered he and Jeremy are cousins."

I snort. "Bernard Briscoe can't be too pleased right now."

"Your councilman had his legal team on it before we had a chance to question the boys. They're not talking." Sanders sounds frustrated. "We have them dead to rights on the murder of Sarah and the attempted murder on you, but I want them to go down for all of the other victims as well."

"Tell me they'll at least be tried as adults," I press.

I know that's not up to Sanders, but I need the reassurance these kids aren't getting off with a slap on the wrist.

"I will do everything in my power," he grinds out, clearly struggling to keep his composure before he continues. "I should go or I'll miss my flight. I'm heading up to Saginaw to talk to Jenny Churchill. I hope she can give me something I can use to drive a wedge between Curtis and Jeremy. All I need is for one of those two punks to talk."

His shoulders droop as he walks out the door.

"I'll be there in a sec," Yanis calls after him, before turning to me and putting a hand on my good shoulder. "Talk to your father?" he asks.

"This morning. He's fine. He's supposed to come by for a visit with my brother this afternoon."

"Good. Any word when they plan to let you go?"

"Maybe tomorrow. I should be able to do some work when I get home, though," I add.

"Not gonna happen. Mandatory two weeks off and then we'll talk."

I'm about to respond when Hillary walks in and Yanis slips out with a few quiet words for her.

"What was that?" I ask her when she leans down on the side of the bed.

"He apologized for yelling the other day."

She grins down at me, appearing almost giddy.

"Good lunch?"

"Well, it was…eventful."

My attention is piqued. “How so?”

She leans down and the first thing I smell is her damn shampoo. My body instantly responds.

“Linda set me straight on something.”

Her dark eyes smolder just inches from my face. My heart starts thundering in my chest and I swallow hard.

“Yeah?” my voice cracks.

“Oh yeah.” I can feel her breath brush my lips. “I’m done holding back, Radar. Done holding up the shields. I’m letting myself fall.”

She kisses me and I groan in her mouth. I wish I could wrap my arms around her, pull her on top of me, but just the taste of her fills me with a sense of belonging.

“I may also have quit my job,” she mumbles against my lips. Before her words register, she’s already distracting me with her mouth.

She abruptly lifts her head at the sound of a throat clearing.

“Sorry to interrupt,” I hear my father’s amused voice.

CHAPTER 26

HILLARY

I PAY CLOSE attention as the physical therapist takes Radar through a few exercises he's supposed to do daily, and I plan to make sure he does.

This morning Rosie dropped by to visit Radar, but as she was leaving pulled me into the hallway. I shouldn't have been surprised somehow word got to her about my confrontation with Karla yesterday—I'm pretty sure Linda had something to do with that—but Rosie offered me a full-time position at the shelter on the spot. I told her I could start right away, but she wouldn't hear of it. Told me I looked like I'd gone a few rounds in a boxing ring and ordered me to take a couple of weeks off to heal up.

She's right; my face looks like someone used it as a punching bag. My eyes and nose bruised, swollen out of proportion, and the stitches across my forehead giving me a unibrow. Radar doesn't seem to care, but I noticed his father and brother doing a double take when they walked in on us yesterday afternoon. I'd offered to give them some time alone, but Radar hung on to my hand and wouldn't let me out of his sight.

I like his family, like the way they don't seem to hold back the love they clearly feel for each other. His dad is a bit of a curmudgeon and carries an air of sadness, but I also noticed he looks with pride at both of his sons. Hugh is the embodiment of what I would expect a big brother to be. Teasing, a tad overbearing when it comes to his family, but very personable with a healthy dose of humor. Still, I can imagine it might not have been easy growing up in his shadow.

"Morning," Hugh announces as he walks in the door, his father following behind.

They'd announced yesterday they'd drive us home since Radar's truck is still at the office and Chris still has my car.

"Ready to get out of here?" Mr. Jansen directs his question at me.

"Absolutely. Just waiting for his discharge papers."

It's almost noon by the time we leave the hospital. Hugh is behind the wheel with Radar beside him, and I'm in the back seat with their father, who insists I call him Chuck.

I'm looking forward to my own shower—the ones in the nurses' locker room suck—and some normal clothes. Hospital scrubs don't quite cut it. It's only been a couple of days, but it'll be weird going to an empty home.

I haven't asked, but I wonder how long Radar's family is intending to stay. For sure he'll need someone looking after him for at least a little while, until he can get back on his feet, but I'm sure they can manage. I don't want to intrude on their family time.

"...pack a bag and we'll go pick up that mutt of yours." I tune in to the conversation from the front seat. "Found a log cabin on the south side of Blue Mesa Reservoir. Booked it for a week. No better time to get our fishing trip in."

"Now?" Radar responds incredulously. "I can't use my arm."

"So what? You've got a spare," Hugh responds dryly.

Beside me Chuck snorts.

"Ne'er mind those two. Been like this since they was tykes."

In the front seat the bickering continues.

"Low, Hugh, even for you. If I didn't know better, I'd think you planned it this way. Are you that desperate to beat my record?"

"Record?" I whisper at Chuck.

"Growin' up Hugh always came out on top, 'cept with fishin'. Radar's got a knack for it. Patience, I reckon. Could sit still for hours, even as a boy. Always pulled out the biggest fish." He shakes his head, but his lips twitch. "Fought about it as kids, still going at it as grown-ass men."

I grin at him and he winks back.

Part of me had looked forward to maybe spending some time with Radar since we're both off work for the next little while, so I'm a little sad, but this'll be good for him. Sounds like this is something of a family tradition.

Hugh pulls into the visitors' parking near the stairs to Radar's apartment. I quickly get out and round the vehicle so I can give Radar a hand.

"You good?" I ask when he sways a little on his feet.

"Yeah. Just tired."

"That's normal. Most people think they're good as new until they actually leave the hospital. Give it a couple of days and let these guys pamper you a bit." I lift up on my toes and kiss him sweetly on the lips. "Hope you have a good time."

I start walking toward my building.

"Where are you going?" Radar calls after me.

"Home. I need a shower and quite possibly a nap." I turn with a forced smile and take a few steps backward.

"We plan to leave between three and three thirty," Hugh announces. "Make sure you pack something warm. The nights can get chilly."

It takes me a second to process before I stop in my tracks, my mouth slack.

"Oh…but I…yeah, okay," I mumble stupidly.

"Don't worry," Chuck says, a grin on his face. "We won't be sleeping in bunk beds. The place is more of a lodge than a cabin, with plenty of bedrooms and a couple of bathrooms. A state-of-the-art kitchen too," he adds.

"Wow. That sounds fantastic. You like to cook?"

Hugh bursts out laughing. “Dad? He’s king of the frozen meals.”

“I don’t, no,” Chuck ignores his son and answers with a shrug and a twinkle in his eyes. “But according to Radar, you do.”

I start laughing too. Cheeky old coot.

“I see, so that’s how it is,” I tease, but the old man makes no apologies.

“Not passin’ up on a chance for a home-cooked meal.”

“I’ll see what I can do,” I promise, and turn my back as I resume the walk to my apartment.

Still smiling I throw them a little wave over my shoulder.

“Three o’clock,” Hugh yells behind me.

Radar

Dad wasn’t kidding. This place is huge.

The main part of the lodge is an open space with a wall of windows in the front overlooking the reservoir, bisected by a ceiling-high, stone fireplace. Three comfortable couches and a rustic coffee table make up the seating area. Behind it is a large open kitchen and dining area. Bedrooms and bathrooms are located in two wings on either side.

When we arrived, Hugh insisted Hillary and I take the master suite and he and Dad would take the rooms in the opposite wing. The two of them disappeared outside with their fishing tackle, but I didn’t have the energy. Instead I laid down on one of the couches for a bit, while Hillary putzed around in the bedroom, and promptly fell asleep.

I hear someone moving around the kitchen, but when I try to sit up to see who it is, my shoulder protests loudly and I can't hold back the vicious curse bursting from my lips. Immediately footsteps approach and Hillary's face appears over the side of the couch.

"Need help?"

"I can do it," I mutter stubbornly.

She raises an eyebrow and folds her arms over her chest. Aware of her eyes on me, I try again, this time making sure I roll toward my good side before I drop my feet down and use my core to sit up.

"I'm going to grab your meds," she announces and her footsteps retreat.

Even though it's on my lips to tell her I don't need them, the pain in my shoulder disagrees so I keep my mouth shut.

"You're a difficult patient, you know that?" she informs me, handing over a couple of pills and a glass of water.

There's so much I could say to that, but in the end, I'd still have to admit she's right. I've done little more than snarl since I woke up in the hospital. Being laid up isn't my idea of fun and it turns out pain makes me cranky. Not being able to work and see this case to the end is messing with my head as well.

I hate being weak, especially in front of my brother and father, but also around Hillary. Shit, I can't even hold her properly; never mind doing what is always on my mind when I'm around her. I should be taking care of her. She was injured herself, and has to be worried about her job situation, and yet she's looking after me.

"Get out of your head." She sits down on the coffee table in front of me and I quickly toss back the pills followed by the water. "I can hear the wheels turning and there's steam coming from your ears." She turns toward the window and watches the two figures on the edge of the water, my dog Phil sniffing around at their feet. "After dinner we do your exercises, and again in the morning. You take your meds as prescribed and by tomorrow afternoon you'll be out there with them."

She turns back and grabs my spare glasses from the coffee table where I dropped them, and perches them on my face before putting a hand on my neck.

"You can be as crotchety as you like, but you're not gonna scare me off. You forget, I deal with pains in the ass like you all the time."

I snort and crack a smile.

"I bet you do."

"Let me help get you back on your feet, and I promise I won't fight you when you want to take care of me."

I'm gonna keep her to that and I'll start by getting her some decent wheels to drive.

Tucking a stray strand of the hair she started wearing naturally—a look I much prefer—I lean in and press a kiss to her mouth.

"I'll take you up on that."

I'm pretty sure my dad was already half in love with Hillary, but his first bite of the Navajo fry bread topped with refried beans, sliced flank steak, sautéed onions, and salsa, sealed the deal.

"Not sure about the wisdom of feeding a houseful of guys refried beans, darlin'," my brother teases. "You'd have to check with my Leslie on that, but this is damn good stuff."

"Your momma teach you to cook like this?" Dad asks innocently, and I check for Hillary's reaction.

"My mother's mother, actually. She and my grandpa raised me. They're Navajo. I don't know who my father is, other than he's clearly black."

"You're a mishmash, like my boys."

Hugh and I look at each other and almost burst out laughing. Dad used to tease us by calling us mutts. He did so lovingly, but I'm still glad he opted for a different term.

"Oh?" Hillary doesn't appear insulted.

"Yup, Norwegian and Dutch on my side, and my Cara was Irish and Italian. The boys got my looks and her temper."

I'm frankly surprised he brings it up. It used to be the quickest way he could rile Mom up. I remember she'd get steamed and he'd laugh at her before wrapping her in his arms, whispering stuff in her ear until she'd be smiling again.

"Mom would threaten you with her rolling pin if she could hear you say that," Hugh comments.

"She would. She didn't take crap from anyone, even me."

His smile is bittersweet at the memory, but it's so much better than the stark pain we saw on his face for so many years after losing her. They had a special kind of love, my parents, and it doesn't surprise me Dad wasn't able to move on from that.

I've only been with Hillary a short while in comparison, but I can't even imagine what life was like before, let alone—God forbid—what it would be after.

Hillary squeezes my knee under the table when she notices my eyes on her. Her look is one of concern.

"You okay?" she mouths, and I smile at her, not holding back any of the emotions I'm feeling.

There are words to share as well, but not at the dinner table with my father and brother in audience. That opportunity comes after, when Hillary leads me to the bedroom for my exercises while the others clean up the kitchen.

She has me lie back on the bed and tells me to relax as she carefully moves my left arm.

"Your dad is sweet," she says, smiling gently.

"Sweet is not the word I'd pick," I point out, wincing at the stretch in my shoulder. "Although he does seem to be sweet on you."

"The feeling is mutual. Your family is great."

The last is added with a hint of sadness, and I grab one of her hands with my good one.

"What's mine is yours," I tell her, noting her eyes

taking on a shine. "Not that I have any say in the matter, they seem to have adopted you all on their own. Took you less than twenty-four hours to steal their hearts." I press my lips to her palm.

"I wasn't trying."

"You don't have to." I place her hand in the middle of my chest and cover it with mine. "You had mine before you even stopped fighting me."

"Honey…" she whispers, bracing an arm on the mattress beside me as she leans close.

"And for the record," I mumble softly. "I haven't just fallen; you've landed me square on my ass."

She's still chuckling when I lift my head to take her mouth. She stretches out beside me and tangles her fingers in my hair.

I feel no pain with her tongue in my mouth, her scent surrounding me, and her sweet curves pressed along the length of my body. I put my functioning arm to good use, sliding my hand down her spine and into the waistband of her jeans to cup a lush asscheek.

"They're in the other room," she mutters, trying to pull back as she catches her breath.

"There's a bathroom, a laundry room and a hallway between. We could be screaming and they probably wouldn't hear."

I enforce my words by sliding my fingers down her crease until I feel her slick heat. Slipping a digit inside her pussy, I press deep, swallowing her moan with my mouth.

She pulls back again, panting hard as she moves

off the bed.

"We're supposed to be working your muscles."

The cocky grin splitting my face is automatic. I'm a guy; my mind can turn anything suggestive.

With one hand I undo the buttons of my fly and pull free my swollen cock.

"I have one in particular that could use some attention," I challenge her.

She may roll her eyes, but her hands are already stripping down her jeans and panties, leaving her in nothing but the dark curls at the apex of her shapely thighs. Her shirt is gone next and I'm momentarily distracted by the sway of her breasts.

"Are you sure?" she asks when she climbs on to straddle me. "I don't want to hurt you."

I grab on to her hip.

"Lady, you're gonna hurt me if you don't."

The next moment I lose the ability to think, let alone formulate words, when she sinks down and takes me deep inside her body.

CHAPTER 27

HILLARY

I STRETCH MY arms over my head.

This is the life.

Phil, who is curled at my feet, briefly lifts her head, only to put it back down on her paws and promptly close her eyes.

I can't remember the last time I've taken a vacation, working diligently toward the goal I set myself many years ago and which is still months and sixty-two hundred dollars away. I've always worked two jobs, lived frugally, and socked away the extra cash to pay down my student loans. St. Mary's provided me with decent medical insurance, the start of a small pension, and some job security, none of which I have now.

You'd think I'd be a wreck without that security, but I'm not. I'm lazing on the front porch of a gorgeous lodge, enjoying a beautiful view, made even better when I look over at where Radar is perfecting his one-armed cast.

The guys are fishing, something they've done daily

since we got here. During the warmest hours of the day, we'd hang on the porch in the shade, talking, and twice we've gone for a hike while Chuck took a nap.

Other than preparing a few meals—which is always better when you cook for an appreciative audience—I have done absolutely nothing. Zip. Nada. And the weird part is, I don't even feel guilty. In fact, I think this may well be the most relaxed I've been in a decade.

The late afternoon sun feels great on my skin, my book is upside down on the table beside me, and I'm perfectly content just being in the moment. I may as well soak it up because tomorrow we're heading back home.

Hugh is flying back to Anchorage—his job and his family are waiting for him—and Chuck wants to be back in Montrose for his Saturday night poker game at the community center. Both Radar and I have at least one more week before we're even allowed anywhere near our jobs, and it'll be interesting to see what life will be like in our regular environment.

This short week has been amazing. Observing Radar with his brother and father has given me a good look at both the man and some of the family dynamics, providing me with even more insight. I can see how he is different from the other men in his family. His dad and brother are all about the physical, where Radar is definitely a mix of physical and bookish. Interesting is that his bookish side disappeared completely during this trip.

I like both sides of the man. Heck, I *love* all of him.

Chuck comes sauntering toward the house. He skipped his nap today because it's our last day, so I'm guessing he's getting tired.

"Any luck?" I call out when he's close enough. Phil immediately wakes up and jumps to her feet, her tail wagging as she waits at the edge of the porch.

The boys had promised fish for dinner tonight. They have a routine of practicing catch and release, except for the last day when—so they tell me—they feast on the day's spoils.

"Couple of rainbows, a brown, and a bucket of perch. Comin' to get a couple'a beers and the fillet knife. Gonna clean 'em."

"Can I help?"

I'm already getting up from my seat.

"Suit yourself," he says with a wave of his hand, and in passing adds, "Hope you've got a strong stomach 'cause it can get messy."

"Chuck," I call after him. "I'm an ER nurse, remember? I've had my hands in body cavities, I think I can handle some fish guts."

It wouldn't be the first time. Grandma didn't just teach me to cook, she made sure I knew how to find and prepare food if ever I was stranded on my own in the wilderness. I used to roll my eyes at that, but she felt it was important for me to learn some traditional skills. I have to say, being able to skin or debone a rabbit or a wild turkey hasn't exactly moved my life along, but it did give me a fascination with anatomy and a strong stomach.

"Well, then make yourself useful and grab the beers while I fetch my knife."

I grin as I watch him walk away. Crusty old coot. I feel like I've been accepted into the fold; he now grumps as hard at me as he does at his sons.

Armed with beers, a decent knife from the kitchen, some old newspapers, and a plastic tub I found in the laundry room, I follow Chuck. Phil sticks close to my heels.

"Hey, Lady," Radar grins, leaning down for a kiss.

He looks good. Relaxed. We lucked out with the weather and the daily dose of sun has given him a bit of a tan. Surprisingly he looks like he belongs out in the elements instead of in an office.

"Nice catch," I comment, checking the haul laid out on a large rock at the water's edge. A bucket sitting beside it holds about six or seven perch. I hand out the beers, set the tub down, and spread out the newspapers on a flat rock. When I straighten up I find all three men looking at me curiously. "What?"

"Wondering what you're doing," Radar asks, a smirk on his face when he looks at the Santoku knife I brought from the kitchen.

"Your dad said you were cleaning fish, I'll help."

Ignoring the doubtful looks, I reach for one of the larger trout and place it on the newspaper. With the tail firmly in my hand I use the blunt side of the knife to deftly scrape the scales off both sides of the fish. I step over to the water and rinse any that stick to the skin off. Then I fold over the top sheet of newspaper so I have a clean slate and cut off the dorsal fin and carefully slice open the belly. The Santoku knife was the sharpest one and, although a thin boning or filleting knife would've been easier, the thin edge slices effortlessly through the tough skin. The innards are easily removed and I make sure the cavity is empty before putting the blade of the knife behind the gills sliding it down to the spine, and then I flip it over and do the same on the other side. All it takes is some pressure with the heel of my other hand to snap through the spine. I toss the body into the plastic tub for a good rinsing in the kitchen, roll up the top layers of newspaper cleaning up my workspace, and reach for the next one.

"Nine minutes," I hear Hugh mumble behind me. "Faster than you, Dad."

"Bullshit," the old man grumbles. "Gimme that fish."

What started off as a little showoff on my part turns into a full-out competition, accompanied by beer, complete with heckling and challenges. The loudest—and only one not competing because he only has use of one hand—is Radar, taking great pleasure in taunting his brother in particular. The result is a tub full of cleaned fish and a sense of camaraderie that feels a little unfamiliar, but warm and wonderful all the same.

Hugh picks up the tub, Chuck grabs the dirty newspapers we'll burn in the firepit tonight, and I carry the empties back to the house. Radar walks beside me and slings his good arm around my shoulders, tugging me close.

"That was hot," he mumbles, his lips brushing my ear.

"You're nuts. I'm covered in scales and fish guts. I stink."

"Oddly, not a deterrent," he mutters amused.

It is for me, and after rinsing and seasoning the fish, I head to the bathroom for a quick shower. The guys announced they'd be cooking tonight and far be it from me to argue.

By the time I get downstairs, a hint of sautéed garlic and spices hits my nose, luring me straight to the kitchen where Hugh is stirring something in a frying pan on the stove. A quick peek out the back doors shows Radar and his father manning the grill.

"What's cooking?" I ask, peeking around him.

"Pan-fried potatoes," he announces, stepping aside so I can see.

It looks amazing; small new potatoes, colored with diced bell pepper, red onions, and chopped spinach tossed together in what smells like a royal amount of butter.

"That smells awesome. I had no idea you could cook."

He chuckles softly.

"I'm a one-trick pony, this is all I can make. It's one of Leslie's recipes and the only reason I learned how to make it is because when we moved to Alaska,

I had to fend for myself for a few months before she came up with the kids." He steps back up to the stove to stir. "It's my favorite and the prospect of eating takeout for two months didn't appeal. I can do this, fry an egg, and I can grill a decent steak, but that's about the extent of it."

"Shouldn't be too hard to expand your menu?" I suggest, grabbing a water from the fridge. "Drink?"

"Please, and as to the other, hell no," he returns. "Not until the boys are grown. Kids are unbelievably picky eaters and harsh critics to boot. Leslie has the thicker skin."

I laugh at the poor excuse as I hand him one of the beers I pulled from the fridge. "Coward."

"You bet I am." He grins and shoots me a wink.

I pull open the sliding door and step out on the deck. The two out here are arguing about the proper way to grill the fish. I step in between and hand Chuck a bottle before turning to Radar and distracting him with a kiss.

"You smell good," he hums, not seeming to care his father is looking on. "Coconut."

"My shampoo."

"I know." He grins down at me. "You told me."

"You, however," I poke a finger in his chest, "still reek of fish."

I hadn't noticed before, I only smelled myself.

"Not washing it off until after dinner," he announces.

"Then I'm sitting next to your dad," I fire back,

taking a step back and hooking my arm through Chuck's, catching another whiff of eau-de-trout. "Scratch that." I release him and take a few steps away. "I think we should eat outside."

For the first time I watch Chuck crack a wide smile, crumpling his face.

"You'll do for my boy, Hilly, you'll do."

Radar

"Gonna miss you, girlie."

Hugh and I look at each other and grin.

Beside the vehicle, Dad is hugging Hillary hard. Or maybe it's the other way around.

"I have one more mandatory week off, Radar probably more, and Montrose isn't that far," she says, releasing my father. "We'll swing by next weekend and you can show me around town. I've only ever driven through, so it's pretty much new to me."

Dad throws her a lopsided grin.

"It's a date."

She waits to get back in beside me until Dad disappears into his trailer with just a wave for Hugh and me.

"You know you could've gotten in the front," my brother says over his shoulder.

"You're a nice guy and all that, Hugh, but I'd rather sit beside my boyfriend."

He mumbles something inaudible from the front seat as he starts the SUV, while Hillary lifts Phil on her lap and snuggles in against my good shoulder.

"I'm gonna miss him too," she whispers.

How my cranky father managed I don't know, but I think she fell faster for him than she did for me. Hillary seems to have effortlessly charmed her way into the hearts of my family too. Even Leslie, who she only briefly spoke to last night when Hugh handed her the phone. Hillary promised to visit Alaska soon too. I believe her exact words were, "Don't worry, I'll drag his ass up there if I have to." I have no doubt she was talking about me.

They've been in Anchorage for three years and I have yet to show my face. Work has always been in the way, but I get the sense I won't be able to wield that as an excuse all the time anymore. Not that I would anyway, now that I have a reason to go home at night.

Needless to say, by the time they hung up, Hillary was Leslie's new best friend.

"I love your family," she says in a soft voice.

I smile in her hair.

"I'm getting that impression."

"It's possible I love you too."

I have to strain to hear her. Tugging her even closer, I use my left hand to lift her face and look down in those beautiful dark pools.

"I figured. Especially after you made the mistake of cooking chili for a houseful of men and still stuck around." I grin at her when she snickers at the memory. "I doubt it escaped your notice that I love you too."

"Yeah…"

I kiss her smiling mouth, feeling like my world that so often seemed off-kilter finally righted itself.

We spend the rest of the drive to Grand Junction quietly snuggling in the back seat, with the only exception when we pass the old motel. Beside me Hillary stiffens and puts a hand on my leg.

"It's behind us, Lady."

Hard to believe that was only last week. If not for the tightness in my shoulder it might as well have been months ago. I have to thank my brother for dragging us all away for that break. It's been good for everyone.

I catch Hugh checking on me in the rearview mirror, a smile on his face. I decide on the spot that as soon as I can, I'm going to load Dad and Hillary on a plane to Alaska.

It's already getting dark when he pulls into the parking lot behind my apartment building. I'm surprised to see my truck parked in its regular spot. I'm guessing one of the guys or Bree dropped it off here at some point. Which reminds me, I need to take Hillary shopping for new wheels.

Hugh has only a small window of time to get to the airport for his flight, so we say goodbye in the parking lot. He gives Hillary a hug first and then turns to me.

"You did good, little brother. Don't mess this up."

Of course he had to add the last bit. Wouldn't be Hugh if he didn't needle me a little.

"You worry about your own woman," I fire back.

He starts laughing and grabs me in a one-armed

hug.

"Happy for you, Bro," he whispers, before letting me go with a punch to my good shoulder.

Then he gets into his rental and takes off.

Hillary

I WAVE AFTER Hugh and turn to Radar, who has his eyes on me.

"What?"

I feel a little uncertain. We've spent a lot of time together, even before he got shot, and I'm not quite sure where to go from here. My apartment is waiting right across the parking lot, but I'm not sure if he expects me to go home or stay here.

"Whose place?" he asks with half a smirk.

The relief is instant as I smile back. The prospect of going to my apartment alone was not an appealing one.

"Yours," I answer right away. "Your building has better water pressure and I really like your bed."

Heat immediately floods his eyes. "My place it is. We have a week to sort out a more permanent solution."

Well, then, it's clear he's not wasting any time. Excellent.

"Let's get these bags upstairs," I suggest, grabbing my tote. "Let's get you some food," I tell Phil, who is waiting at my feet.

In Radar's apartment I get started on our laundry while he looks after the dog. I'm going to have to grab some clean clothes from my place because everything I brought is in the washer.

Radar is clipping the leash on Phil when I walk out of the laundry room.

"I'm just taking her for a walk."

Just then his phone rings from the kitchen.

"I'll take her, I need to grab a few things from my place anyway. Take the call."

He drops a peck on my lips in passing. Then he snatches his phone off the counter and answers as I step out the door.

"Come on girl, we'll head around the block first."

As usual Phil sniffs every blade of grass, every lamppost, and pees about twenty-three times before we round the final corner to my building. She's a little confused when I start up the stairs to my place, but where I go, she follows, like she's done this entire week.

Funny, I never had a pet in my life, it didn't even occur to me. Not with two jobs and long hours. I knew there was no way I could care for an animal, so it wasn't on my radar. Apparently I missed out.

"You hang out here while I get my stuff," I mutter at the dog, who continues her sniffing inside my apartment.

In the bedroom I toss a few things in a bag, grab a new book from the shelf—I finished the one I took with me—and head to the bathroom to get my straightener. I haven't used it in a while.

I pick it up and catch sight of my reflection in the

mirror. My hair is big and a little wild, and for many years I carefully controlled it with flat iron and product, but I'm actually starting to like its unpredictability. Radar likes it too.

I twist the cord around my straightener and toss it determinedly into the trash. From now on I take life as it comes.

I find Phil lying on the front doormat and pick up her leash as I turn off the lights and step outside.

I'm pulling the door shut when Philomena starts growling, but before I can move cold steel is pressed to the base of my neck.

"Finally. *Bitch.*"

CHAPTER 28

Radar

"SO? HOW WAS the trip?"

I drop down on the couch and plant my boots on the coffee table.

"Great," I answer Dimas. "How did you know I was home? I just walked in the door."

"Lucky guess. Shoulder coming along?"

I lift my arm and test the joint a little.

"Better. Can't lift my arm over my head yet, but I'm getting there."

"You will, but don't push too hard. Do exactly as much as your PT instructs you."

Dimas would know. He lost part of his leg his last deployment and set himself back in his recovery by trying too much too soon. Now you can't even tell he has an artificial limb.

"Fair enough, but after I see the surgeon this week for my follow-up, I'm hoping I can at least get back to work."

"You'll have to get that past my brother first. He'll

want you in tip-top shape. According to him you're the company's brain and we'd be lost without you."

I'm silent for a beat. Yanis isn't one to compliment and I had no idea he regarded me like that. Feels fucking great, even if I'm hearing it second-hand.

Clearing my throat, I look to change the subject and ask, "What's happening with the case? I feel like I've been out of the loop. Was that girl in Saginaw any help? Jenny something?"

"You bet. She handed Sanders the thread and the FBI has had their hands full unraveling this shitshow ever since. She admitted to meeting up with Jeremy and Curtis at that convention in Dallas, along with eight other kids. Didn't take long to figure out they were chosen for their vulnerability. Some were victims of bullying, some were abused, some got lost in their parents' contentious divorces. It was a virtual smorgasbord of angry and angsty teens. Perfect little subjects for his sick game. *Lock&Load - Revenge* was presented as a platform that would empower them and they were told they'd be the first to test it.

"Curtis spent a few months grooming them like some fucking cult leader, building them up and manipulating them before he sent them out to recruit more kids. That gave those kids a sense of power, especially when Philips started calling them his 'original ten.'"

"Jesus," I mutter.

Gives me chills, thinking how clever he was to gain control over the group by pushing exactly the right buttons. What's even fucking scarier is that Philips is no more than a snot-nosed punk himself, but clearly one with genius-level skills.

"Let me guess," I continue. "The murders were some sort of a loyalty test? If you fail, you get booted from the top tier?"

Dimas chuckles, but it doesn't sound lighthearted.

"That, and initiation for the next recruits. They had some other tests they had to complete beforehand—acts of vandalism, issuing threats, that kind of stuff—before they were asked to complete the big one. After each completed task, they would hashtag a message with a Bible verse before moving on to the next one. For the attack on the girl who bullied her in school, Jenny said she had to bring a second, who'd be there to 'learn.'"

"So other than the five murders we know of—not including Sarah or the homeless guy—did you connect any others?" I want to know.

The shelter resident was likely killed because he'd seen something, not because he was an intended victim. I'm sure Sarah was killed, and I would've been, because we were closing in.

"Two more. One in Biloxi and the other in Rochester, New York. Similar MO and Jenny was able to line them up with two of the kids she met in Dallas."

"Holy shit. Tell me they've got the other ones?"

"Yeah. She was able to give Sanders the names of the remaining kids and the FBI has picked them up for questioning."

"Can you imagine being one of those parents? I'd lock my kid up myself."

"No kidding," Dimas agrees. "There's a lot still to sort out, but there's enough to throw the book at Curtis. Armed with Jenny's testimony, Sanders was able to put pressure on Jeremy Loman. Guess his lawyer saw the writing on the wall and went into negotiation mode to have the kid tried as a minor. He'll get ten years max."

"Not enough," I grind out.

"No, it isn't, and as it turns out he's the one who shoved the homeless guy off the bridge because Curtis still has his arm in a cast, but the claim is he was coerced into it. He was also complicit in the murder of the waitress at the diner, who apparently was Curtis' intended victim."

"Why? What did she ever do to him?"

"As I understand it, Emily Philips worked at the diner until she was fired eighteen months ago for skimming the till. Gina Castillo was the one who reported her to the owner. Philips and his mother hit some hard financial times until Curtis won that BAFTA Award. It came with some prize money he used to develop *Lock&Load*."

"The buy-in for the game was a hundred dollars," I remind Dimas. "Even if just five hundred kids bought in, that would make for a nice little chunk for a teenage kid."

"Except it looks like we're talking thousands, and

not just from the US; from all over the fucking world. And apparently not only kids either. Lots of people were looking for the next big thrill in violent gaming and apparently *Lock&Load* was starting to be a hot commodity. Even for a dark web game."

"The shit people do for a thrill," I observe.

"Or for money." Dimas adds. "Whatever Philips' motivation may have been at the outset; money definitely became another drive. Feds are having a hard time finding it, though."

"What? The money?"

"Yeah. The kid has some serious skills. Too bad none of them are being used for the good."

That comment could've easily been made about me if Yanis hadn't pulled me out of that world. Unfortunately, it is way too late for Curtis Philips.

"Have they talked to his mother yet? I find it hard to believe she'd be completely in the dark about this. Especially after that murder at the diner."

"They're still trying to find her. One train of thought is she took off with the money. She could easily be in Central America somewhere by now, sitting pretty."

"With her son in jail?"

"The kid gets the cold heart from somewhere." I can't argue that. "Hang on a sec."

I hear some muffled voices in the background and then Dimas is back on the line.

"Jake's asking for Hillary to give his wife a call. She's been trying to get through to her. Maybe her phone's out of juice."

In my mind's eye I can visualize Hillary taking the leash from my hand and on her way to the door grabbing her phone from the small table in the hall.

"Yeah, maybe…" I mumble, making my way to the window and peeking through the blinds. I don't see anyone in the parking lot. "I better go," I announce in a firmer voice. "She should've been back from walking the dog by now."

I hang up before he has a chance to answer and head straight for the door.

Hillary

I STRUGGLE TO place the whispered voice.

It's a woman, I can tell that much.

"What do you want?"

My mind is scrambling and the only reason I'm fighting my instinct to swing around, so I can see her, is the cold pressure of what I'm guessing is a gun on my neck. Phil adds a bark to her growl.

"Shut that mutt up," she hisses.

Phil barks again in response.

"What do you want with me?" I repeat, a little louder this time, in hopes someone is around to hear me.

"Get inside." The barrel of the gun slides up my neck to the base of my skull. "Now."

The hope of being seen deflates and I apparently hesitate a second too long. I'm forcefully shoved against the door, which flies open. My bag is knocked from my hand as I stumble inside and trip over the dog. The second I hit the hallway floor, I twist around to find a woman dressed in a black hoodie standing over me with a gun aimed at my face.

For a second the gun has my complete focus, before I pay attention to the person wielding it. Recognition dawns, but I still shake my head in disbelief.

"Mrs. Philips?"

"None of this would've happened if not for you," she spits vehemently.

I have a hard time reconciling this enraged woman with the outwardly shy and timid mother, who walked into her son's hospital room and caught me talking to him. I had a hard time seeing the family resemblance then, but I can sure see it now.

"I don't know what you mean." I scoot back on my ass, trying to increase the distance, but she takes a step forward in response. The door behind her swings shut but gets stuck on my overnight bag.

Behind me Phil still growls softly as she presses her trembling body in the small of my back. Despite being as scared as she clearly is, I appreciate the show of support, even though part of me wishes she wasn't a cute, little fluff ball. I make up my mind on the spot if I get through this; I'm getting a dog, a big mean-looking one.

"It's *your* fault my baby is behind bars. We were doing fine until you stuck your nose where it didn't belong."

She's swaying back and forth on her feet, her body angled toward me, but the barrel of that gun continues to be aimed unwaveringly at my face.

"I'm sorry, I—"

"Sorry? You're sorry?" She laughs hysterically and that scares me even more. "He is my life!"

I quickly scan my immediate surroundings to see if I can find anything to use as a weapon, but the only thing within reach is a pair of athletic shoes.

"Not so high and mighty now, are you? You're nothing but an instigator looking for attention. Even that nurse said you like to cause trouble." That gets my attention and she must've seen my reaction and snickers. "Oh yeah, no love lost there, she was all too ready to point me in your direction, wrote down your address and all. Been waiting to look you in the eye when I make you pay. No one hurts my boy and gets away with it. No one. Not even his daddy. He found out the hard…"

My God, she's batshit crazy.

I stop listening to the ranting woman and start inching closer to the running shoes, but my eyes stay fixed on hers. There's no doubt in my mind she means to harm me, but I sure as hell don't intend to go down without a fight, even if my only weapon is a pair of Nike Flex.

"…I said stop moving!"

The moment her voice penetrates, I launch myself toward the shoes, but before I can reach them, she fires the gun.

Everything happens in slow motion as I hit the ground. The door is kicked open and Philomena jumps over my legs, just as Emily Philips swings her gun around on Radar who barges in. She never gets a chance to fire before the dog charges her and clamps her small jaws on the woman's ankle. A well-aimed kick from Radar knocks the gun from her hand and he takes her to the ground.

"Lady! Are you okay?" he yells in my direction, as he struggles to keep Emily pinned to the ground with one arm.

Things have moved so fast I haven't even had time to take stock of my body. I'm buzzing with adrenaline; so I don't feel anything, but to make sure I visually check myself. I may have a few bumps and bruises, but I look to still be in one piece.

"I'm good," I assure him, catching his worried gaze.

He lets out an audible sigh and closes his eyes.

"Thank fuck for that."

CHAPTER 29

RADAR

MY EYES FOLLOW her around the room as she hands out fresh beers.

I haven't let her out of my sight once since I barged into her apartment and tackled her attacker the other night. I'd locked my eyes on her and didn't look away until Jake and Dimas piled through the door; the cops close on their heels.

They'd torn out of the office the moment I'd hung up to go in search of Hillary. I was more than relieved when they showed up, keeping the spitting-mad woman pinned to the ground had been taxing, despite Phil's assistance.

I chuckle at the memory of my eighteen-pound mop of a dog snarling and growling as Emily Philips tried to dislodge her from the ankle Phil clamped onto. After the boys took control of the woman, it had taken me a minute or two of coaxing before the damn dog would let go.

The woman was taken in by the cops and Dimas

notified Sanders, who showed up twenty minutes later to take Hillary's statement. Not long after Jake called his wife to let her know Hillary was okay and he'd be home in a bit, Rosie stomped in the door, Tessa on her hip, demanding to see for herself. It was a little chaotic and by the time we got everyone out the door and the two of us walked back to my apartment, we'd both been exhausted.

Phil slept on the bed with us that night, and the night after. I'm afraid we've set a precedent there is no return from.

"With antifreeze?" Hillary responds disbelievingly to something Jake shared as she sits back down beside me.

I tune back into the conversation.

Jake had shown up with Yanis half an hour ago to give us an update, and I suspect to check on our welfare. I had my follow-up appointment with the surgeon this morning, who seemed pleased enough with my recovery. He thought I should be ready for work in another two weeks, but warned me that with regular physical therapy it might be another couple of months before I'd feel close to a hundred percent again.

"Fed it to him in his chili, apparently," Yanis responds. "The woman is so far gone it's scary. She seemed proud to share she made it extra spicy so he wouldn't notice. The man was a raging alcoholic and it didn't surprise anyone when she said she woke up to find him dead in bed. He was cremated just days after."

"And Curtis was how old?"

"Twelve. If she's to be believed, both she and her son were beaten regularly. I'm pretty sure it wouldn't be hard for any half-decent lawyer to make a claim for insanity. She's off her rocker."

Hillary scoots a little closer and I drape my arm over her shoulder, enjoying the feel of her body seeking comfort from mine. The corner of Yanis' mouth twitches as he eyes us.

"The kid himself is clammed up tight, though," Jake contributes. "He hasn't said a word, but it doesn't really matter, the others—starting with his cousin, Jeremy—are talking enough. Sanders is pushing to get Philips tried as an adult and thinks he'll be lucky if he ever sees the outside again."

As much as I believe it's what he deserves, I can't help feeling a pang of sympathy for the kid. Sounds like he never had a chance.

"They probably shouldn't give him access to computers in jail," I caution. "With his set of skills, he doesn't need to be on the outside to be able to create some serious damage. The kid is smart."

Yanis grins. "That's pretty much what Agent Dunlop mentioned in the briefing. Good to know we have some brilliant minds on the right side of the law as well. If not for you, Sarah Dunn, and Matt, I don't think we'd have been able to resolve this case."

My job is of the quiet variety, not rife with heroics or bravery and rarely in the spotlight, and I'm fine with that. I'd like to think I'm beyond craving praise, but I have to admit, it feels damn good to get a pat on the back.

"So..." Jake pipes up, perhaps sensing my unease with the compliment. "What did the doc say?"

Not long after I give them my medical update, they take off. Hillary walks back from showing them out and stops in front of me.

"Have I ever told you I think brilliant minds are incredibly sexy?" she points out with a twinkle in her dark eyes.

I drop my head back and smile up at her.

"I don't think you have."

She puts a knee in the couch and swings the other leg over my lap, straddling me. The cool fingers of one hand run through my too-long hair while she plucks my glasses off my nose with the other, setting them on the armrest.

"It's probably easier if I show you," she murmurs, her mouth already descending on mine.

"Good idea," I barely manage before she slips her tongue between my lips.

I grab her hip with one hand and look forward to properly holding on to her again. This past week I've let her take the lead, and I'm far from complaining, but I'm getting frustrated I'm limited in the ways I can repay her.

My mind doesn't linger there for long when she reaches for my jeans and deftly unbuttons me. I groan down her throat when her hand closes around my cock, her thumb stroking the tip with just enough abrasion to raise goosebumps on my skin.

She breaks our kiss and runs her tongue down my jaw, flicking my earlobe, before nipping the tendon in my neck.

"Jesus, Lady," I groan when she slides off the couch and kneels between my legs.

Looking down, I watch as she slips my erection between her lips, taking me deep. She hollows her cheeks as her head bobs back up, leaving a sleek trail on my cock. My hips buck involuntarily, chasing the heat of her mouth as she teases me with slow, languid strokes.

My fingers tangle in her tight curls, trying to take control but she's not giving up.

"Please…I need to fuck you," I grind out, holding on to the release building.

The moment she lets me slip from her lips, I grab my dick, squeezing right below the crown to force my climax back.

"Where do you want me?" she asks, a teasing smile on her slick lips.

I'm almost beyond caring but indicate the armrest, and the next thing I know she's naked and bent over, her gorgeous ass in the air, wet glistening. I can't resist a taste of her while I wrestle my jeans down with one hand. Then with one foot on the floor and a knee in the couch behind her, I line myself up and surge deep inside her.

We're both more than primed and in minutes I can

feel her pussy flex around me as she throws her head back.

"Harder…"

I dig my fingers in her flesh and power my hips to the sound of heavy breathing and skin slapping, until finally she cries out. I follow seconds later and collapse over her back.

"Fuck…" I pant, barely catching my breath, "… but I love you, Lady."

HILLARY

"I NEED TO stop in at the hospital."

Radar looks up from the newspaper he's reading on his laptop with his eyebrows raised.

"Why? Did you leave something behind?" He starts to get up from his seat and slaps his laptop closed before announcing, "I'll come."

I should've known he wasn't going to let me go by myself. I've barely been able to move out of his eyesight. I had to take my phone into the bathroom so I could finally have a private chat with Linda this morning.

He's going to be pissed I kept this from him, but I'd been afraid he'd take the information and run with it. I really wanted the gratification of confronting Karla myself first.

It was obvious it hadn't been Linda the deranged woman referred to, but I wanted to make sure she'd be around when I talk to my former boss and had a request to make. I guess Radar will be too, since I don't think I'll be able to stop him from coming.

"It may get ugly," I warn him, which only serves to make him more confused, so I quickly explain, "Emily Philips mentioned something that night about talking to a nurse who didn't like me much. In fact, she supposedly wrote down my address for Emily."

"And you didn't think to let Sanders know? Heck, to tell me?"

Oh yeah, he's not happy.

"I did think of that, but I want to look her in the eye when I inform her the pointless resentment she has for me could've easily cost me my life."

"Damn right it could've."

I put an appeasing hand in the middle of his chest.

"I know, honey, and I want her to bear some consequences for that. Besides, other than her giving out my address, which is against hospital regulations, I don't see there being any law against what she did," I justify.

He covers my hand with his own and some of the anger drains from his eyes as one corner of his mouth pulls up.

"You want revenge," he accuses in a soft voice.

I shrug. "Not that, per se, but some accountability for her behavior, yes. She's made my life difficult long enough and I was never in a position to call her out on it. Now I am, and she's taken it a step too far."

"Fair enough, but you're not going alone."

It's my turn to grin. I'd never admit it out loud, but I kind of like it when he thinks he can order me around.

"I figured as much."

I WAS RIGHT. It was every bit as satisfying as I imagined it to be.

She was caught off-guard when I confronted her and started denying it when Radar piped up and told her it would be easy to confirm with Mrs. Philips, since she was already singing like a canary. I guess it was enough for her to turn her anger on me and slip up, saying she was sorry I apparently walked away unscathed.

That's when the director of nursing—who'd been alerted by Linda at my request—walked into her office and dismissed her on the spot.

Petty? Perhaps, but after years of walking on eggshells around the woman and putting up with her abuse, I felt it was no more than she deserved.

"Feel better?" Radar asks me when we get into his truck.

My car is still in the lot at the mechanic, where he's agreed to take me next so I can finally pick it up.

"Yes, and not only because I enjoyed watching her get her dues, but also because she might well have used her position to bully someone else. She's just a mean and vindictive person."

He gives my knee a squeeze with his hand before putting the truck in drive.

"You're going the wrong way," I tell him when he turns left instead of right at North Avenue. Chris's shop is on the east side of town and we're heading west.

"I just need to make a quick stop," he says, pulling into a Honda dealership.

He doesn't say much else, but I have my suspicions when he coaxes me out of the truck and has me look at a couple of Honda CRVs that just came off lease.

A salesman is following us around, eager to tout each vehicle's features if we show any interest. He's annoying me and apparently Radar as well, who abruptly turns on the man and in no uncertain terms tells him we need some time to ourselves.

As soon as the guy is out of earshot, I face Radar.

"What are we doing here?"

He puts his hand on the side of my neck, lightly curving his long fingers at the back.

"Moving forward, I hope," he says, a barely-there smile and mellow eyes softening his face. "What do you think we're doing?"

I grab on to his wrist and tilt my head toward his hand.

"Buying a car I can't afford?"

"Aside from that," he presses. "You ready to move forward?"

My stomach is instantly assaulted by an army of butterflies and a hint of panic is setting in. I know what he means, I'm not an idiot, but am I ready? What will it look like? Am I supposed to give up my apartment? Is he? What if it doesn't work out, or after a month we can't stand each other, what then?

"Relax, I can practically hear the panic wheels grinding. Let me make it easier for you." He leans his forehead to mine. "I love you and I want a future with you. Now I'm okay waiting for you to be ready to take the next step, but I'm already there. After these past few weeks, I can't see us going back to sleeping alone, even some of the time. I want to make this permanent—move in together—and I don't care where. Your place, my place, somewhere new that can be ours. We'll figure it out as we go." The butterflies turn into melted goo inside me and a lump forms in my throat. "But if you want to w—"

"I don't," I cut him off, covering his lips with my fingers. "No need to wait. Let's look for a new place." With my momentary panic gone, I'm on a roll, my mind going a mile a minute. "Maybe a little house with a yard for the dog. Oh." I catch myself smiling up at him. "Make that dogs, because I want to…"

I was about to say 'adopt one' but Radar swallows the words as he kisses me with such passion, I'm pretty sure we could get cited for indecency.

"Done," he says, grinning when he finally lets me up for air.

My own face is cramping, I'm smiling so big.

I'm really doing this.

We're really doing this.

There's only one more thing to clear up.

"But why are we looking at cars?"

CHAPTER 30

HILLARY

"OH, MY GOD. It's so pretty!"

I throw Rosie a dirty look as she admires my brand-new Honda CRV.

"What color is this?" She runs her hand over the shiny, light, blue-gray paint.

"Sonic Gray Pearl," I grumble.

It had been a month-long, ongoing argument that ended this morning when I left for work to find the SUV in the spot where I left my silver Honda Civic last night. Fine, I had been driving around with a hole in my muffler for a week and it sounded like NASCAR came to town.

It's not like I couldn't afford to fix it. I'd received a certified check in the mail last week from one Bernard Briscoe. You could've struck me down with a feather. Apparently, his stepson admitted to defiling my car on orders of his cousin. I guess the check was Briscoe's last step in an attempt to wipe the slate clean, after he apparently filed for a divorce from the boy's mother.

I'm sure the fact municipal elections are on the horizon has nothing to do with that. Not that there's any chance I'd vote for the weasel.

Anyway, this new car was waiting for me this morning. Radar left before I did and apparently took my old keys out of my purse and replaced them with the SUV's. I had about fifteen minutes to get to work and he wasn't answering his phone when I stood fuming in the parking lot. I had no choice but to drive it to the shelter, where Rosie was waiting for me at the front door.

Apparently, *someone* had been in the know and failed to warn me.

"Some friend you are," I complain, as she walks around the vehicle oohing and ahhing.

"Don't be a grump," my best friend says. Although that's a title I'll seriously have to reconsider. "Cars are a guy thing. Believe me. Remember when Jake tricked me and bought me my SUV?"

"Yes," I hiss. "Which is why it's a mystery to me how you could be complicit in this. If I recall correctly, you were furious with him."

She smiles one of those swoony smiles she reserves for her husband.

"I was, and then I wasn't. I have a better understanding now."

I snort and plant my hands on my hips.

"Really? Pray share."

She flaps her hand. "Oh, like I said, it's a guy thing…an honor thing. They can't have their woman drive around in a crap car or someone might think they don't know how to take care of them." She puts a hand on my arm. "Trust me, girlfriend, you may wanna throw this battle, there will be plenty of far more important ones ahead."

She starts walking inside and I grab my purse and lock the doors, unable to resist a last glance over my shoulder at the pretty color. Rosie is grinning with the door open when I head in.

"Admit it. You like it," she whispers when I walk past her.

"Shut it."

Her giggle follows me to the cafeteria, where I load up with a large coffee and one of Brad's muffins. I'd better be careful now I've started full time, pastries every day will definitely start to pack on.

Rosie has already disappeared into her office and I slip into mine, closing the door—save a crack—so I can hear what's going on outside. Then I sit at my desk, take a big swallow of coffee, and grab my cell.

"Lady," he answers, a smile evident in his voice.

"Murray Jansen," I say in my sternest voice. "You don't play fair."

He chuckles softly.

"Something had to happen, babe. We spent too much time bickering over the same thing, not getting anywhere, when we both know this was going to be the result anyway."

"It was not," I protest, but he's right. I was only hanging on because I didn't want to give in.

Now he's full-out laughing.

"You're a shit liar, you know that?"

"Whatever," I grumble.

"Do you like the color?"

It's on my lips to say no, but I can't bring myself to disappoint him. It was the color I would've picked if I'd been there and it makes me feel good he knows me well enough to get it just right.

"Yeah. It's pretty."

"Good."

His voice goes warm and deep, and I wish he were here so I could thank him properly. I'll have to tell him instead.

"Thank you, honey," I whisper.

"My pleasure." I can hear him smiling. "Now can we move onto the next thing?"

"Which is?"

"I found a house."

That takes me by surprise. I'd gone to month-by-month two years ago, but Radar just signed the initial lease on his apartment a couple of months ago. We'd agreed it would make sense for me to give my notice, put surplus furniture in rental storage, and stay in Radar's place for the duration of the lease. I have to vacate my place by the end of June.

"I don't understand. What about your apartment?"

"That's for later worry," he says easily. "Look, I have a meeting I've gotta get to, but how about we go have a look at it tonight?"

"Yeah, but—"

"Sorry, Lady, I really have to run. See you later."

He hangs up before I can respond.

Radar

"You're in so much trouble."

Bree shakes her head as I make my way through the main office.

Jake has a big mouth.

He's the one who noticed the For Sale sign and alerted me a couple of days ago. I made him swear not to mention anything to Rosie until I had a chance to have a look at it.

It was something Dad said when we visited him a couple of weeks ago that got me thinking. He asked now that I found myself a *good* woman when I planned on making an *honest* one out of her. I told him hadn't thought that far ahead, but he reminded me I wasn't in my twenties anymore and neither was Hillary. He made it clear he expected to see some grandchildren before he was too old to enjoy them.

Dad was never one for tact, but at least he waited until Hillary was out of the room before he opened his mouth.

It did get me thinking, though, which is why when Jake mentioned the house, I jumped on it. Before I ask her to share the rest of her life with me, she needs to know I'm serious and can take care of her.

The CRV was first, the house is next, and the most difficult hurdle will be getting rid of her remaining student loan. It's a drop in the bucket for me, but it is a matter of pride for her. I foresee many discussions on that subject.

I flip Bree the bird over my shoulder and wish Lena a good evening before I walk out into the parking lot. Hillary will likely already be home and have taken Phil for a walk. I'm late today because of the new job Yanis has me working on. I'm eager to get home but I have one stop to make.

Twenty minutes later I pull into my parking spot, check the back seat to make sure the blanket covers my surprise, and hop out of the truck.

She's in the kitchen, Phil sitting at her feet waiting for her dinner. Already my dog has picked Hillary as her new favorite person and barely looks up when I walk in. Little traitor.

"Where are we going?" she says, setting down Phil's food before straightening up to face me.

"Well, hello to you too," I counter, reaching for her.

I can tell she's still a tad peeved, but that doesn't stop me from pulling her flush against me and laying a heavy kiss on her. Her body relaxes in my arms and her hands curl in the shirt on my chest.

When I release her mouth, her lids are heavy and her eyes are soft.

"Hey," she whispers, and I tap the end of her nose.

"Much better," I share, and immediately see I should've just kept my mouth shut, because just like that the fire is back in her eyes.

"Now will you tell me where we're going?"

"Come on." I grab her hand and pull her to the door. "It's better if I just show you."

I had the restaurant double wrap everything, but I can still smell the food when I open the truck door for her. Luckily Hillary is too annoyed and distracted to notice.

"Are we going to Jake and Rosie's?" she asks when I turn onto 28 Road.

"Nope."

I bite off a grin when I catch her glaring at me from the corner of my eye.

I drive past our friends' house and make the next left onto Beechwood Street. About halfway down the block, I pull into the driveway of the stone and wood paneled, two-story, two-door-garage home with the For Sale sign stuck in the front lawn. I put the truck in park and glance at Hillary.

Surprise and what I hope is a happy smile brightens her face.

"Are you serious?"

"Wanna go have a look?"

"You mean we can just go in?"

I fish the key the realtor—who happens to be a friend of Yanis—lent me and dangle it in front of her.

"Nobody lives here. The owners moved out four days ago as a result of a job transfer and are hoping for a short sale."

What I don't tell her is that Mitch, the real estate agent, already has a provisional offer, which I hope I can give him the go-ahead on tonight. It all depends on Hillary's response, which so far looks positive.

She gets out of the truck, taking in the mature trees surrounding the property, the well-maintained front yard, and the modern, yet rustic appearance of the house.

"Open concept main floor with a separate den. Three bedrooms and two full baths upstairs." I round the truck and hand her the keys. "Have a look around. I'll be right behind you."

The interior of the house could use a few improvements I hope she'll be able to see beyond. To facilitate the quick sale, the price is quite a bit below market, even with the marginal overbid I offered on it.

I also counted on the fact it's right around the corner from Rosie and Jake's place to be a selling point.

I watch her open the door and tentatively step inside before I start gathering the bottle and glasses I hid under my seat, and the bags and the blanket from the back seat of the truck. Instead of heading inside, I round the side of the house to the backyard.

As well maintained as the front, the backyard is like a little quiet oasis. Surrounded by mature trees that provide privacy, the yard also has a rock garden, complete with pond and small waterfall. The sound of the water drowns out what little traffic noise you'd hear and only adds to the sense of a rustic hideaway.

I'm unpacking the containers with tapas I picked up on my way home, when I hear the sliding door open and Hillary steps out on the small deck.

"This place…" she starts but doesn't finish.

I walk over to her and take her hand to lead her over to the small stone patio under the trees, where I set up our dinner. I glance over but can't really gauge the expression on her face.

Suddenly nerves hit me. As I watched her go in the house earlier, I was so damn confident she'd love it. I'm not so confident now.

"So what do you think?" I can't help asking when she lets me help her down on the blanket but stays silent, her eyes on the food and the bottle of wine.

"My grandparents lived in an apartment on the main floor of a noisy, old building that has since been demolished. That's where I grew up." I notice the hitch in her voice, and I grab for her hand. "When I got myself through college all I could afford was a bedroom in someone's basement."

"Lady," I start to interject, but she sharply shakes her head.

"Let me finish. The apartment in our building is luxurious compared to some of the places I've lived." Then she lifts her head and I see tears pooling in her eyes. "A house—an actual house with stairs, and a garden, and no neighbors knowing every move you make—was always a dream of mine. Something I could strive for, work toward, once I paid off my loan." She turns away and looks around the garden and up to the house. "This is so much more than the little modest home I'd imagine myself growing old in. I'm overwhelmed," she admits, her eyes coming back to me.

My fingers tighten around hers.

"Remember I told you this was a short sale?" I wait for her to nod before I continue. "We can get this place well under market value. It's a great investment, because even if we flip it back on the market right away, we'd make our money back and then some."

I lose her eyes when her head drops again.

"I have enough set aside for emergencies, but not for a down payment on a house or even part of it."

"I've been lucky. Lucky enough to be able to sock away some money. At this price I'm able to buy it outright. I love you, let me give you your dream," I plead.

She shoots me a sad smile.

"As sweet as that is, and as much as I love you back and would love to call this place home, it wouldn't feel that way if I hadn't contributed to it."

I lean closer and take her face in my hands.

"I figured you'd say that, which is why I came up with a plan B. I put down sixty-five percent of the purchase price…in ratio to my income," I have to add quickly when I see her frown. "We take out a mortgage for the remaining thirty-five percent, which you can pay."

Her face lights up.

"I can do that. It wouldn't be any different than paying rent."

Jesus, what a relief. I wasn't sure how to combine my need to look after her and hers to retain her independence and didn't know if she'd go for my proposal.

I grin at her and try to contain my happiness. It's either that or forget about the food and the wine, and toss her down on the blanket to show her how fucking thrilled I am.

The fact I plan to put an amount equal to the mortgage payment into a college fund for our kids I keep to myself for now. I don't want to push my luck.

Thank God the wine bottle has a screw top because the way my hands are shaking, I don't think I could've managed a corkscrew. I pour us a glass and hand her one before lifting mine.

"So, are we a go?"

She shakes her head and for a moment I worry she's changed her mind, but when she lifts her face and is smiling wide through her tears, I don't even have to hear her resounding, "Yes!"

EPILOGUE

Hillary

I DON'T THINK I've ever inhaled air this clean.

Radar was right, I can feel the bite of frost and pull my winter jacket close. I'd laughed at him when he told me to pack it. It's only the middle of September, but apparently in Alaska that means winter.

We're sitting on a rock in the wide riverbed, a short walk from our camping spot, looking at the stunning fall colors of Denali National Park. It's still surprisingly bright for nine o'clock at night.

This trip was Chuck's idea. I still have to smile at the blatantly obvious way he guilted his son into conceding by playing the I'm-not-going-to-be-around-forever card. Not that it's a lie, trips like this one might well be the last of its sort, but overall the old man is in pretty good health.

We spent five days in Anchorage with Hugh, Leslie, and the boys, and it had been Hugh's suggestion we rent an RV and get a true taste of Alaska here in Denali for a couple of days. It's an experience I don't think any of us will ever forget. So raw, so unspoiled, and so breathtakingly beautiful I've been in a state of overwhelmed the entire trip.

We spent a good chunk of the day driving around on a bus that runs all the way to the end of the park, where private cars can't go. Some of the roads were hair-raising, it felt like the old school bus was hanging off the edge of the cliff, but the views were unparalleled. We stopped at the side of the road at some point and saw a grizzly bear with two young, fattening up for the winter on the slope of a hill.

The many impressions of the day had Chuck tuckered out and he called it a night right after the hamburgers we grilled back at the campsite. Radar asked me to go for a walk since it's our last night out here before we have to return the RV. We'll spend one more night with his brother and then we head back to Colorado.

I shiver against the cold and Radar moves behind me, stretching his legs on either side of me and tucking me into his body for heat.

"This was the best day ever," I tell him, leaning my head back against his shoulder.

"Mmm, it's up there for me too. If I'd known this place was so beautiful I'd have visited before."

I tilt my head so I can look up at him.

"We'll just have to visit again." One of his hands rests low on my stomach and I cover it with one of mine. "More beauty than you've already given me to look forward to," I add.

"How about for our honeymoon?" he asks, producing a small box he holds up with his other hand.

My vision is instantly blurred with the tears that seem to come too easy these days. All I can see is a sparkle when he smoothly flips up the lid with his thumb.

"I can't remember my life without you in it, and I even don't want to. Marry me, Lady."

I twist my body so I can look him straight in his beautiful, warm eyes.

"Of course I will."

He picked a perfect time and an unforgettable location, and I'm not about to take this special moment from him.

My news will wait for a day or two.

THE END

ACKNOWLEDGMENTS

As always there are a great number of people without whom this book would not have been possible. The people who keep me on track, correct my mistakes, support my endeavors, and promote my words. I consider every one of these people my friend;

My editor, Karen Hrdlicka, and alpha reader and proofreader, Joanne Thompson. These women are my touchstones, my co-conspirators, and my friends.

My agent, Stephanie Phillips of SBR Media who is an absolute treasure and believes in me without reserve.

My publicists, Debra Presley and Drue Hoffman and my PA Krystal Weiss of Buoni Amici Press. I am so grateful for this amazing team for making me look like I know what I'm doing, when in all reality I don't have a clue.

My beta readers—Deb Blake, Pam Buchanan, and Petra Gleason. Three good friends and faithful readers who are not afraid to give it to me straight, which is exactly what I need.

My Barks&Bites folks who make for an amazing cheering squad, a comforting shoulder, a good laugh, and a soft place to land.

Every single blog and early reviewer taking the time out of their days to support my stories, your work and your efforts are so appreciated.

But most of all I'm grateful for YOU, my readers.

Where would I be without you? Your enthusiasm for my words feeds my muse and your feedback is invaluable.

I love you all!
Freya

ABOUT THE AUTHOR

USA Today bestselling author Freya Barker loves writing about ordinary people with extraordinary stories.

Driven to make her books about 'real' people; she creates characters who are perhaps less than perfect, each struggling to find their own slice of happy, but just as deserving of romance, thrills and chills in their lives.

Recipient of the ReadFREE.ly 2019 Best Book We've Read All Year Award for "Covering Ollie, the 2015 RomCon "Reader's Choice" Award for Best First Book, "Slim To None", and Finalist for the 2017 Kindle Book Award with "From Dust", and Finalist for the 2020 Kindle Book Award with "When Hope Ends", Freya continues to add to her rapidly growing collection of published novels as she spins story after story with an endless supply of bruised and dented characters, vying for attention!

https://www.freyabarker.com

If you'd like to stay up to date on the latest news and upcoming new releases, sign up for my newsletter:
https://www.subscribepage.com/Freya_Newsletter

CPSIA information can be obtained
at www.ICGtesting.com
Printed in the USA
BVHW071104100221
599730BV00002B/228

9 781988 733593